The WORLD'S STRONG[...] REARGUARD | Labyrinth C[...] Novice S[...]

D0556886

GREEN HALL

The location of the Upper Guild and the base of operations for Arihito's party after they moved up to District Seven.

Coordinating with his allies, Arihito used his rearguard powers to boost each and every one of their attacks!

"Everyone, I'll support you!"

YEN ON
NewYork

The WORLD'S STRONGEST REARGUARD
Labyrinth Country's Novice Seeker

3

Tôwa

Illustration by Huuka Kazabana

NORTHERN PLAINS
PUBLIC LIBRARY
Ault, Colorado

The WORLD'S STRONGEST REARGUARD | Labyrinth Country's Novice Seeker 3

Tôwa

Illustration by **Huuka Kazabana**

Translation by Jordan Taylor
Cover art by Huuka Kazabana

This book is a work of fiction. Names, characters, places, and incidents are the product of the author's imagination or are used fictitiously. Any resemblance to actual events, locales, or persons, living or dead, is coincidental.

SEKAI SAIKYO NO KOEI -MEIKYUKOKU NO SHINJIN TANSAKUSHA- Volume 3
©Tôwa, Huuka Kazabana 2018
First published in Japan in 2018 by KADOKAWA CORPORATION, Tokyo.
English translation rights arranged with KADOKAWA CORPORATION, Tokyo through
TUTTLE-MORI AGENCY, INC., Tokyo.

English translation © 2020 by Yen Press, LLC

Yen Press, LLC supports the right to free expression and the value of copyright. The purpose of copyright is to encourage writers and artists to produce the creative works that enrich our culture.

The scanning, uploading, and distribution of this book without permission is a theft of the author's intellectual property. If you would like permission to use material from the book (other than for review purposes), please contact the publisher. Thank you for your support of the author's rights.

Yen On
150 West 30th Street, 19th Floor
New York, NY 10001

Visit us at yenpress.com
facebook.com/yenpress
twitter.com/yenpress
yenpress.tumblr.com
instagram.com/yenpress

First Yen On Edition: June 2020

Yen On is an imprint of Yen Press, LLC.
The Yen On name and logo are trademarks of Yen Press, LLC.

The publisher is not responsible for websites (or their content) that are not owned by the publisher.

Library of Congress Cataloging-in-Publication Data
Names: Tôwa, author. | Kazabana, Huuka, illustrator. | Taylor, Jordan (Translator), translator.
Title: The world's strongest rearguard: labyrinth country's novice seeker / Tôwa ; illustration by
    Huuka Kazabana ; translation by Jordan Taylor.
Other titles: Sekai saikyo no koei: meikyukoku no shinjin tansakusha. English
Description: First Yen On edition. | New York, NY : Yen ON, 2019– |
Identifiers: LCCN 2019030466 | ISBN 9781975331542 (v. 1 ; trade paperback) |
    ISBN 9781975331566 (v. 2 ; trade paperback) | ISBN 9781975331580 (v. 3 ; trade paperback)
Subjects: CYAC: Fantasy. | Future life—Fiction.
Classification: LCC PZ7.1.T676 Wo 2019 | DDC [Fic]—dc23
LC record available at https://lccn.loc.gov/2019030466

ISBNs: 978-1-9753-3158-0 (paperback)
        978-1-9753-3159-7 (ebook)

10 9 8 7 6 5 4 3 2 1

LSC-C

Printed in the United States of America

CONTENTS

The Hidden Side of the Labyrinth Country

The souls of those who died in that sudden accident on Earth received a second chance at life in the Labyrinth Country. Even with the authority I do have, it's impossible to tell which Seekers have potential at the "reincarnate introduction" stage. I can, however, get a sense of how effectively they will use the new life given to them, or how long they'll stick around, by examining their lives before they were reincarnated—hence why I enjoy observing the reincarnates with my own eyes.

Guiding these newcomers is entirely unnecessary, but I do it simply because I get fed up with waiting and waiting. And there's one other reason: Arihito Atobe. I find it fascinating to watch the lives of interesting Seekers like him, from the very beginning to the very end. I was honestly quite pleased when I received the report that he'd moved up to District Seven, though I had to double-check that my own eyes weren't deceiving me. At the same time, I thought it could be just as bad if things went too smoothly. So many promising Seekers end up satisfied staying in the novice-inclined District Eight and quit seeking, with all their hard work and promise amounting to nothing.

We can never have too many excellent Seekers. Thankfully,

Arihito—I already like him and so have decided I can call him by his first name—is surrounded with the most hopeful and competent companions possible.

There's Theresia, a highly skilled Rogue well suited to the midguard position. As a demi-human, she has certain advantages that a human would normally lack. Considering how she came to join Arihito's group, you can easily call her the most valuable of his companions.

Then, there's the very capable Valkyrie, Kyouka Igarashi, who has all the capabilities necessary to be a leader herself but instead puts those capabilities to use as the party's deputy leader, in a sense. She did use Arihito for her every whim before they were reincarnated, which is one of the things about her that I quite dislike, but I may be able to let this slide if she continues to contribute to his party.

Additionally, there's Suzuna Shiromiya, whose abilities weren't widely acknowledged in her previous life, but she has been able to use her evil-banishing Shrine Maiden skills to great effect here in the Labyrinth Country. Her friend Misaki Nitou is blessed with the unseen talent of good luck and was able to choose the Gambler job, which makes good use of that.

They are joined by Elitia Centrale, whose talents in swordsmanship flourish here in the Labyrinth Country, despite the risks inherent to the cursed sword she wields. Her skills work well in tandem with Arihito's, and she is the party's primary attacker.

Finally, there's Cion, the silver hound; Madoka, the Merchant; and Melissa, who is well suited to be a vanguard but selected the less-than-desirable job of Dissector. Arihito is truly blessed; he was also assigned to one of the Guild's best caseworkers, Louisa.

Most important of all is that these individuals are "chosen" Seekers in the truest sense of the word. Any Seeker who finds the key to a reliquary is granted both the authority and the duty to view the hidden side of the Labyrinth Country—the side that no one knows exists.

They'll be here soon, at the path that leads from District Eight to District Seven. I already know what I will say to them: It shall be both a blessing and a guiltless curse.

CHAPTER 1

Starting in a New District

Part I: Those Who Forge Ahead and Those Who Fall Behind

The same purple-haired girl who had introduced us to the Labyrinth Country when we'd first been reincarnated now walked beside us as we continued down the pitch-black path leading from District Eight to District Seven. I looked at my license and saw that District Eight, which we had been in for less than a week since getting reincarnated, was shaped like a slice of a pizza, with the Labyrinth Country as the entire eight-slice pie. Or actually, maybe it was more like a donut—the Labyrinth Country's central region didn't have any information displayed other than GUILD-CONTROLLED ZONE. Perhaps that was where all the walls that divided the country came together.

It was only natural that we still had so much to learn. As I walked the path to District Seven, I felt a sensation similar to when we were teleported down the stairs into a labyrinth—

"...Your face tells me you've noticed something," the purple-haired girl interrupted. "I could just hide it, but I don't want you to suspect me of anything. So I'll explain."

"No, you don't have to do that… I just felt like something was off," I replied.

"Are you sure? That's unfortunate. I'm just so happy you've all come this far, and I wanted to explain some things to you." She was pretty cute but made some biting remarks. Maybe this wasn't the right analogy, but it was almost like she was a clown in disguise.

"I was just asking Ellie if we'd teleported since it was so dark this whole time, but then, we saw a light up ahead and… Uh, wh-what's the matter…?" Igarashi started to say, but the guide looked really annoyed, like she'd wanted to tell her, *I was going to tell him myself.*

"Haaah. Why are busty women always so insensitive? I bet all their energy is concentrated on maintaining the *larger* things, and there's not enough left for the finer ones."

"H-hey…! You were our guide when we got reincarnated, just like you were for Atobe, so why are you so nice to him but so rude to us…?"

"I'm not rude to *all* of you. Just you. I know all about your life before you were reincarnated. You'd always drop Arihito into the middle of projects because he was so good at what he did. If it were me, I'd have respected his own pace more…"

"Um, e-excuse me… No, actually, listen. Quit trying to mess with our party like that. Igarashi's already apologized for what she's done, and I've forgiven her." I didn't think she would have listened if I was more polite, so I spoke a bit more forcefully than usual. I thought I'd offend her, but she seemed amused and studied my face. I wasn't particularly wary of her, but I felt trapped when she closed the distance between us.

"You're so kind, Arihito," she said. "As your guide, I sincerely hope you don't lose that kindness here in the Labyrinth Country."

"I-I'm not kind… You're exaggerating a bit, don't you think?"

"It's no exaggeration. Kindness is about avoiding quarrels with others and wanting to protect your neighbors. Not everyone in the Labyrinth Country is like that. The more people there are, the more likely you are to meet someone who doesn't think like you do… I just want you to stay who you are, even when that happens." She faced forward, looking toward District Seven. It seemed to have a completely different atmosphere from that of District Eight—more oppressive. "I think we've chatted enough. I'll let Louisa show you around District Seven."

"Oh… Y-yes… Of course," said Louisa.

"No need to be so nervous, Louisa. Compared with *some others*, I'm very much an ally of the Seekers." The purple-haired guide looked younger than Louisa but didn't address her with *Ms.* or a formal title. Louisa seemed hesitant to even open her mouth in front of her.

"Um… I know it's rude to interrupt, but we're just so curious, so we have to ask," Misaki began.

"Who exactly are you…?" asked Suzuna. "You led us here and stayed with us until we got to District Seven. Why would you do that for us?"

"…You talk about Arihito like you're friends—do you like him?" asked Elitia.

The purple-haired guide straightened her cap before answering the questions that the three girls flung at her in succession.

"Couldn't you ask the same thing about anyone in the party? We simply wish to show our highest respect for the parties at the head of the pack. Keep advancing, rookies."

"Before you go, can I ask one thing?" I said. "What's your name? You seem to know about us, but we still don't know much about you. I'd like to at least know your name."

"Ha-ha... You're not all that smooth when it comes to women, I see. That argument isn't enough to sway me." It seemed even getting her name would be difficult. Despite that, the more she tried to hide it, the more curious I became. "I suppose you can call me Yukari. It's not my real name, but a fake one I've decided to use. How's that?"

"But why do you need to use a fake—? No, I get it. We'll just call you Yukari until we learn your real name." The name unexpectedly sounded like it might be Japanese in origin, but it wasn't totally unsuited to her. I couldn't do anything about her holding the real information back, so I just needed to remember to call her Yukari for the time being.

"No need to worry about something like my name right now. I'll give you a handsome reward if you meet my expectations and fly through District Seven the way you did in District Eight."

"Looking forward to it... I'll just leave it at that. Thanks for seeing us off."

"You're welcome. I do like how considerate and proper you are."

"Wha—?"

Mysterious and cryptic to the very end, the girl who called herself Yukari turned and headed back to District Eight. There really must be a teleportation spell in the path, because she disappeared suddenly.

"......"

Theresia seemed anxious about Yukari, because she was turned around, staring back at where she'd disappeared, but I tapped her on the shoulder, and she finally faced forward.

"What was that about…? I mean, she knew how incredible Atobe is. Maybe the people in whatever public organization the Labyrinth Country has are expecting a lot from him?"

"*Public organization*… Do you mean people on the management side of things? Louisa, is there an organization like that? Like a government?" I asked.

"There isn't a government per se, but there is a body that oversees all of the Labyrinth Country in place of a royal family," explained Louisa. "The Administrative Department, which oversees the walls that divide the districts, is a legislative organization that also manages the Guild. Which means that lady was one of the people who helps govern the Labyrinth Country."

Why would someone like that guide new reincarnates and also take a particular interest in us? Maybe there wasn't anyone who could mentor them other than someone in the Labyrinth Country's management. Regardless, Yukari didn't seem likely to tell us anything about the Administrative Department as long as she was still treating us like rookies.

"I'll lead you all to the Upper Guild in District Seven now," said Louisa.

"An upper guild? …There are multiple Guild locations in District Seven?" I asked.

"Yes. District Seven has a particularly high population compared with the other districts. There are approximately ten thousand Seekers."

"Ten thousand...?! That's almost three times the size of District Eight. Does that mean there are also three Guilds in District Seven?" asked Igarashi, and Louisa replied with a nod. Just as Igarashi said, there were multiple Guilds, and we were going to be working out of the highest one.

"I'll add that those ten thousand people are those who are continuing to work as Seekers in order to move up to the higher districts," continued Louisa. "There are an additional forty-two thousand people staying in District Seven... If you don't go on an expedition for a certain amount of time, your contribution points decrease. There are quite a few people who will then raise their contribution points slightly before letting them drop again over and over. Those people are counted in the total population of the Labyrinth Country, but they are not included in the ranking for District Seven." Meaning we ranked 294 out of 10,000 active Seekers, but there were another 42,000 whose contribution points would fluctuate and were therefore excluded from the ranking.

"If there are forty-two thousand Seekers, then...is it really that difficult to move up to District Six?" I asked.

"It is. The monsters in the District Seven labyrinths are significantly stronger than in District Eight. Many people are unable to handle even one of the labyrinths in District Seven, so they commute to District Eight or find a way to make their living outside of seeking expeditions. If they continue like that, their rank stagnates, and they're never able to make first rank in District Seven in order to move up to District Six."

It was almost impossible to climb the ranks in District Seven if you had to go back to District Eight to make a living. If you couldn't even make a living as a supporter, there was no way you could hope to make it to the higher districts, and you'd probably enter the labyrinths every once in a while to make some cash. I couldn't blame anyone who did that; better to live a normal life than to push your luck and get killed.

Our first fight with the monsters here would likely let us know whether this district would be a harsh ordeal for us or not. Even if it did turn out to be a difficult battle, we'd have to find some way through it. We had to advance to the higher districts no matter what.

"Arihito, I've already advanced to District Five once before, so let me take down any monsters from the front lines. If you can analyze the enemy while I'm attacking, we shouldn't end up stuck."

"Thanks, Elitia. We'll have to make sure we catch up to your level!"

We could live safely and happily in District Eight, but apparently, you couldn't rent lodging here if you were already renting in District Seven. However, if you bought a house, you could have multiple bases in different districts. That said, the average Seeker wasn't able to buy a house unless they'd opened a Black Box like we had.

The housing units in District Seven were taller than the ones in District Eight and built even closer together. The road leading to the Upper Guild was packed with people and lined with an inordinate number of adult entertainment shops, which clearly had no connection to seeking. I peered down one of the alleys branching off from the main road and saw a raunchy sign for one of them. I knew what kind of store it was but tried not to say anything stupid.

"Wooow, look at all the shiny signs everywhere! Arihito, is that one for a naughty store?" asked Misaki.

"Uh, I—I don't really know... I guess it's possible, b-but it's not necessarily anything n-naughty..."

"Well... As it happens, the Administrative Department allows all sorts of shops, some for men, some for women. I've only been to District Seven once for training, though, so I don't really know much about it," explained Louisa calmly, despite her blushing cheeks. I thought it'd be better if they kept the entertainment district out of the center of town, but maybe the population here was just too dense to really make that feasible.

The area we were walking through appeared to be home to a lot of people who'd dropped out of the ranking, but not many in the crowd looked like Seekers. There were even people sitting outside the taverns, starting their drinking this early in the day.

"There are thirteen labyrinths in District Seven," said Louisa. "These many labyrinths allows the district to support the large population on the goods from the labyrinths. Of course, they also purchase items from the other districts, given how many people reside here."

"Thirteen labyrinths... So are they really crowded?" I asked. "Labyrinths are pretty big to begin with, but I feel like that's too many people."

"Yes. That's why the Lower Guild issues numbered tickets,

which allow entry to a fixed number of people at a time. They provide tickets for six of the thirteen labyrinths, and only a total of one thousand people can enter per day."

In other words, if the people in the Lower Guild didn't do very well, they wouldn't be able to go into the labyrinths as much as they'd like. If they failed an expedition, they wouldn't be able to level up, and it'd turn into a vicious cycle.

Well, that was probably better than risking death. We had our own goals of turning Theresia back into a human and saving Elitia's friend, but plenty of people didn't have things they wanted to accomplish. They had no reason to push themselves and risk death on expeditions just so they could climb the ranks. All reincarnates were forced to become Seekers, but we could all choose how exactly we went about seeking.

"Seekers are divided into those who forge ahead and those who fall behind," said Elitia. "District Eight has a high proportion of the former, but you need more than the will to fight monsters to advance beyond District Seven."

At that, I turned around to see the people filling the streets around the Lower Guild. I wouldn't say their eyes looked as dull and empty as those of a dead fish, but none of them seemed full of life. They had no strong interest in trying their hand at the labyrinths; instead, they were focused on other things. They had found value in their lives in the Labyrinth Country. Would the day come when I'd break down and think of how I could live a simpler life?

My musings were interrupted when Igarashi cautiously whispered, so no one else could overhear, "We jumped up the ranks, so we're starting off at the Upper Guild, right? If so, we need to take every advantage of that environment. I'm sure we'll do great."

"You're right... I was just surprised at the number of people who'd given up. That's out of the question for us," I replied.

"Arihito, please don't hesitate to come and talk to us if you're ever feeling unsure," Suzuna offered. "I want to do everything I can for you. If it'll help you feel better, I'll even do what Ariadne suggested—"

"Nooo, Suzuuu! If Arihito takes you seriously, you're gonna be in real trouble... Ack, not you, too, Theresia! Curse youuu, Arihito!" cried Misaki.

"Listen to yourself, Misaki... Do you really think I'd do something like that?" I was pretty certain they all trusted me in that regard, so I was confident when I spoke, but for some reason, everyone looked at me funny.

"...You'll all be nearly inseparable, living under one roof going forward. As the only man in your party, Mr. Atobe, don't you think there would be certain, um...challenges?" Louisa asked me.

"...I'd be lying if I said it would be perfectly easy, but for better or for worse, I'm the party leader," I replied.

"You see yourself as a leader first and a man second...? I admire your resolve, Atobe... O-okay then, I'll do my best to be a Valkyrie before anything else, even a woman," said Igarashi, balling her hands into fists as she offered me encouragement. That's how we as a party formed our unbreakable, ironclad pact, which was something like a treaty banning any illicit sexual relationships.

I'm the only one the ban explicitly applies to, though... Besides, the girls don't worry about me struggling with any "challenges"... Or do they? Maybe some of the younger girls do...

"......"

Theresia was staring at me while these ridiculous thoughts ran through my head. I looked at her, but Igarashi was able to figure out what she was trying to express faster than I could.

"Theresia's fine as an exception. Even if she joins you in the bath, she knows you won't get any weird ideas. You're harmless."

"Kyouka, you reaaally do know Arihito super well," said Misaki.

"Er... N-no, not really... Atobe's an honest person, so I just figured that was the case." Honestly, I thought any man who felt absolutely nothing from a woman joining him for a bath was a problem in itself, but saying anything along those lines right now would surely backfire on me.

"I think it's less that he's harmless and more that he's trustworthy," corrected Louisa. "I wouldn't even worry about drinking too much with him around." Whichever was actually true, they didn't feel the need to treat me as a potential threat. I'd have to work really hard to support them and make sure not to lose their trust... Actually, I needed to commit myself to the highest possible standards.

More importantly, though, how were we going to tackle District Seven?

We approached the street that the Middle Guild was on and saw people talking outside equipment stores, people buying portable food to take into a labyrinth, people haggling down prices at an expensive potion shop, and a lot of Seekers with the spark of

ambition in their eyes. After continuing a short while, we could see the Upper Guild on the easternmost edge of District Seven. The first thing I wanted to do was see what the Seekers near our rank were like.

Part II: A New Encounter

The Upper Guild in District Seven took up multiple buildings. It was an attempt to prevent congestion, since it would be difficult to serve the number of Seekers here with one building. The building we'd be using was called Green Hall. As the name would suggest, its roof was painted green. Green Hall stood three stories tall, and every floor was divided into meeting rooms for Seekers and their caseworkers. We would be allowed to use the first floor. Parties ranked in the thousands used the second floor, while parties ranked in the two-thousands had to go up to the third floor—at least, that was the general rule, but a party could move between the various floors if they requested it.

"Good thing reception's on the first floor. That way, we won't have to bother moving around as much," said Igarashi.

"Especially since Arihito always does the reports on his own. The quicker he can come home, the happier we are!" said Misaki.

"…Hmm? You're not joking around? That's rare," I teased.

"Heeey, what's that about? You think I always just say ridiculous things?"

"That's the general impression I get, yeah. But maybe I'm wrong."

"How dare you! …Oh, are you trying to hide your embarrassment? You are, aren't you? You wouldn't say that seriously."

Perhaps we were so keyed up because we had just arrived in a new district, but it didn't seem all that bad if it led to this sort of sweet connection.

She continued, "You'll have to look after Suzu for me while I'm taking my break from seeking. In fact, I was hoping you'd get started on that right now."

"It'd be nice if the party could have more than nine people. Ellie, is there a reason we can't?" asked Igarashi.

"Any skills that work on your fellow party members won't work on more than eight people at a time. The ninth person could just be in their own party—but I don't think Arihito's skills would work on them that way, either."

I would have to use far too much magic to target a ninth person with Outside Assist, my skill that let me assist people outside the party. Anyone without my support would be at a significantly higher risk, so the safest move was to only go in the labyrinth with one party of eight. That wouldn't apply if we managed to get more members and could form a second party, of course.

"…Well, that's an option. We could consider going in as multiple parties. Louisa, did anyone do that in District Eight?" I asked. She seemed nervous in her new workplace but smiled happily when I spoke to her.

"Yes. Some people regularly go into the labyrinth with multiple parties—and not just to defeat powerful monsters like with Juggernaut. Larger groups like those often call themselves an 'alliance' or 'brigade' and act as an organization where Seekers help one another."

Elitia had been a member of the White Night Brigade before. We could join a group like that, or we could always create our own. Including me, we were already up to nine members. Depending on the circumstances, we could grow even further.

"Beginning in District Seven, parties often band together on labyrinth expeditions in order to reduce any risks," continued Louisa. "That doesn't necessarily mean they always work together, but having another party to collaborate with in the same labyrinth can completely change the outcome."

"A higher ranked party might ask for compensation for joining us, but we could probably team up with a party of a similar rank without having to worry about that sort of thing," added Elitia. "But the higher you go in the districts, the more likely there's going to be a clash of interests, and that makes it harder to build equal relationships." Maybe that was why Elitia was unable to find any parties willing to help her save her friend. I had a hard time imagining belonging to a brigade that refused to help people. After all, that would instead force those people to find other parties that were willing to accept the risks involved.

It would definitely be encouraging to know there were parties that you could work with. I didn't know if Polaris would be following us up the ranks, but I hoped we would meet other groups and build a friendly rapport.

So far, we haven't managed to get much info out of other parties. If possible, we should recruit someone who's good at negotiating and talking to people...

I suddenly looked at Louisa as the thought crossed my mind. I realized that as a Receptionist, she probably had a real knack for the art of conversation.

"Um... M-Mr. Atobe, if you have something serious to discuss with me, could we leave it until after work? My workplace here is still quite new to me."

"Oh... N-no, that's fine. Did I really look that serious?"

"Atobe, for a little while now, your eyes sometimes get this really sharp expression. Is that a skill or something?"

"Well, I have this skill called Hawk Eyes, so maybe that's it... It must be pretty scary to see me glaring all the time. I'll be more careful." I didn't know if it was because I was the only man in the group, but now that I was in an all-female party, my number one priority was gaining their trust. No matter how curious I was about Louisa's skills, I couldn't appear greedy.

"...Mr. Atobe, I am your party's caseworker exclusively. Please don't hesitate to ask if you have any requests of me."

"Exclusively?" I repeated. "Oh, I guess that makes sense. You moved up with us from District Eight."

"Yes, and I would like to continue doing so. The Guild has given me priority since you are such a promising group of new Seekers." Did this priority mean her work overseeing us would be put first? That would be nice... There were so many people in District Seven that I could imagine waiting for anything would be a hassle.

"All right," I said. "I won't feel bad about asking you for help since you're our exclusive caseworker. We're still new to this, but I do understand the value of our time as Seekers."

"That's good to hear. Because I work with only your group, I am also allowed to use the same lodging as you. I could live with you if you have the space for one more person."

"Oh, that sounds great. Then we could have evening meetings if we needed to."

"Y-yes... I'm sure you'll continue to be very busy, so please contact me whenever you need my assistance. I will add my contact information to your license." That contact function might be the single most useful feature our licenses had, but not everyone could use it. You needed a special skill. "My job, Receptionist, gives me a number of communication-related skills. I can only contact parties I've registered. I haven't registered any particular parties yet, so that shouldn't be an issue now that I'm exclusively working with you."

"Thank you very much. I'm really glad that we'll be able to consult with you whenever we need to."

"Y-yes... Me too... Even if it's not work-related...," said Louisa in such a low voice that I couldn't really make out what she was saying. Maybe she was just trying to tell us she was happy to keep working together as Receptionist and Seekers.

"Hey, Kyouka, what do you think this Contact skill does?" asked Misaki. "Like, will they be able to chat constantly and have a secret relationship...?"

"U-um... Atobe just said *consult*. It's fine—they'll just be using it for work."

"Your face doesn't say you think it'll be fine... Kyouka, if there's something bothering you, then you should just speak up and say it," said Elitia.

"E-Ellie, you're the one who looks bothered…," retorted Igarashi.

"Contact with Arihito… If I ask for Ariadne's help, then…," said Suzuna.

All the girls were talking secretly to one another. They were probably impressed by how handy this skill would be.

To be honest, though, I couldn't believe the day would come when a girl actually asked me for my number… Although, it was just for work, so I shouldn't read too much into it.

We entered Green Hall and waited in the lobby while Louisa prepared a room for us.

"There's more people with strong-looking equipment than there was in District Eight… I wonder where I can buy a spear like that," said Igarashi.

"The quality of goods sold here is better than what's sold in District Eight, but it's still not better than what you can find in chests or make from materials you get in the labyrinths," replied Elitia. "It is nice, though, to be able to buy replacement gear if yours breaks… Oh, but if you get a silver weapon, you could probably buy a new one. It's not a very hard material, but it's good for dealing with ghost-type monsters." Since she was the most experienced member of the group, we all listened to her explanation attentively. Her mention of materials made me realize something.

"Our Savior Ticket is made from a metal called crystium. Is that a metal that can be used for equipment? Not that we'd smelt it down."

"Very few forges have a furnace that can handle crystium, but I've heard it's a better material than the high mithril my equipment's made from. It can be found in a certain number of ores, but there's so little of it produced that it's very valuable. It's a bit wasteful to use it for equipment, so they use other, more widely available materials in the higher districts. There's glowing gold and heaven steel... Obviously, those are valuable as well, though." There were a number of metals more valuable than gold... Someday, I wanted to try out a slingshot or armor made of something like high mithril or better.

"Atobe, look... That big group of people over there—they seem like one of those party collectives we were talking about," said Igarashi.

"You're right, they do... Twenty-four people—that's three parties."

One of those people, a young man with gray hair, was talking to a group of girls standing in front of the notice board in the lobby.

"Kaede, are you still talking about finding other companions? Haven't I told you that if you join our alliance, we'll help bump you up to District Six?" he said.

"And I've told you that we'll find our own partners to work with. It's your fault that labyrinth's first floor is taken up by all your people and we can't get in," replied the girl.

That girl with the long sword, plus those two others... They look like they could be Japanese. Haven't seen too many Japanese people since coming to District Seven...

"Quit it, Kaede. Sorry about that; it's just, we've decided to recruit on our own...," said one of the other girls. The one called

Kaede appeared tough, which gave her a mature air, but she actually seemed to be around Misaki and Suzuna's age. Her black hair was pulled back in a ponytail, and the long sword she carried made her look like a kendo practitioner. The girl who'd stepped in to mediate when the gray-haired man and Kaede seemed about to get into an argument had short hair. Her outfit was reminiscent of a martial arts uniform, and she wore hand and wrist protectors. I figured she must be a Martial Artist.

"The most efficient way for you to get contribution points is for you to join our alliance and help us defeat monsters on the first floor of the labyrinth. If Roland's party passes the advancement test, they'll move up, and the space will be open in the ranking here. Just repeat the process and..." It sounded like he was suggesting they gang up on any old monster that showed up. Sure, it was safer to attack first whenever possible, but this just seemed *too* efficient.

"I'm sure that method would work, but we have no way to compensate you for allowing us to participate," said a third girl, gently mediating the conversation. She had sun-bronzed skin, and, well, I wasn't sure how else to say this, but she basically wore bikini armor. I wondered if that was really enough protection. She looked like a former competitive swimmer or beach volleyball athlete.

The fourth and final girl wasn't Japanese. She was young with very faintly blue-tinted silver hair and a leather case on her back in a very peculiar shape— Maybe it was some sort of club?

"Hey, that's just how my boss operates. Nothing I can do about it. C'mon, what's the harm in just joining me for drinks every once in a while if it means you'll be able to move up to District Six?" said the gray-haired man.

"Hmph… Out of the question. You think we're too stupid to see you're just using your leader as an excuse to get your hands on every girl in District Seven?" said Kaede.

"S-stop, Kaede, we don't want to cause trouble," pleaded the short-haired girl.

"Ibuki… Ugh, it just pisses me off so much! They can't just take over a labyrinth for themselves!" replied Kaede.

"We haven't taken it over; we're just being strategic. A Seeker will do anything to go up even one rank, right? We just prioritize efficiency—nothing wrong with that. All we've done is maybe make it a bit harder for other Seekers to hunt there."

"Tsk… The hell are you saying? You completely shut all of us out of the hunting areas! Everyone wouldn't have such a terrible time surviving if we could just hunt the crabs, but you—"

"You're only angry 'cause you're too weak. Weaklings only get in the way, taking up more of our time, even if they do repay us. Or do you disagree?"

"…This is ridiculous…!"

"I'm not trying to upset you. If you want to keep up the Seeker life, you can join our alliance for a little bit. But you'll have to think long and hard about how to make it up to me for all this time you spent turning me down."

That was about where I considering stepping in, but as the girl named Ibuki said, I had to be careful about causing trouble.

"Atobe… Hold back for now."

"Igarashi…" I looked at her. She was gripping the upper part of her left arm hard, like she was using the pain to hold herself back. Apparently, she was just as angry as I was.

"Fine. Our alliance will just stay in the Beach of the Setting Sun for another two weeks. Shouldn't be a problem if we just *happen* to kill all the monsters that appear there... Ha-ha-ha-ha!"

"Rrgh!"

I got the basic gist here: Kaede and her party had probably just come up to the Upper Guild and couldn't yet handle the more difficult labyrinths. Out of all the labyrinths that the Seekers at the Upper Guild could go to, the one that was best for efficiently earning contribution points was being taken over by that guy with the gray hair and his "alliance." He would let them join if they went out for drinks with them, but Kaede refused. I could see why. The gray-haired man wanted them—their bodies—in exchange for the convenience they'd get. He was being so brazen that he didn't even try to hide it.

"If you change your mind, you'll have to come to me this time. I won't let you talk to Roland even if you put me in a good mood... Ha-ha-ha-ha!"

He probably never thought he'd be able to convince Kaede and her party on his own. He was trying to have his way with them by using the power of his organization.

"...I can't stand it. Unbelievable that his group is one of District Seven's highest-ranked...," fumed Igarashi, as angry as if she were in their situation. The rest of the party seemed to feel the same, and that included me. I couldn't just oust all the people at the top of the ranks—something that felt extremely dubious to pull off.

So what could we do? First off, we needed to choose which labyrinth to start with. We didn't have to worry about this alliance if we could manage somewhere that wasn't the one they'd set up in. If we did end up in the same place as them, we'd need to figure out how we'd earn contribution points and handle the labyrinth. Would we be able to help Kaede and her party if they ran into a problem? We'd have nothing useful to offer if we weren't secure on our own two feet to begin with.

"…What should we do, Kaede?" asked one of the girls.

"No way I'm gonna butter up to those guys, sorry. I'd rather go back to District Eight and take the time to improve my skills if that's the only alternative."

"But…the monsters in District Eight don't give much experience. We wouldn't be able to spend much time resting between expeditions. We'd be working all the time but never getting strong."

"Look, Ibuki. You think you could stand letting them do whatever they wanted with you? I know I can't. I'd rather die than let a man I don't like put his hands on me. Right, Ryouko?"

"I wish I could say that won't happen here, but Roland's built himself a bad rap as long as he's been in District Seven… Although, I doubt they'd try and go for an old maid like me. You guys, on the other hand…"

"Ryouko, you're only twenty-eight. That's nowhere near old maid status."

"Thanks, Anna. Maybe it's all the new stuff I've been eating since becoming a Seeker, but my skin just seems way more youthful than it used to be…"

"Haaah… Ryouko, I know your skin is important, but first, we gotta figure out our plan of action," grumbled Kaede.

"For sure… Hmm… Ah!" said Ibuki, the girl with short hair, as she noticed us in the lobby with them.

"…Those folks new? That guy's weapon looks crazy strong…," wondered Kaede.

"Y-yeah, probably… Looks like they just got here."

"Hey… Think this is our chance? There's a lot of girls in the party and just that one guy in the back… He seems harmless… Or actually, he looks pretty serious. Don't you think so, Ibuki?"

"Huh? …I—I mean, not really. He doesn't seem nearly as chatty as that other guy from before. More like…some sort of dark and mysterious man in a suit…"

"No way… Ibuki, is he your type or something? You're not supposed to fantasize about real men once you're past middle school."

"N-no, that's…that's not what I mean. But we'll never be able to get more people to join us and go up against the Alliance if we don't trust any man at all…"

"We could try negotiating? I'm pretty much for it. I don't want to ask someone like Gray for help."

Well, I guess that was that guy's name, though I wouldn't have expected a gray-haired man to literally be named Gray. I really wanted to give him what was coming to him, but that wasn't what we did as Seekers.

I was about to head toward the notice board when Kaede and the three other girls walked in our direction. Kaede was in front, looking serious and knowing how important this matter was for them. It would end up being just as important for us.

Part III: A United Front

I couldn't tell which of the four girls was the oldest: Ryouko, the leader, or Kaede, the one up front. Louisa came back while I was pondering, but she guessed I was about to start a conversation with Kaede and the others and walked over to wait beside Elitia at the back of the party.

Kaede had what looked like a *tachi* sword hung behind her, but the shape of the grip was clearly different from that of a typical Japanese sword. I'd seen that shape before... That, along with her long, black hair that was pulled up into a ponytail, which made her look like a fairly sporty girl, gave me an idea of what her job might be.

Maybe a swordswoman...or kendo master? Some sort of Japanese sword user, if that's a thing here.

"Um... E-excuse me... W-we, we..."

"Sheesh... Kaede, you're so tense that you're walking funny. Not that I'm one to talk."

"Kaede, let's just calm down now. Remember, the Alliance is hogging the area where the crabs and fish appear, and we got attacked by those spiders and praying mantises when we went farther inland... We've hit our limits in terms of strategy."

"That labyrinth just has a ridiculous setup, that's all. How can it be called the Beach of the Setting Sun yet have so little beach? And everywhere else, you run into monsters way more powerful than the crabs." If there was a lot of fish and other sea creatures in the Beach of the Setting Sun, then we'd probably see them at the dinner table sometime. District Eight had sea monsters of its own, but there wasn't a huge variety. It'd be nice to try something new for a change…but maybe that was a concern better left for later.

"It's nice to meet you. My name is Arihito Atobe. We just came to District Seven today."

"Huh…? T-today? We…we only managed to get to the Upper Guild after working hard in District Seven for six months…"

"Back then, people said we were pretty fast, but I guess there's always someone better. By the way, this here is Kaede, and my name is Ibuki."

"Wh-what the heck, I was gonna do the talking! I'm not even that nervous! It's just that I was thinkin' he looks like an upstanding kinda guy!"

I'd found clothes to wear in the Labyrinth Country that were somewhat like a suit, and layered over that was my leather armor. I supposed I did look pretty formal.

"I'm sorry you had to witness that exchange earlier. You've only just arrived here, and you're already seeing us get in arguments with others."

"N-no… It's all right. Seekers are always competing. I imagine it's normal," I replied as Ryouko moved in front of the four girls. She was wearing a long boa coat made of fur, but under it really was bikini armor. She must get cold around town but seemed perfectly comfortable, like it was her usual equipment. I had a hard time finding a safe place to look. "You'll have to excuse me for strolling about in equipment like this at my age," said Ryouko. "This armor is surprisingly good for what my job can use. I wouldn't gain anything by changing. It's quite water-resistant and lets me move more quickly underwater…"

"I see...," I replied.

"Quit staring so much. She just told you some people need to wear equipment like that!"

"Erk... I-Igarashi, you don't understand—I'm actually trying *not* to stare..." Maybe I was a little too flustered just because it was a woman in a bikini. I turned around and was stung by everyone's glares. I really was more suited to being a rearguard and not being in the front.

The four girls looked to Igarashi with surprise.

"That armor of yours—it's so beautiful and strong-looking," gushed the one named Anna. "Kaede, you were talking about how you'd like some new armor soon. Would you want something like that?"

"Totally. So badass... I'm jealous. I still only have leather armor. Maybe that jerk from before wouldn't have given me such a hard time if I'd been wearing somethin' like that."

Since we had been lucky enough to find that in a chest, I hadn't realized how valuable other parties would see it. It really did seem that Igarashi's Ladies' Armor was quite priceless. Anyway, small talk was necessary for building good communication, but we had more important things to discuss.

"Forgive me, but I did happen to overhear what was going on earlier. So the group that man belongs to has taken over the good hunting grounds?" I asked.

"Y-yes. That's why we thought we would form a group with other Seekers, but since we've only just come to the Upper Guild, no one would join us...," said Ibuki, leaning forward as she expressed her frustration. She looked a bit boyish with her short hair and martial arts uniform, but she seemed innocent and unused to interacting with men, because her face was flushed red, and she wasn't entirely composed.

"We were thinking of checking out some of those places as well, but it would probably be a better idea to go into a different labyrinth if that one has been taken over. I would have thought monopolizing a labyrinth would be against the rules, so to speak, but I guess not."

"Y-yeah... But that labyrinth is something of a stepping-stone to greater achievements," replied Kaede. "The Guild even suggested we go there, but when we went, we couldn't actually do anything. It's ridiculous..." Normally full of such strong spirit, she slumped her shoulders forward, dejected that their plans had been ruined. Ryouko wrapped her arms around her and consoled her, so Kaede finally wiped her reddening eyes and smiled bravely.

"...All right, I've decided. I don't necessarily want any animosity between us and Roland's group, but how about we go into that labyrinth and hunt something other than the crabs?" I suggested.

"Uh... Bad idea. They're super strong. Like, way stronger than you'd think. We'll just end up hurt if we don't gain a level or two before fighting them again," said Kaede.

"We used a Return Scroll once when we were being chased by those monsters. They're far stronger than any of the other monsters we ran into while we were in the Middle Guild," added Ryouko.

There were monsters that were easy to earn from and others that were too dangerous, both on the same floor. If that was the case, we really were better off going into a different labyrinth. If we didn't raise our level and prepare good equipment, any attempt to beat the difficult monsters while we waited to find the monsters that gave good rewards would come with high risks. If possible, we could go do some test runs at one of the labyrinths that the people from the Middle Guild could go into as well. Besides, we'd only just come to District Seven.

"All right, it sounds like it'll be better to train ourselves in a different labyrinth first. Which ones have you explored so far?" I asked.

"We were looking for a sheep that has a material that I need for my weapon," said Anna.

"A sheep...?"

"There's a labyrinth called Silvanus's Bedchamber. The sheep's a monster that's supposed to appear on the second floor there. The Middle Guild suggested it, so we're allowed entry, but most people are too afraid to venture too deep. They usually stop at the first floor. We kept going to the entrance of the second floor and pulling back if it got too dangerous."

"Okay, do we want to try it out together?" I suggested. "It sounds like the monsters outside of that one group's jurisdiction in the Beach of the Setting Sun are too dangerous. I'd prefer we go somewhere safer so we can get a feel for working together. Afterward, we can think about how to deal with Roland and his group taking over that labyrinth."

"Ah... W-well...," Kaede stammered, her eyes wide.

I turned to Igarashi and the others in my party to see how they felt about the idea.

"Louisa, we don't have to go into the more difficult labyrinths just because we jumped over the other Guilds, right?" I asked.

"Of course not. Actually, the Beach of the Setting Sun is a

three-star labyrinth. Kaede's party and Elitia have met the requirements necessary to enter, but you and the rest of your party haven't. You'll have to earn a certain amount of contribution points in District Seven first." Elitia had told me that in order to become a three-star Seeker, you had to earn ten thousand contribution points through the Guild in District Seven. My total contribution points were over ten thousand, but that was what I had earned in District Eight; I'd need to earn that much in this district alone.

"In that case, we'll have to go into Silvanus's Bedchamber or a similar labyrinth anyway," I said.

"…Teaming up with us will likely make those people from before see you as an enemy. Are you sure you really want to work with us?" asked Ryouko.

"They'll probably move up to District Six and be out of that labyrinth if we wait, but I don't want to get stalled here," I said.

We needed to get to District Five to save Elitia's friend, who was still in the labyrinth there, and then we needed to get to the cathedral in District Four to turn Theresia back into a human. I didn't want to let Roland's alliance make us falter or even get us stuck in one place. Their method of climbing the ranks by bringing a large number of Seekers to hunt these crabs might be efficient, but we could consider going into other labyrinths.

"Thank you, Arihito," said Kaede. "None of us have any specialized skills; we mostly focus on attack skills. Even so, I hope you won't mind working with us…"

"We're the ones who'd be grateful to work with you. Would you mind having a meeting before we head to the labyrinth?"

"Of course not. I'm Kaede Akiyama, by the way. Nice to officially meet you," she replied, holding her hand out. I shook her hand, and she beamed happily.

Louisa let her coworkers know she was leaving before showing us to a meeting room. She gave us enough water for all twelve of us, plus a bowl of water for Cion to drink from, and we watched as he lapped it up. Ibuki and Anna both liked dogs and were happy to watch.

"Um, Kaede, are you and the other girls about our age?" asked Misaki.

"Yep! Ibuki was saying the same thing before. I was in the kendo club, and she was in karate club. Ryouko's a swimming instructor, and Anna's a tennis player."

"Ha-ha, guess this means I've got even more daughters now," joked Ryouko.

"H-hey... I'm around the same age as you. I'd feel better if you called me a little sister instead of a daughter...," Igarashi protested.

"Really? I thought you weren't that far off from the other girls. Ha-ha, in that case, we'll be the grown-up ladies." Ryouko was only twenty-eight, one year younger than me. Her confident sexuality must be thanks to various life experiences.

As of now, we weren't having any problems working together, but I reminded myself we'd likely need time to adjust fully to the situation.

"Your party has such a variety of members, Mr. Arihito. You even get along with a lizardman, which is quite remarkable. We hired a mercenary once before, but he couldn't communicate at all," said Anna.

"All he did was listen to our commands, which made me feel bad. Theresia's totally different from him, though. Sometimes, he'd look at us like we were slabs of meat. If it weren't for that ownership symbol he had, like with other demi-humans, I thought he might get angry at the people who hired him," said Kaede.

"Wow, really...? Theresia and I worked really well together from the very beginning, so I decided to add her to the party. She's a good person."

"......"

I said that in hopes of relieving any negative impressions they might have toward demi-humans, but I could see Theresia turn red. Everyone else noticed and smiled awkwardly.

"I'm surprised you can say such embarrassing things with such a straight face. No way I could," said Kaede.

"Nothing embarrassing about it. I think it's incredible... Oh, by the way, I just had a thought—since we're all younger than you and we're going to be working together, you don't need to be so formal with us. I think it's nice that a man like you would try to be so polite, but there's no need," said Ibuki.

"Well, sure, if you're okay with it. You and Kaede seem really close; did you guys know each other before you were reincarnated?" I asked.

"We got reincarnated around the same time, and I started talking to her in the square outside the first labyrinth I was about to go in. It was kind of hard, though, since Kaede can be really shy around strangers."

"Hey, what're you talkin' about? *You* were the shy one, Ibuki! She's got a great punch, but she's as gentle as a baby deer."

"We met these two in the Sleeping Marshes labyrinth. Anna and I had been working together for a while before that...," explained Ryouko.

Anna added, "I'm ever so grateful to Ryouko. I owe her my life."

Every Seeker had their own history leading up to this point. That was normal, of course, but hearing it like this made me feel something; it made me remember the time I spent with my party.

"A lot has happened for us, too. I don't think I can ever pay Atobe back for what he's done...," said Igarashi.

"Yeah, yeah, you two can't just make your own little world. Stop fawning over each other in front of people we just met; they'll never be able to trust us if you do. It'll aaall just blow up in your faces!" said Misaki.

"Ha-ha, how I wish I was that young. Just watching you lot makes me think of my earlier days," said Ryouko.

"Y-you know... Atobe is twenty-nine, so he's older than you."

"What...? N-no way... I was sure he was barely old enough to be a new college graduate or something." She gave me the impression she was more interested in older men, but it wasn't really my place to be analyzing her.

"I know everyone is still getting to know one another, but I'd like to start the preparations necessary for you all to head into the labyrinth," Louisa piped up. "When you go into Silvanus's Bedchamber, each party's contribution points will be calculated separately. There is a bonus for working together, but I will explain that once you've returned." I had a faint feeling that she might have interrupted to rein in Ryouko, but maybe I was just assuming it was about me.

The parties we were working with were displayed on our licenses. I let Theresia view mine since she didn't have her own, while I checked out the information on Kaede and the others.

```
◆Cooperating Party 1◆
Party Name: Four Seasons
1: Kaede    Kendo Master         Level 5
2: Ibuki    Karate Master        Level 5
3: Anna     Tennis Player        Level 4
4: Ryouko   Swimming Instructor  Level 5
```

CHAPTER 2

The First Labyrinth of District Seven

Part I: Prior Information

Kaede Akiyama, Ibuki Kasuga, Anna Winters, Ryouko Natsume—the inspiration for their party name, Four Seasons, came from their own surnames: Akiyama was written with the kanji for *autumn*; Kasuga with *spring*; and Natsume with *summer*; then obviously, there was Anna's last name.

"We didn't notice for a while after Ibuki and I joined together. Once we met Ryouko and Anna, we thought, *Wow, what a coincidence!*" said Kaede.

"Arihito, your party doesn't have a name yet, does it? It isn't showing on my license," said Ibuki, very casually letting me see. Their licenses indicated the parties they were working with as well, so our party would be displayed there. My job would probably be displayed strangely. Ibuki didn't really react to that, though. I didn't think there was anyone who had written and been accepted as a rearguard before. Maybe she just wasn't that concerned with other people's jobs.

"Arihito... What is this job? The words on my license have gone strange," said Ryouko.

"Huh? ...What does it say?"

◆Cooperating Party 1◆
Party Name: Unregistered
1: Arihito   ○□—×   Level 5

It looks different... But the display still won't show it. Guess it really isn't an ordinary type of job.

Regardless, it appeared *rearguard* wasn't going to be displayed even when looking at it on other people's licenses. Whoever was in charge of selecting a Seeker's job in the Labyrinth Country was a mystery to me, but I must've put down something it hadn't considered...or maybe I was reading too much into it.

"Arihito's job is one where he protects everyone from behind. He's a really dependable leader, so that's sorta his job...or something like that. Even Kyouka's accepted him as our leader. She goes on and on about how great he is behind his back, so he's pretty awesome," said Misaki.

"H-hey, that may be true, but you can't just go saying that in front of people. You could just leave it at *she really trusts him*," said Igarashi.

"Oh... S-so, is that really true?" asked Ryouko.

"I just knew they were a couple! They really do give off that vibe," said Anna.

"We're not," protested Igarashi. "We just used to work at the same company. Then, we both ended up in the same accident, a lot of stuff happened, and Atobe let me join his party," she explained calmly. She folded her arms and glanced at me every once in a while, but all I could do was try to show her I didn't have a problem with what she was saying. The others didn't need to know what a strict boss she had been for now.

The first thing we needed to do in order to be able to use the hunting grounds in the Beach of the Setting Sun, or to secure other means of fighting in the labyrinths, was to quickly get a sense for how it felt to work together. That's what I was thinking when I realized Anna was staring at me. She was quite petite, so it felt like she was looking up at me, directly into my eyes.

"When you say *protect from behind*, does that mean you have a support job?" she asked.

"Yeah, you can think of it like that. By the way, I feel like Tennis Player is a pretty rare job... Do you fight with tennis serves and smashes?"

"Yes, I generally hit a ball with a racket. I need some rare materials if I want a better racket, so it's been pretty difficult. I used a wooden one in the beginning, but the strings were weak, and I couldn't hit with my full force."

"I've heard serves can be very fast, so you would likely improve your strength a lot if you could get good equipment. The rest of your party have sports-related jobs, too... Since you're a Kendo Master, do you know sword skills?" Elitia asked, and Kaede pulled the weapon from the sack on her back. "Is that sword...wooden?"

"Yep. I can use steel swords as well, but I find a bamboo sword the easiest to use. Wish they made bamboo ones here. This is a Wooden Sword + I found in the labyrinth, so it's not as easy to break as you'd think," explained Kaede. If she could increase her damage through skills, she didn't necessarily need to use a sharpened steel sword. We had Misaki, who used dice to fight, and I wouldn't call her damage so low that it was useless.

There was also Ryouko, the Swimming Instructor, who wasn't even carrying a weapon. The Labyrinth Country had magic, so she could probably use special skills related to water.

"I can't use my skills if there's no water, so I always carry a bottle of water with me. It's best if there's water in the labyrinth already, though…"

"The Beach of the Setting Sun is a place where Ryouko can best use her abilities. She's superfast when she swims. Even if we were to run as fast as we could, she'd swim faster," said Kaede. A swimmer in the Labyrinth Country wasn't a simple athlete. It was exciting to imagine she'd be even more powerful in battles that take place in the water. Although, to be honest, I wanted to avoid fighting aquatic monsters as much as was humanly possible.

"So your party has made it this far from exploring labyrinths that had water?" asked Suzuna.

"Both District Eight and District Seven have labyrinths with water in them. Silvanus's Bedchamber is a field, but it's got some bodies of water here and there. Since we've met Ryouko, we've been choosing those kinds of labyrinths. One of the reasons we've come this far is because we've been able to earn contribution points where others might not be able to," answered Ibuki.

I wanted to ask about her job as well, since I had the chance. It was more normal to see Seekers who used weapons. People rarely fought barefisted.

"Ibuki, you fight using karate, right? Is that... I mean, how do you actually fight like that?"

"Ha-ha, you need courage to fight a monster without a weapon, don't you? Well, what I've been using since I've come to the Labyrinth Country isn't your normal martial arts. Boxers can shoot punches by using magic. I can do something similar, so I've managed to get by."

"Do you mean you shoot out laser beams and stuff?! Whoooa, that's so cool! I wish I could shoot laser beams now that I've been reincarnated," said Misaki.

A lot of characters in fighting games carry similar projectile weapons, but I bet there were a lot of people who fantasized about being able to shoot out beams if they pushed their mastery of a martial art to its limits. In reality, it appeared there were Martial Artists who could use their aura or magic or whatever to do it—I was starting to see Ibuki's abilities in a new light.

"Oh, u-um... It's really not that cool."

"Don't be silly, Ibuki! Your Wave Thrust is awesome for taking out monsters. You've saved our skins so many times," said Kaede.

"B-but...it's only helpful because it ignores a portion of the enemy's defense," said Ibuki. I could see from their conversation that they'd used their own individual strengths to make it this far.

"Arihito, I've been thinking. Could I maybe join Four Seasons for a bit so we can all seek together?" said Misaki.

"I thought you were going to take a break? If you're feeling worn out, it's better to rest than to push yourself."

"Are you sure you won't need my skills while you're seeking?"

"Well... Are you really okay?" I could still support her if

needed since I had Outside Assist, but I would worry about her if I couldn't keep an eye on her at all times.

"I'm sure. I'll just be tagging along; I won't get in the way. Would everyone in Four Seasons be all right with me joining for a little while?" asked Misaki, standing up straight and speaking properly for once. Kaede and the other girls agreed.

"Since we'll be seeking in two parties, we won't have monsters coming from behind as easily. It should be fine as long as you stay in the rear," replied Ryouko.

"Ibuki and I will make sure the monsters don't get past us to you. You can just support us when you think you can," said Kaede.

"Okay! I'll be really careful and do my best to help! Arihito, cover me if you can manage it!" said Misaki.

"Well, if push comes to shove, I can do that. Just make sure you stand in front of me." I reminded myself that I could support Kaede and her party with Outside Assist if I needed to as well. I would have to pay attention to where I was in relation to everyone else, though, since my skills wouldn't activate if I wasn't behind them.

Louisa wrote a letter of introduction for us, and we headed to Silvanus's Bedchamber with the Middle Guild's permission. There was an open square in front of the entrance to the labyrinth, which was south of the center of District Seven. It seemed like one of the more popular labyrinths from among the ones that the Middle Guild suggested, since there were a lot of food stalls in the square. They filled the area with the scent of baking bread and roasting meat. We had a quick meal at one of the stalls before we went, then bought some portable food and water to take with us.

Madoka possessed a requisite Merchant skill called Inventory 1. Apparently, it let her put up to fifty items into her rucksack, regardless of their size and weight. Since water was a necessary item, we could ask her to carry it without getting weighed down.

"That's an amazing skill... Did you use it to load up and carry around all your equipment back when you were selling stuff at your stall?" I asked.

"Yes, I did. Roughly fifty or so items were enough to cover almost anyone's needs in terms of weapons and armor. Every day, I'd make a few adjustments to what I brought before setting up my stall."

"...I can carry defeated monsters with my Dissector skills," said Melissa. "We get a Repository skill, so I can do almost the same thing as Merchants. I can't send living creatures, though. That could be abused. You have to use special tools to send living monsters to the Monster Ranch." I thought both skills were incredibly useful, but it meant there was overlap. Neither had doubts about taking it, though; they were required for both of their jobs. And thanks to that, our lives as Seekers had gotten way easier. So far, we had just sent things to our storage unit if we weren't able to carry them, but that meant you couldn't retrieve them easily if you wanted to use them. Now we could have Madoka bring potions so she could get them to us quickly.

"Arihito, mind if I tell you about the monsters on the first floor before we go in?" Kaede offered.

"That'd be great... You sure, though? Info like that has to be really valuable."

"We're the ones who wanted to work with you—I'd feel bad if I didn't do this at least. Don't worry 'bout it." Kaede pulled a notebook out of her bag. When she opened it, I saw a number of drawings that looked like monsters, with notes on what kind of enemy they were.

Is this...a mole? It kinda looks like it's wearing a helmet...

"Don't mind the pictures too much. I ain't that good."

"No, these are great! You get a real sense of what the monster actually looks like."

"Y-you think...?" Kaede had a fiery spirit, but she looked cute and innocent as she blushed from my compliment.

I realized Suzuna was staring at me with a cheerful expression as I talked to Kaede. It was her normal bright smile, but for whatever reason, I felt kind of intimidated.

Part II: Silvanus's Bedchamber, First Floor

I continued to flip through the pages of Kaede's notebook until I found one monster that looked like a rhinoceros beetle.

"This one's called a Fake Beetle. Looks like a huge rhinoceros beetle," explained Kaede. "We haven't beaten one yet 'cause they fly away if you approach 'em directly. I've heard they need to gather a lot of nutrition during their breeding season before they'll attack anything."

"Freaky... Hey, let's have Suzu take those down for us with her bow," said Misaki.

"Arihito's slingshot should be able to hit enemies at a distance as well," Suzuna replied. "But if there's no need to fight it anyway, it's probably best to just leave it at that…"

Kaede's drawing wasn't very detailed, perhaps because she only saw it from far away. There was a note saying, *It flew away so I didn't get a good look.* I assumed the handwriting was Kaede's. The uniform size and shape of the characters showed a methodical side to her.

"We've gone as far as the second-floor entrance… Once you get there, sheep-type monsters begin to show up," said Anna. "The material I need for my racket is actually the intestines of that monster."

"Really…? Oh, right, like catgut," I said.

"Um… So what kind of special attacks can all of you use?" asked Ibuki. "They say it's best if you can put a monster you've never encountered before to sleep, or slow it down, but we aren't good at anything like that. Ryouko's the only one who can use attacks that inflict status ailments."

"I can add a number of different effects to my attacks through magic stones," I replied. "I can also stop an enemy's attack by Stunning them. I can Confuse them, Poison them… Just leave all that stuff to me."

Everyone in Four Seasons was staring at me in admiration. We'd found quite a few magic stones, but maybe they hadn't been lucky enough to find any.

I was thinking about how chests usually contained magic stones when I remembered: We'd gotten quite a few stones from the Black Boxes, but we also had two red chests and one wooden chest, which was dropped by a Fear Treant, none of which we had opened yet.

"What's wrong, Atobe? You look bothered," said Igarashi.

"No, something just slipped my mind. We'll set it aside for now and take care of it when we get back."

"Wooow, Arihito, you sound so capable and cool!" gushed Misaki. "Like you're gonna get real serious. Ooh!"

"Misaki, you're going to be joining another party, even if it's just temporary. Maybe you should tone this down a bit...," I said after rustling her hair.

"...Must be kinda nice gettin' your hair tousled like that," said Kaede.

"So lovely, so youthful! I'm trying to remember if anyone ever did that to me... Guess not," said Ryouko. I had been trying to warn Misaki, but for some reason, the members of Four Seasons were all blushing and looking at me. Maybe I'd gotten caught up in Misaki's behavior and done something the girls considered stepping over a line—I gotta hold myself back a little more.

"......"

"...Theresia?"

Theresia stared at me, then touched the top of her lizard cap with her hand, though I couldn't really stroke her head. Actually, I had no idea that was what she actually wanted.

"Oh, right," said Kaede. "You guys cool with making this just a day trip? A lot of parties in District Seven do multiday expeditions, but..."

"Yeah, that's fine for now," I replied.

"Don't forget, I can carry camping equipment in my Inventory should we need it," Madoka reminded me. If, for some reason, we did need to stay in the labyrinth during an expedition, we'd start to have problems with day-to-day necessities like changes of clothing, but…the girls did seem prepared for those issues to an extent. I didn't think anyone would be entirely against doing that if we needed to.

"We'd need a change of clothes at the very leeeast… Don'cha think, Kyouka?" said Misaki.

"F-for me…I'd at least want to be able to take a bath and not just cover up any smells with perfume," replied Igarashi.

"…Good. I'm glad we're all in agreement about that. I mean, some people think it's totally fine not to take a bath every day," said Elitia. She seemed to place a lot of importance on cleanliness, but I didn't think we'd have many opportunities to take a bath in the labyrinth. If only there was some sort of portable changing-room-type equipment—I bet Seekers would kill to have something like that when camping.

The entrance to Silvanus's Bedchamber resembled a cave. There was light coming from the other side, and it felt like we teleported when we passed through, because the atmosphere seemed different. The Field of Dawn had been a fairly flat and vast field, but this labyrinth had hills, dips, and valleys. The sun shone brightly from high in the sky, and the sky itself was so blue that I felt like it snapped me awake. Flowers bloomed throughout the field, adding dots of purple amid the plentiful green grass.

"It's a bit like the lavender fields in Furano."

"Yeah, that's what I thought, too. I've been there once before, but I don't remember much since I was just a little kid then."

Maybe it was a little off the mark to call a labyrinth *picturesque*, but it was only in that moment that I realized this could be one of the perks of the Seeker life. The Shrieking Wood had been really unsettling, so I was thankful this labyrinth was bright and sunny instead.

"What should we do, Arihito? Should we start by fighting a monster?" asked Ibuki once we'd all stepped into the field. "Not that you can afford to drop your guard around here, though."

After Theresia confirmed with me that no monsters had entered her scout range, I answered. "For now, let's head toward the entrance to the second floor and deal with any monsters we run into on the way."

"Sounds good. That way, we can get experience while making progress," said Kaede.

"All righty, Arihito, we're off... Oh, Cion? Nooo, you're in Arihito's party! You can't follow me," said Misaki as she and the other party took the lead. Cion, our guard dog, seemed concerned. Actually, I would feel better if Cion did go with Misaki.

"Cion, use Covering to guard Misaki if anything targets her, but only if you can," I ordered, and Cion replied with a woof before taking the lead to protect Misaki. If one of my party members was moving along with another party, I could still support them if I needed to, as long as I was still behind them.

I was the very last in the battle formation. In front of me were Suzuna, Madoka, and Melissa. Madoka held a *sasumata*, a Japanese polearm used more for controlling the enemy's movements than actually killing them. She still didn't have any attack skills, so I told her to use Hide if we started fighting.

We had been walking for a little while when Suzuna turned back to me and smiled. As the leader, I probably should tell her to focus on seeking, but I decided I shouldn't be so strict.

"What's up? You've been in a really good mood since this morning," I said.

"Yes, thanks to you. This place is so beautiful," she replied.

"Yeah, it is. I'd want to take a nice stroll around the place if there weren't any monsters..."

"......!"

Theresia was the fastest to react thanks to her Scout Range Extension 1 skill. I had thought the skill only increased her range a small amount, but she noticed the enemy before the leading party with Kaede did.

"Ah... Wh-what the...? The ground is shaking!" cried Igarashi as she nearly lost her balance, then activated Mirage Step when she sensed the incoming danger. Elitia had readied herself to use Sonic Raid at a moment's notice.

"—Okay, guys, let's do this! Be careful; the enemy's underground!" I shouted, activating Morale Support 1. Mounds of earth formed on the surface as something came our way.

"—Shit, they're working together! There's two coming!" called Kaede.

"Wha—?!"

◆Monsters Encountered◆
GRAND MOLE A
Level 5
Dropped Loot: ???

```
Grand Mole B
Level 5
Dropped Loot: ???
```

The rumbling that shook the ground was joined by another tremor. The first monster erupted from the ground in the front, near Kaede and the others. The ground mushroomed up as the second crossed toward us from the right, on a path to attack.

"GRRAAAAAAHHH!"

"Urgh...!"

"Elitia, I'll support you!"

```
◆Current Status◆
> Arihito activated   Defense Support 1   ⟶  Target:
                                             Elitia

> Grand Mole B's attack hit Elitia
No damage
> Grand Mole B followed with Mud Blast  ⟶  Hit
                                            Elitia
```

"Guh!"

The attack got through. The monster was able to do more damage than what Defense Support 1 could reduce. Either that, or my skill only applied to the first attack. There was a huge difference between whether this Mud Blast did over eleven points of damage or if my Defense Support 1 didn't work on the second hit.

Elitia still had plenty of vitality left, but she was clearly wounded. Even single-digit damage left scrapes and bruises on her.

No attack is too small to ignore... Best to avoid taking a direct hit whenever possible. No, better yet—keep the attack from happening in the first place!

"Grrr... You won't get away!" shouted Elitia as she tried to counterattack, but the mole looked at her with what was almost a taunting smile before diving back into the earth. The fact that it could toy with her like this likely meant she'd worked her way up to the higher districts through the other labyrinths, without having fought this monster. Whether or not you knew how the enemy moved could have a huge impact on how much of a threat it was.

Is it a good idea for us to try and lure out an enemy that can hurt even Elitia? ...Wait, Four Seasons has fought this monster before! They ought to have a good strategy we can use.

"Guys, fall back!" yelled Kaede. "I'll make us an opening! ...Yaaah!!"

"GRROOOHHHH!"

The mole—which was significantly bigger than a human and more like a bear—burst from the ground, scattering dirt everywhere and slashing out with its claws. Just as I thought it was going to hit someone, Kaede, sword in hand, leaped backward so fast that she left an afterimage in her place.

◆Current Status◆
> KAEDE activated GO NO SEN ⟶ Will move first
> KAEDE activated KAKEGOE ⟶ Intimidated GRAND MOLE A
> KAEDE activated HIKI KOTE ⟶ Hit GRAND MOLE A
> GRAND MOLE A's attack strength fell

"GRROOOH!"

A loud crack pierced the air, followed by a horrific roar that you wouldn't believe came from a mole. Kaede's attack threw off the Grand Mole.

"Kaede, switch with me!" shouted Ibuki.

Kaede yelled back, "No, you won't make it!"

◆Current Status◆
> Ibuki activated Brick Break
> Grand Mole A activated Burrow ⟶ Nullified Ibuki's attack

"Aw man, I was so close...!"

"Get back! We'll take the next opening!" called Kaede.

It was hard to get the timing right for a sequential attack since the enemy could evade so quickly. Misaki and Cion were keeping a close watch on the monsters' attacks, in order to prevent the girl from getting in harm's way.

"Uh, um... Any little bit helps... Hyaa!" she hollered.

◆Current Status◆
> Misaki activated Dice Trick
> Misaki activated Lucky Seven 1 ⟶ Success
> Grand Mole A's speed fell

"...Doesn't it feel like it's gotten slower?" asked Ibuki.

"Now we might just manage this...," said Kaede. "Next one's on you, Anna!"

"Got it!"

The monster swam through the ground, veering every which way. My concentration jumped up a notch when I tried to see the members of my party in the distance, so that I could support them if need be.

◆Current Status◆
> ARIHITO activated HAWK EYES ⟶ Increased ability
  to monitor the situation

Nice—now I'll be able to take advantage of opportunities to support them as well... But first, we need to handle this one!

"Come forth, Demi-Harpies—come!"

◆Current Status◆
> ARIHITO summoned HIMIKO, ASUKA, and YAYOI
> HIMIKO activated LULLABY
> ASUKA and YAYOI activated MUSICAL ROUND
> GRAND MOLE A resisted SLEEP
> GRAND MOLE B fell ASLEEP
> MUSICAL ROUND continued LULLABY's effects

"Whoa... Did Arihito just summon a bunch of monsters?!" asked Kaede.

"It's all right; these Demi-Harpies are our allies! Don't worry about them and keep fighting!" I replied. The Demi-Harpies took to the air and circled above us as they began to sing. However, they only managed to put one of the Grand Moles to sleep.

"Die—!"

"…!!"

"Here I go!"

"Do it, Arihito!"

The underground beast that had been trying to attack us stopped in its tracks. Everyone understood without me having to tell them that we needed to take it down with our combined attacks right now.

Trying this out here is risky…but let's see how far Attack Support 2 will go!

The set damage from Attack Support 1 had been invaluable up to this point, but this time, I used my newly learned Attack Support 2. This would let me stack my attack onto my allies'. I could learn plenty just from trying to add my magic stone strikes and seeing exactly what that would do.

"Everyone, I'll support you!"

I pulled back my slingshot, envisioning what a follow-up attack was going to look like in tandem with everyone else's. I could even select what support method to use.

◆Current Status◆

> Arihito activated Attack Support 2 ⟶ Support
  Type: Force Shot (Stun)

> Elitia activated Double Slash

> Kyouka activated Double Attack

> Theresia activated Wind Slash

> Suzuna activated Auto-Hit ⟶ Next two shots will
  automatically hit

We could pull off some incredible stuff using Cooperation Support with attack chains like this... I really want that skill!

I imagined what we would be capable of with that, but for now, I was just shocked at what happened when I used Attack Support 2. I'd followed my allies' attacks with a full-strength blast of my own, adding my Force Shot (Stun). It was almost like one of those laser beams Misaki talked about had appeared from thin air to join with my companions' attacks.

◆Current Status◆

> Total of 7 attacks hit Grand Mole B ⟶ Attack Support 2 activated 7 times

> Grand Mole B was Stunned 4 times ⟶ Stun time increased

"GROOO...OHHH...!"

Elitia came from the left, slashing the mole twice. Igarashi charged it from the front, jabbing it two times with her spear, and Theresia threw a Wind Slash at it from the right before falling back again. Suzuna pierced it with two arrows shot in quick succession. The monster snapped out of its slumber and let out an enraged roar, but it was Stunned, leaving it defenseless.

Elitia was about to lash out again to finish it off, probably planning to use a Blossom Blade to make sure she put an end to it, but that would take too much of her magic, considering this was our first battle in the labyrinth.

"—Melissa!"

She should have been near me, but she had rushed quite far

ahead. She brandished her butcher's knife and caught up to the mole instantly.

"I can do this... I'll split that thing's helmet...!"

◆Current Status◆
> Melissa activated Knife Artistry ⟶ Increased
  probability of Partial Destruction
> Melissa activated Helm Splitter ⟶ Destroyed
  section of Grand Mole B
> Grand Mole B's weak spot was exposed
Additional Force Shot (Stun) attack
Weak spot attack
> 1 Grand Mole defeated

"GRO...OOOOOH..."

Melissa struck the Grand Mole's head with her butcher's knife, splitting open the helmet-like structure on top. Following right behind was a hit from my Attack Support. It seemed Dissectors were skilled at finding and exploiting the enemy's weaknesses. Also, Melissa's butcher's knife was a far stronger weapon than what any other level-3 Seeker might wield—another factor in this attack's success.

There was one mole left. It was slowed by Misaki's skill but still trying to attack, this time heading for Cion as it dug through the ground. But Cion was ready for it.

"GARGRAAAH!"

Let's use a different status effect this time... How about Confusion?

◆Current Status◆

> GRAND MOLE A attacked
> ARIHITO activated ATTACK SUPPORT 2 ⟶ Support Type: FORCE SHOT (HYPNOSIS)
> CION activated TAIL COUNTER ⟶ Hit GRAND MOLE A
> GRAND MOLE A was CONFUSED by ATTACK SUPPORT 2

"GRAR... GAH..."

Cion's attack was powerful enough to send the Grand Mole flying backward. After it skidded across the dirt, it started to move differently from before. That was the Confusion kicking in.

"Let's use the chance Cion gave us!" shouted Ibuki.

""""All right!"""" replied the rest of their party, piling attacks onto the mole before they lost their opportunity. First up was Kaede.

"Haaah!"

"Here we go!"

◆Current Status◆

> KAEDE activated KI-KEN-TAI
> KAEDE attacked GRAND MOLE A
Critical hit
> RYOUKO formed AQUA BALL
> ANNA activated AQUA FLAT SERVE ⟶ Hit GRAND MOLE A

"GAARAARRR!!"

Kaede landed a solid strike with her wooden sword, then Ryouko formed a ball, drawing the liquid from her bottle, which

Anna served straight into the mole. The moment the Aqua Ball smashed into the shrieking monster, it exploded into a pillar of water. They had incredible coordination.

◆Current Status◆
> GRAND MOLE A deployed an emergency evasion
> GRAND MOLE A activated GROUND STOMP

"Agh!"

Just when I thought they'd be able to defeat the creature with their series of attacks, the mole started stampeding around. Ibuki had been moving in to attack and couldn't stop herself.

"GRAAAAAH!"

"Please, God...!"

I decided I needed to use Outside Assist to protect Ibuki with Defense Support, but in that moment, I heard a voice.

"Master, might I suggest that the best defense is a strong offense? I'd like you to use me to test out Attack Support 2."

It was Murakumo, the sword strapped to my back. I drew the sword without a second thought.

"Ibuki, I'll back you up!"

"Rrgh... Take thiiiis!"

◆Current Status◆
> ARIHITO activated OUTSIDE ASSIST
> IBUKI activated WAVE THRUST
> ARIHITO requested temporary support from ARIADNE
> ARIHITO activated ATTACK SUPPORT 2 ⟶ Support
   Type: GUARD BLADE (BLADE OF HEAVEN AND EARTH)

The mole shook the ground and slowed the attacks coming at it, but even so, Ibuki's strike came in a moment before the monster could react. Right when I swung my sword down, the earth split at the mole's feet. The slash from my blade had struck the enemy from above, before gouging a hole into ground. However, that wasn't enough to split the mole's helmet-shaped head.

◆Current Status◆
> Grand Mole A was hit
> Attack from Guard Blade (Blade of Heaven and Earth) ⟶ Hit Grand Mole A
> 1 Grand Mole defeated

The earth shuddered with the impact, and the Grand Mole collapsed backward.

"Did we...do it...?" asked Kaede.

"I—I thought it was gonna get me...," stammered Ibuki. "Why is the ground so smashed up...?"

"...I heard Mr. Arihito's voice, and then, something happened the same time you attacked... So did he do this...?" wondered Anna.

"I-incredible... Who knew a job like his even existed?" said Ryouko. "And I was so rude because I didn't understand it..." They had supposedly fought a Grand Mole before, but all of Four Season's members seemed relieved they had finished the fight without injury. My party managed to come out unscathed as well. Elitia's scrapes had healed completely once Recovery Support 1 kicked in. She sheathed her sword and turned to me with a smile.

"You really can help us out with any weapon… I knew you'd be able to use your slingshot, but you can even use that sword…"

"Atobe!" called Igarashi.

When I used Attack Support 2, it consumed enough magic for one strike and added it to all my allies' attacks. That was nice to know, but just a single use of Blade of Heaven and Earth drained quite a lot of my magic. It was so low, I almost passed out.

"……"

"O-oh… Sorry, Theresia," I said. "I'm always making you worry…"

"……"

She ran to me and propped me up right as I was about to fall over. Madoka also came out from where she'd been hiding. She opened her eyes wide when she checked my status on her license, and she handed me a blue potion.

"It doesn't matter how much vitality you have; you can't go on with your magic that low," she said.

"Sorry, I'll be more careful… I think this sword will have to be a last resort." I was happy that Murakumo had suggested I use the sword, but now, she'd become quiet. I guessed she also hadn't realized how much of my magic it would consume.

Even though potions were so valuable, I couldn't very well do without one, so I accepted it from Madoka and drank it. I only needed half to bring my magic up to full.

I think my max magic is up to about sixty points after having eaten the Apple of Wit. That means one use of Outside Assist with Force Shot uses about five points, and Blade of Heaven and Earth uses around twenty points…

Attack Support 2 could drain my magic quite a lot depending on what attack I was supporting with. It made me realize how convenient Attack Support 1 was, but the addition of status ailments could greatly affect the flow of the battle. It was vital that I understand when it was best to use which skill.

"Oh… I-it dropped a wooden chest! Arihito, a chest—it dropped a chest!"

"It's been a while since I last saw one of those…but really, it belongs to Arihito and his party. They helped us out so much," said Ryouko.

"No, it's fine. You keep it, since it's such a find. If there's any equipment in there that we want, we can negotiate for it," I said. It was the mole they'd been fighting that dropped the chest, so I thought it would be obvious that it belonged to them…but for some reason, all four girls were looking at me incredulously.

"B-but, it's a *chest*! You basically can't improve your equipment without the equipment or magic stones that come from chests, right?" said Kaede. "Everyone would be scramblin' to get their hands on this."

"Ah-ha-ha… And we're no different," said Ibuki. "But we only beat that monster thanks to your party."

"You should actually just let us negotiate if there's anything we want. This chest is yours, Mr. Arihito," said Anna. I should probably keep quiet that Misaki being there made it more likely for chests to appear. Seeing how valuable they were, other parties would try to force her to join them if they found out about that ability.

"How about we decide who takes what when we get back? We don't need everything, so we can decide later," I suggested.

"That sounds good. Thank you. Ah, Atobe, I'm so embarrassed; I can't believe I decided you were harmless just based on your appearance...," said Ryouko. In the beginning, she'd just called me by my first name, but now, she was being more respectful and calling me by my last name. Maybe part of it was that she learned I was older than her. It actually made me pretty happy, since she made the switch after fighting with us.

"It was kinda reassuring to hear a manly voice cheering us on. Thanks, Arihito," said Kaede.

"I'd like to thank you as well, u-um... Teacher!" said Ibuki.

"...Is this the latest trend, calling Mr. Arihito by different names?" asked Anna.

Perhaps Ibuki was calling me Teacher since I supported her and split the ground with my attack. But that was only because of Murakumo's high attack power; my own wasn't nearly that powerful. I had a feeling she got the wrong idea there. I couldn't very well tell them all about the Hidden Gods, though, so I couldn't correct her.

Speaking of which, I wasn't sure it had been a good idea to show them the protection we received from a Hidden God, as well as my trump card that was Guard Blade...but considering how the Grand Mole would have hurt Ibuki while she was in danger, I didn't regret doing it.

"B-by the way... I get the feeling that skill you used when you saved me is...probably your secret technique, so I definitely won't tell anyone about it! I will always keep your teachings safe!" said Ibuki.

"W-well, uh... Thanks, I appreciate that. But really, calling me Teacher is maybe just a little bit much."

"S-sorry... It's just, you saved me, and I really respect you..."

I got the impression there was another reason why she started calling me that, but pressuring a girl and her emotions wasn't wise.

Anyway, I used the key for our storage unit to transfer the chest. I spoke with Kaede and her party about what to do with the materials from the moles' bodies, and we decided to put them in Melissa's Repository.

"One of them is almost completely intact. We'll get good materials out of it. The broken parts can't be used, so I will be more careful for next time," said Melissa.

"You were so brave, Melissa! You just came in and hacked that mole's helmet apart with your butcher's knife before Ellie and I could get another attack in," Igarashi cheered.

"Yeah, I was surprised," agreed Elitia. "I can't believe you have that much attack power at only level three!"

"It's because of this knife. My dad got it to save my mom," said Melissa.

Her mother was a demi-human who was currently seeking with another party in hopes of finding a way to lift the curse and make her human again. Rikerton probably got that weapon for seeking so that he could save her himself, and that goal was passed down to Melissa. I truly hoped both Melissa's mom and Theresia could return to their former selves.

Even the Demi-Harpies didn't have unlimited magic, so I sent them back to the Monster Ranch for a rest. The Fake Beetles here were a higher level than them, so they would be in danger if the insects attacked from the air.

"...Speak of the devil. Is that a Fake Beetle over there?" I asked.

"Ah… And there's a Grand Mole, too," said Kaede. "It'll probably come this way if we end up in a fight again."

"All right, let's split up… Misaki, mind joining us again?" I asked.

"Suuure! I feel like I was at least a little helpful back there!"

"You really were. Come and fight with us again sometime," said Kaede. It might have helped that they were close in age, but they seemed to be getting along quite well. When they thanked her, Misaki blushed like crazy before coming back to join us.

"Atobe, since I have Wolf Pack, should Cion and I transfer to their party together?" suggested Igarashi. Her Valkyrie skill Wolf Pack increased her abilities as long as she was in the same party as Cion. If possible, it would be best to keep them together.

"Yes, but be careful. I'll support where I can. Let's do our best, everyone!"

""All right!"" the girls replied as they gathered around—they couldn't be too loud or they'd attract nearby monsters. I activated Morale Support to shore up their spirit. I was hoping to save the Morale Discharges for the sheep monster on the second floor. Things were going well at the moment, but I wanted to keep moving forward with caution.

Part III: The Paradox

After defeating the two Grand Moles, we continued carefully across the uneven ground. There was one Grand Mole at the top of a hill on our right and a monster flying directly ahead of us. I was able to clearly tell how far away it was thanks to my Hawk Eyes, but it looked far more massive than any beetle I'd ever seen.

"Just how big can Hercules beetles get...?" I grumbled absentmindedly.

Suzuna dutifully answered, "U-uh... Maybe about six inches, I think...?"

Misaki and Elitia heard the exchange as well and chimed in while they looked at the airborne monster.

"I mean, it's called Hercules, right? I thought they could get up to, like, a whole foot."

"...I think the largest is closer to eight inches. Right now, that monster might look like a speck of dust, but when it gets closer... it'll probably be bigger than us..."

We'd fought quite a few monsters that were bigger than us so far, but this Fake Beetle was way bigger and a different color from any rhinoceros beetle I'd ever seen. The shape was pretty similar, though. What really threw me for a loop was the additional horn sprouting from its back.

...So is it fake? Like a rhinoceros beetle but not really? We won't get anywhere just looking at it, though.

"......"

Theresia turned to Four Seasons, Igarashi, and Cion, who were surrounding the Grand Mole to our right. Igarashi must have discussed her position with Kaede and Ibuki, who were vanguards in the party, because now she was in the midguard position. I wondered what they were going to do, then saw that she made a doll with her Decoy skill and used Force Target to draw the mole's attention, before they leaped at it with a joint attack.

"—GROHHHH!!"

"—It worked! Now's our chance!"

"Let's go, Ibuki! ...Hyaaa!!"

"Haaah!"

"I'll support you guys!"

I tacked Attack Support 2 onto their assault as they rushed in, and I also added the status ailment Confusion, which I now knew was effective on Grand Moles.

◆Current Status◆

> Arihito activated Outside Assist

> Kyouka activated Decoy

> Kyouka activated Force Target ⟶ Target: Decoy

> Grand Mole attacked Decoy

> Kaede activated Suri-Ashi

> Arihito activated Attack Support 2 ⟶ Support Type: Force Shot (Hypnosis)

> Kaede activated Enpi ⟶ Hit Grand Mole

> Ibuki activated Crescent Kick ⟶ Hit Grand Mole

> Attack Support 2 activated 2 times ⟶ Grand Mole was Confused

They could keep the battle under control as long as they could get that status ailment in. Since the mole was Confused, Anna and Ryouko guessed it might activate Ground Stomp, so they racked up damage from afar. Cion avoided an attack from the Confused mole, then hit back with a Tail Counter. They could win safely with how things were going.

"Suzuna, let's attack that thing. Can you manage from this distance?" I asked.

"I'll try... Countless Gods, I ask you to guide my arrow with the light of the sun..." There was no way an arrow would make it that far if shot normally, but if we took the explanation for her skill Auto-Hit as it was, we knew that her next two shots were "guaranteed to hit their target." Since it was our one and only attack before it came at us, I added Attack Support 2 to it. I couldn't use the Blade of Heaven and Earth since it drained too much of my magic, but I was prepared to take it out if push came to shove.

As I ruminated over our battle plans, Ariadne's voice called out to me.

"For humans who have not trained much with the Stellar Sword, a certain amount of time must pass after activating it before you can use it again. There is no limit to the number of times you can use Guard Arm, but it does consume magic every time you do. Also, once your party's combined level reaches twenty, you will gain Guard Variant, a higher skill, though you can only wield its full power if you have the shield part and someone equipped with it in the party."

"Guard Variant"? I should keep that in mind... Guard Arm and Guard Blade are more than enough right now, though.

I wanted to practice attacking with the Stellar Sword—if only I had the time. I could normally use my slingshot to attack, which didn't take any magic, then improve my sword skills for when we needed it. It made me realize how convenient it was that my rearguard job let me equip any weapon, regardless of whether it was close- or long-range.

But for now, I needed to deal with the enemy in front of us. Four Seasons would likely come rejoin us once they'd defeated the mole they were up against, but there wouldn't be anything wrong with beating our target before they did.

Suzuna took in a deep breath and nocked an arrow. I heard the string stretch as she pulled it back. After a moment of tension, she opened her eyes and released the arrow.

"Strike your target!"

"I'll support you!"

As long as she used Auto-Hit, two consecutive arrows would hit their target. If I activated Attack Support 2 both times, I could hit the monster with two different status ailments.

It takes a lot out of me, but since we don't know how strong the enemy is, we need to do everything we can in the first volley!

◆Current Status◆

> Suzuna activated Auto-Hit ⟶ Next two shots will automatically hit

> Arihito activated Attack Support 2 ⟶ Support Type: Force Shot (Hypnosis)

> Suzuna's attack hit ?Out-of-Range Monster

No damage

> Arihito activated Attack Support 2 ⟶ Support Type: Force Shot (Poison)

> Suzuna's attack hit ?Out-of-Range Monster

> Attack Support 2 activated ⟶ ?Out-of-Range Monster was Poisoned

It was so far off in the distance that I wouldn't have been able to tell what happened without my Hawk Eyes, but I could see that both of Suzuna's arrows hit the Fake Beetle.

Confusion didn't affect it...but Poison did!

I didn't know how much it would reduce its vitality points, but I expected it to help. Or maybe, since it was so far away, we could even wait from afar until it was weakened—

"Here it comes...!

"......!"

Something was wrong. I didn't know what, but the size and shape of what I saw with my Hawk Eyes sent a shiver of dread running down my spine. I regretted not checking with Kaede and her party what the monster was.

```
◆Monster Encountered◆
★PARADOX BEETLE
Level 6
Hostile
Dropped Loot: ???


◆Current Status◆
> ★PARADOX BEETLE activated SCREW DIVE
```

We didn't have long to savor our advantage when the attacks hit at long distance, because the massive beetle came hurtling straight at us, fast as a meteorite plummeting to earth.

"Wh-what...?" said Kaede. "We...we n-never saw this thing here before..."

"R-run! Teacher, an enemy like that will kill you!" shouted Ibuki. It wasn't the Fake Beetle we thought it was. It had a ★ before its name, meaning it was a Named Monster. For better or for worse, we'd grown used to encountering Named Monsters. But the same couldn't be said for Four Seasons.

The beetle crashed down at full speed, whipping up a gale in its wake. I could tell by the four girls' terrified expressions that they were certain we would die.

◆Current Status◆
> KAEDE, IBUKI, ANNA, and RYOUKO were FRIGHTENED

"Y-you guys... Run! Your party, too, Atobe! Hurry!" Ryouko shouted to us.

"Mr. Arihito, this enemy is too strong! It's too dangerous to fight it!" called Anna. Just because they'd been reincarnated and fought countless monsters didn't mean they were immune to fear. Actually, their reaction was appropriate. We simply weren't capable of taking an attack like that.

We could remove their Fear status with Mist of Bravery... No, first, we need to survive this next attack... That should give Four Seasons some of their courage back...but who...

"Nooo—it's coming again! ...Everyone, run!"

"M-my feet won't move!"

"Kaede, Ibuki!" called Ryouko.

The massive beetle loomed over them almost like it were laughing at them, their Fear status having rendered them immobile. The monster flapped its transparent wings rapidly and rose again into the air.

```
◆Current Status◆
> ★Paradox Beetle activated Screw Dive ⟶ Target:
                                              Theresia
```

"Run, Theresia! It's after you!" I cried.

"......!"

My heart skipped a beat. I instinctively knew that if I made the wrong decision, I could lose my friend.

I won't let that happen!

My vision went red—I didn't even have time to breathe before my brain kicked into overdrive and I made my decision.

"—Ariadne, I request your help!" I shouted.

```
◆Current Status◆
> Arihito requested temporary support from
  Ariadne ⟶ Target: Theresia
> Ariadne activated Guard Arm
Blocked ★Paradox Beetle's attack
```

I definitely saw it—the moment before the beetle struck, a mechanical arm appeared in the monster's path in response to my request. There was an earsplitting boom from the high-speed collision as it veered off course, plummeting into the earth somewhere to the side of its target, Theresia.

"Ack!"

The impact was powerful enough to form a crater in the ground. I protected everyone from the resulting blast with Defense Support, but I couldn't support myself. However—

"......!"

—Theresia stood in front of me, covering me as she held her targe up. The moment the attack had been deflected, Theresia's highest priority was protecting me.

◆Current Status◆
> Screw Dive produced Blast
> Arihito activated Defense Support 1
> Elitia, Theresia, Suzuna, Misaki, and Melissa took no damage

"...The heck was that just now...?" asked Kaede.

"Arihito shouted... And its attack was knocked off course...," said Ibuki.

"...Was it luck...or did Atobe do something...?" wondered Ryouko.

Four Seasons stood there dumbfounded. They had no idea what had just happened. If so...

"I'll protect you all even if that thing comes after you," I told them. "We ought to be able to win this if we take it seriously... So please, don't be afraid and help us fight!"

"...Mr. Arihito... Why would you go this far for us...?"

◆Current Status◆
> Kaede, Ibuki, Anna, and Ryouko recovered from Fear status

We managed to get past the first major threat, but the battle was just beginning now that they knew I could still stop the enemy's attacks.

The beetle was upside down, its gigantic horn thrust into the ground. It was covered in a thick, glistening carapace, all the way to its feet, which ended in sharp, hooked claws. It looked just like a rhinoceros beetle with heavy armor on. It used its arms as much as it could, barely managing to reach the ground as it dragged its claws into the dirt to extract itself. It flung its body over and righted itself, brandishing its vicious horn. Its carapace was a silvery color, and it glittered like it was made of a metallic substance.

"L-look at that massive crater... Urrrgh...," Misaki muttered in total shock.

"I doubt people regularly run into monsters this powerful here... Otherwise, there'd be far more victims," said Elitia. I could see from her profile that the blood had drained from her face, but she immediately collected herself and drew the Scarlet Emperor from its sheath.

This monster was most likely a Named version of the Fake Beetle. I looked at my license and saw that it had a surprising name. We should have been more cautious when it had just come up as *Out-of-Range Monster.*

"......"

"...Theresia."

She seemed to guess what I was thinking just by looking at me, because she shook her head, then pressed her fist to her chest. She was saying she'd follow my orders.

"Thank you for covering me. You really saved my neck back

there… We don't want to have to come across a monster like this twice."

"Should we test to see if it can hurt me even with your support, or should we just avoid it…?" Elitia asked me.

"If we leave it be, it'll attack anyone who comes in the labyrinth after us. It doesn't sit well with me knowing we made it hostile and then ran."

"…Madoka, you hide. I might hinder the party as well, but I have a skill called Partial Destruction that's effective against bug-type monsters. I want to try it," said Melissa. The other party had been wearing down the Grand Mole. I checked how far they'd gotten it down before the beetle attacked, but they would likely still need another ten or twenty seconds of fighting.

We need to keep this thing from targeting that party. We need to flank it. Should I go ahead and try…?

"Uh, Arihito, the monster seems…different," said Suzuna.

"Huh…?" I looked up and saw that its entire surface was turning purple. Even its eyes, sitting at the base of its horn, were purplish.

◆Current Status◆
> ★Paradox Beetle took damage from Poison
> ★Paradox Beetle was affected by Poison ⟶ Took damage equal to 10% of its maximum vitality

A weak cry came from the creature's mouth, and I made a guess.

"…It's heavily armored, but maybe in exchange, it actually has fairly low vitality?" I wondered.

"Oh, that's right…"

"Ellie, did you just remember something?" asked Igarashi.

"…I've never defeated an enemy with Poison, but I have heard that monsters with strong defense are often weak to it. Some people Poison them, then buy time until their targets die. That's why long-lasting poisons are sold for more than poison runes on the market," she explained.

I wasn't sure I would generally choose to use that strategy of waiting while the Poison slowly wore down the monster's vitality, but I guess there really was no reason to directly fight a monster this large and heavily armored.

"If that's what we're going with…let me bring up the rear as we disengage."

"You can't stack Poison, so I do think that's the best option while the current Poison works at it. I'll use Sonic Raid to lure it while everyone else runs ahead."

"Um… We'll be fine as long as we're in front of Arihito, right?"

"Yeah. If it goes after you, I'll get Ariadne to help protect you like I did before… This battle is one of patience. Let's go, everyone!"

"""Okay!""" they chimed back, coming to an agreement. Elitia was the only one who faced the enemy now, moving so fast that she left a blur in her wake.

"—I'll tear you to shreds…!"

◆Current Status◆
> Arihito activated Attack Support 1

```
> ELITIA activated SLASH RIPPER
> ★PARADOX BEETLE activated PROTECTION SHELL
> ★PARADOX BEETLE nullified ELITIA's attack
```

I had a feeling an enemy like this would appear eventually. It blocked Elitia's blade with its armor, as you would expect from its appearance, and it used a special skill to defend against the set damage of my skill.

"Grr... Not another monster immune to physical attacks!"

"It's okay, we just need the Poison to wear it down! Pull back, Elitia!"

"Understood...!"

"—KYEEEAAA!"

Elitia deflected the beetle's attack, leaped backward, then came next to me, sped up by her skill. I signaled with my eyes, and she moved ahead of me. The ten-foot-tall beetle followed easily, flying low in the sky, but that's where my weapon and skills would be useful.

"Stop right there!"

```
◆Current Status◆
> ARIHITO activated REARGUARD GENERAL  ⟶
   Abilities improved based on the number of
   party members
> ARIHITO activated FORCE SHOT (STUN)  ⟶  Hit
   ★PARADOX BEETLE
> ★PARADOX BEETLE was STUNNED
```

The magical bullet from my black slingshot struck the beetle's face with a sound like gunfire. Even though that magical bullet was strengthened from the effects of Rearguard General, I saw it strike the enemy's carapace and bounce off. The Stun from the gaze stone that I added to the shot apparently activated even though the damage done was negligible. The beetle's wings stopped moving, and it dropped to the ground, indenting the soil of the field where it landed.

If we just keep that up... No, doesn't look like it'll be that easy!

◆Current Status◆
> ★Paradox Beetle countered with Anti—Magic Shell
> Reflect Magic trait added to ★Paradox Beetle's shell
> ★Paradox Beetle was damaged by Poison

"Uh, wha...? Arihito, what's happening...?"

"—Magic won't work on it anymore! Meaning, run! We'll let the Poison take effect!"

"Okay...!"

"......!"

Thankfully, it hadn't targeted Madoka while she was hiding. No other parties had come into the labyrinth yet, either. I didn't like the idea of this beetle thing going after someone who happened to be here at the same time.

I turned back while I ran and saw Igarashi with her spear and Cion on top of a hill in the distance.

I'll back you up!

"Let's do this, Cion!" urged Igarashi.

"Woof!"

"—Ryouko!" called Igarashi.

"Yeah…!"

◆Current Status◆

> Arihito activated Outside Assist, Attack Support 1

> Kyouka activated Double Attack

> 2 stages hit Grand Mole

> Cion activated Wolf Rush

> 4 stages hit Grand Mole

> Total of 6 stages hit Grand Mole

66 support damage

> Ryouko formed Aqua Ball

> Anna activated Aqua Scud Serve ⟶ Hit Grand Mole

Blindside attack

11 support damage

> 1 Grand Mole defeated

The Grand Mole took a total of six attacks from Kyouka and Cion as they worked together. Anna and Ryouko then circled around behind the mole and shot a ball of water at its back. This was different from Ryouko's previous move—it followed a straight path and made a fierce impact. The mole took it right in the back of its head, before falling flat on its face.

I'd been able to successfully support their party when they needed it. Now we just needed to finish what we started. The Poison on the Paradox Beetle cut its vitality by 10 percent of its maximum amount every ten seconds, which meant we would be able to beat it if we could just outrun it for a little under a minute and forty seconds—but right around when we were taking a quick breather, we saw something different about how the beetle moved.

◆Current Status◆
> ★Paradox Beetle activated Accelerated Metabolism
> ★Paradox Beetle's status ailments were removed
> ★Paradox Beetle transformed

"The Poison is gone…!"
"KYEEEAAAAH!!"
Its entire body glowed red like it was on fire, and bits of its carapace broke off—actually, it was intentionally removing unnecessary parts to speed itself up as much as possible.

◆Current Status◆
> ★Paradox Beetle's attack power and speed rose sharply
> ★Paradox Beetle's defense fell
100 seconds until annihilation

It must have been close to dying…but now it's brought its remaining time up to 100 seconds!

It was determined to chase us down. We all felt dread looking at the changed beetle. Monsters in the Labyrinth Country really didn't ever want to give us an easy time.

"Arihito!" cried Suzuna.
"Ugh…!"

```
◆Current Status◆
> ★Paradox Beetle activated Blast Horn
> Arihito evaded
Additional damage from impact
```

If my abilities hadn't received a boost from Rearguard General, that would have been a direct hit. I reacted immediately when Suzuna warned me, but the arm of my suit jacket was torn, and I felt pain. Did it vibrate its horn to generate a sound that it attacked with? Thank goodness no one was running in front of me. A line had been carved into the field from the invisible attack.

I don't know if I can dodge the next hit... I can't simply rely on my allies' intuition to warn me about incoming attacks. What should we do...? What can we do...?!

"......!"

"—Theresia!"

```
◆Current Status◆
> Theresia activated Double Throw
> ★Paradox Beetle activated Horn Swipe ─→ Nullified
  1 long-range attack
> 1 stage hit ★Paradox Beetle
No damage
11 support damage
```

"—GYEE!"

For some reason, it wasn't using its arms—only its horn to

swipe away the dirks Theresia threw. She had staggered her throw, hitting it with the second dirk and making it flinch ever so slightly as it took the set support damage.

Wait... Something's off. It still has armor on its arms, but it only defended with its horn. Is that thing particularly sturdy or— No... it's something else, something...

I recalled the beginning of the battle. Did something happen when I added Attack Support 2 to Suzuna's first attacks? The second arrow hit and poisoned it, but I couldn't see an arrow stuck in the monster's body or a wound from where the arrow struck. It was called Paradox Beetle. It had developed arms it could use for defense but didn't. Was that because it couldn't react that fast with them? If so, why?

Suzuna's arrow struck the thing's front... So this entire time, what I thought was the monster's back is actually its front!

The part that Suzuna's arrow and my Attack Support 2 hit was, from where we were, its back, which we couldn't see. We should be able to take it down if we piled attacks on there. I didn't know exactly how fast it could move now, but it was worth aiming for its weak spot since I knew it was there.

"Elitia, the spot Suzuna's arrow hit should be on that thing's back," I said.

The fire grew in her eyes before I even asked if she could hit it.

"...Someone would need to draw its attention. I won't force anyone to take that risk."

"You're right... I'll leave it to your best judgment. If we fight it straight on like this, it'll still take damage from my support. Its horn can't stop more than one attack at a time."

"Good suggestion, but we don't know what it'll do when it's

backed into a corner. We should finish it off as quickly as possible... Yeah." She grinned. Even in tragedy, she would not despair—her expression was graceful and powerful, and just looking at her gave me courage.

"I'll lure it. Arihito... Things might get dicey, but just hold on until the end."

"Yeah. We'll probably end up leaving the labyrinth after this fight... But we need to make sure we finish our first joint seek with a win."

Could the level-9 swordswoman, admittedly stronger than what you'd expect in this district, surpass a level-6 monster that was fighting with its every last ounce of strength?

I took a deep breath so I wouldn't mess up our final attempt. There was Theresia, Suzuna, and Misaki, who was gripping her dice in trembling hands after having done nothing but flee. The other party was running this way from behind the Paradox Beetle, which was trying not to waste any of its remaining time left. Elitia readied her scarlet sword and rushed straight toward it, her golden hair fluttering in the wind.

Part IV: Beneath the Underside

"—Let's do this, you piece of shit!"

Elitia raced off like a golden gale, plenty fast enough at her base speed, but she let out a dauntless shout not quite suited to her appearance and sped up even more with her skill.

It may just be Elitia's personality, but people do seem to change in battle… It brings out their fighting spirit. I couldn't ask for more!

"Elitia, I'll support you! Everyone, stay on your toes!"

"""Got it!"""

◆Current Status◆
> Arihito activated Attack Support 2 ⟶ Support Type: Force Shot (Stun)
> Elitia activated Sonic Raid
> Arihito activated Morale Support 1 ⟶ Party members' morale increased by 11

I can't get their morale up to a hundred in this battle, but I have to keep it up!

Just then, the unarmored Paradox Beetle started emitting a bloodred steam. It wasn't the sort of thing that had an effect on the things around it—it was more like the steam from an engine that was fueled with the creature's own life.

"—KYEEEEAAAAAH!!!"

◆Current Status◆
> ★Paradox Beetle activated Final Stand ⟶ Vitality decreased; attack power and speed increased
> ★Paradox Beetle activated Razor Horn

It was fast. I couldn't make out its attack even while trying my best to follow it with Hawk Eyes. Yet somehow, Elitia, sped up with

Sonic Raid, managed to barely avoid the attack by swinging herself up into the air. The beetle's horn looked like it sliced through the head of the afterimage she left in her place. Everyone held their breath. I was the only one who could see that she had actually evaded, counterattacked, and gotten out of there.

"—Ellie, it still has a decent amount of time left! Finish it if you can!" I shouted.

She was around the side of the beetle, but her follow-up attack was terrifying. Right before her Sonic Raid cut out, she leaped up, then activated another Sonic Raid, before lashing out with a series of counterattacks into the gaps in the beetle's defenses that no normal person would ever be able to see.

"FREEEEEEZE!"

◆Current Status◆
> Elitia activated Blossom Blade
> Stage 1 hit ★Paradox Beetle
Resisted Stun
> Stage 2 hit ★Paradox Beetle
Resisted Stun
> Stage 3 hit ★Paradox Beetle
Resisted Stun

"GYEE... GYEEE..."

The Stun wasn't working. Was it immune to status ailments now? Only one Stun needed to work out of the twelve stages, then the other party closing in from behind would have a clear shot at its weak spot.

"...I always... Right at the most crucial moment... Rrgh!"
I could feel her anger and frustration; even now, I could see her
fragility—and yet, she never felt inferior, and she never gave up.

Our party always fought together; it had always been that way,
and it was how we'd gotten through as much as we had.

"Ellie, I'll help you! ...Strike your target!"

"Here's a Dice Trick and a Lucky Seven! Cheating is awesome!"

"......!"

The three girls combined their long-range attacks and struck
the Paradox Beetle after it bounced back from Blossom Blade,
before it could return a counterattack, and they used what skills
they could.

I'll support you all!

◆Current Status◆
> Arihito activated Attack Support 1
> Suzuna activated Auto-Hit ⟶ Next two shots will
  automatically hit
> Misaki activated Dice Trick
> Misaki activated Lucky Seven 1 ⟶ Success
> ★Paradox Beetle's status ailment resistance fell
> Theresia activated Double Throw
Threw two small dirks
> Total of 4 long-range attacks hit ★Paradox
  Beetle
No damage
44 support damage
> Blossom Blade stage 6 hit ⟶ ★Paradox Beetle was
  Stunned

Misaki rolled her dice, and I could see the aura surrounding the beetle fade. The support damage threw it off-balance, and it fell to the ground, Stunned.

"We did it!"

"—Melissa!"

"That horn is...all mine...!"

◆Current Status◆
> MELISSA activated KNIFE ARTISTRY ⟶ Increased probability of PARTIAL DESTRUCTION
> MELISSA activated Lop Off ⟶ ★PARADOX BEETLE dropped materials

"GYEEEAAAAA!!!"

Melissa wielded her huge butcher's knife with two hands and cleanly chopped off the beetle's shiny horn, which tumbled through the air before piercing deep into the ground as if to demonstrate how truly sharp it was.

By that point, Igarashi and Four Seasons had gotten close enough to attack. I didn't just tell them it was weak on its back and let them go in for the attack. I had a hunch, and I gave Igarashi one order based almost entirely on that hunch.

"—Igarashi, use Decoy first!"

"A decoy... All right!"

"Wait, wh-what...?"

"Kaede, trust Arihito's orders!" yelled Ibuki. "I'm sure he's right!"

Kaede pulled back, slowing her attack. Igarashi immediately activated her Decoy skill.

"Human form born from the earth, imbued with my magic! Rise up and be the vanguard to draw the demon's gaze!" The small doll that Igarashi needed to use Decoy absorbed her magic and grew larger and larger until it was the size of a human, then closed in on the beetle.

◆Current Status◆
> ★Paradox Beetle activated Backstabber's Guillotine ⟶ Decoy was destroyed

"Eeeek!!" Igarashi was so surprised that she shrieked. Guess it was a good thing I decided to be extra cautious. The decoy was sliced in half by the massive set of pincers that sprung out from the Paradox Beetle's back. The front of the Paradox Beetle worked like the back of a normal rhinoceros beetle. Its pincers were hidden inside its armor, but really, this monster was more of a stag beetle than a rhinoceros beetle.

"Ew, gross... The heck was that?!" cried Kaede.

"Holy crap, that scared me... Don't do that!"

"It looks like a rhinoceros beetle, but that's all a trap... It's actually..."

"...A stag beetle...? Those are huge pincers."

Each member of Four Seasons looked shocked and afraid. I couldn't blame them; a human caught in those pincers wouldn't get out with just some cuts and bruises. They'd probably be chopped in two and die instantly. However, it looked like once the pincers closed, they couldn't be used again for an attack immediately. The Paradox Beetle had lightened its armor and sacrificed defense. Now Igarashi, Cion, and Four Seasons concentrated their direct attacks on it.

"—Cion, everyone, let's go!"

"Bowwooow!"

""""Yeah!"""""

◆Current Status◆
> Kyouka activated Mirage Step
> Kyouka activated Double Attack ⟶ 2 stages hit
  ★Paradox Beetle
22 support damage
> Cion activated Wolf Rush ⟶ 4 stages hit
  ★Paradox Beetle
44 support damage
> Kaede activated Nidan-Tsuki ⟶ 2 stages hit
  ★Paradox Beetle
22 support damage
> Ibuki activated Flying Eagle Claw ⟶ 2 stages hit
  ★Paradox Beetle
Weak spot attack
Flinch
22 support damage
> Anna activated Jump Smash ⟶ Hit ★Paradox Beetle
Critical hit
11 support damage
> Ryouko activated Aqua Dolphin
> 1 ★Paradox Beetle defeated

Igarashi used Mirage Step just to be on the safe side, then made the first attack. The damage from her spear wasn't that great, but it was followed by Cion's rush, then a series of thrusts from Kaede's wooden sword, and flying kicks from Ibuki, which struck the stag beetle right on its head. Anna saw the creature flinch and leaped up as high as her small frame would take her, before smashing her racket right into the beetle's face. Last up was Ryouko, who brought forth far more water than could fit in her small bottle; she summoned an aqua dolphin and launched it at the beetle.

"...GYEE...EE..."

It was hostile to the very last moment. It finally managed to open its pincers again and tried to catch someone in its grasp...but it lost the last bit of its strength before it could and stopped moving.

"...Did we do it...?"

"...Whoooa! Awesome! So cool! I can't believe we beat such a powerful Named Monster!" At first, Kaede was dumbstruck, but it wasn't until she looked at her license and saw that it said we'd defeated it that she let out a cry of joy, finally realizing what we'd done.

Elitia looked at their party but then turned and walked back toward us. "...Looks like I did my part. I wasn't sure I'd be able to at first."

"You did great. Um, also... Sorry I accidentally called you Ellie in the middle of combat," I said.

"Uh... N-no, that's...that's fine with me...," she said. Then, in a voice so soft that scarcely anyone could hear her, she whispered, "Besides, other people call me that, too." Her face was bright red. "...I don't really mind if you call me that anyway. It's just, Ellie was my nickname when I was a kid, so it feels a little awkward getting called that now."

"G-got it... Guess I ought to stick to calling you Elitia, then."

"Geeeez, Arihito, why so formal?" teased Misaki. "Ellie says it's fine, so you should make an effort to call her by that name. Right, Suzu?"

"M-Misaki... You'll just embarrass Ellie if you make fun of her like that."

"I-it's all right. Thanks, Suzuna. Arihito, you can just...call me whatever you like, I guess... Wh-what?"

If this had been Igarashi, she would have started apologizing out of sheer habit, but Elitia was different. Even though she could be stubborn, she had her timid side and her fragile side. Maybe she had been lonely until she'd met Suzuna. Now she might be trying to avoid being too pushy for fear of upsetting me.

What I needed to do, as the leader and the oldest in the party, was maintain my composure. I had to work to make sure Elitia felt comfortable and at ease.

"In that case, how about I sometimes call you Ellie?"

"Th-that's fine...," she started, and then added under her breath, "...but only *sometimes*?" Suzuna and Misaki heard and exchanged smiles with each other, although Suzuna seemed hesitant.

"People like you are so quick to tease others. Misaki, come with me to the Guild later."

"Eep! ...F-forgive me! I'll do anything you say! But just know that Arihito's my boss!"

"Should the three of us discuss it again? I'd like to talk to Ellie about it once more...about Arihito," said Suzuna.

"A-about me...? Look, if you have any complaints, I'd rather we hash them out in the open. You can talk to me about anything—improving working conditions, party policy..."

"…Ha-ha, it's nothing," Elitia replied with a laugh. "Let's go gather the loot, you two. We shouldn't leave it all to Madoka and Melissa."

"All right," replied Suzuna.

"Ooooh, I wonder if we got something good. Oh-ho, these here are the culprit's footprints!" said Misaki. There wasn't anything like that, but I wasn't sure it was appropriate for a girl her age to crawl on the ground looking for loot. I couldn't help turning a little red at that.

Just as I was struggling finding a spot to look at, Igarashi and Cion came over. Cion had done such a good job that I made sure to spend some time petting her head and back. She swished her fluffy tail back and forth, wagging it happily.

"Atobe, you're normally so cool and composed, but then you react to this sort of thing… I—I mean, it's fine and all. It's just a little strange…"

"W-well, I'm getting to the age where I should start settling down… Uh, not that I should be saying that in front of everyone."

"…Actually, don't you think it'd make everyone worry that you're getting on in years?"

"Th-that's a little harsh, wouldn't you say? There's so many girls in the party, so of course I'm going to lose my composure, but my age is another conversation altogether…"

"……"

It wasn't just Igarashi; even Theresia was looking at me. They weren't really worried about me, were they? I would have thought everyone would feel more comfortable with me being old, but maybe I needed to rethink that assumption.

"Hey, Arihito, c'mere! There's another chest! A red one this time!" called Kaede happily. Of course, we weren't going to get a Black Box. I had hoped a monster like this would have one. Chests were so rare, but they were pretty much guaranteed to drop from a Named Monster, so I wasn't surprised by them anymore. Thinking back, this labyrinth was called Silvanus's Bedchamber, which was connected to the sheep monster. Maybe if we ran into a Named version of one and defeated it... Or maybe it's all up to chance.

Guess we'll have to keep Misaki in the party permanently... I have to make sure she's well protected. Theresia's currently covering her right now.

Without Misaki's luck, our seeking efficiency would drop drastically. I couldn't let her quit just because she didn't have good armor. I wanted to give her some enhanced armor. I could say that about the rest of the party as well, though.

"Good work, Teacher! Our first time working together went so well, and it's all thanks to you!"

"Kyouka and Cion helped out, too. Your party is full of excellent Seekers," said Anna. She and Ibuki were excited, their cheeks tinged pink. They were a powerful party capable of working their way up to the Upper Guild in District Seven, but their faces were as innocent as you would expect for their age.

Ryouko came up from behind them. Something about her seemed different from before. She'd always been ladylike, but now she was even more graceful and reserved.

"All of you have incredible offensive skills," I replied. "You included, Ryoko. You looked like a magician."

"I...I used to help out with a dolphin show, which, I think, is why I have these dolphin-related skills now... You were watching me, Atobe?"

"Of course. You dealt the final blow, after all; it was really cool."

"Ah... W-well... S-say, Ibuki and Anna are such good kids—they were talking about how they'd love to have a party with you to relax from all this work...right?"

"Huh? We didn't say... Oh...!"

"Y-yes, yes we did. We haven't yet encountered the sheep monster we're looking for, but we defeated a strong monster, and we thought it might be a good idea for us to go back to town for a bit and maybe...have a little get-together, or some such... How does that sound?"

Based on Ibuki's and Anna's reactions, they hadn't talked about this possibility, but Ryouko smiled in satisfaction, her hand to her cheek as she beamed at Anna's suggestion.

"Well, uh... I did consider going back for a little bit," I responded. "We were probably a rare example of a group that could land a hit on that Named Monster. It most likely would be unthinkable for others in similar situations. Yet, we managed to pull it in and ended up in a battle with a particularly tough opponent. I think everyone's a bit worn out after that. Anyway, we've managed to do some research on the monsters on the first floor, and if we go back now, we can make it to the second floor fresh next time."

"All right. We'll let your party decide how to divide the loot," said Ryouko.

"Okay, we'll make a list later, then you can let us know if there's anything you want. We can negotiate who gets what if we both end up wanting the same thing..."

"What're you saying, Arihito?" chided Kaede. "You guys beat a monster we'd never stand a chance against. This is all thanks to your party. We'd owe you for life if you even give us any of the loot."

If that's how they really felt, then I didn't need to feel bad about using the materials to strengthen my party. Based on how they fought, I imagined the Grand Moles' headgear, claws, and perhaps even fur would make good materials. And the Paradox Beetle's entire body was likely a lump of extraordinary materials.

Melissa was trembling, her arms wrapped around her butcher's knife. She ran her tongue over the blade, then brandished it, her face one of ecstasy. What was with this sensuality? She was just going to dissect some monsters.

"...Oh! I was just about to do the dissection now. Or should I do that after we take them back...?"

"Could you do some here and send the rest to your Repository?" I asked.

"I can. If I dissect immediately after the monster is defeated, I can use my skill Preserve Freshness to keep meat from going bad. Named Monsters are delicious. This one might make a really tasty dish."

Eating monster meat didn't particularly concern me, but if there was some meat that had additional effects, I suppose I'd have to try it whether or not I liked it.

"...A-Atobe, do I need to eat it, too?" asked Igarashi.

"N-no, no, I won't force you. But there might come a time when we all need to eat something like that."

"……"

Theresia pressed a hand to her stomach, and I heard it gurgle. She didn't seem to have any food preferences outside of lizard-type monsters. She'd probably enjoy eating this one. In that case, I could have her eat it, too. Then we'd both be in the same boat, sailing across a sea of unknown flavors.

"Arihito, we're done collecting the dropped loot!" called Madoka.

"Ah, thank you. And sorry you didn't get a chance to fight… We have to find a way to make sure you level up."

"No worries; support members get a small amount of experience even if they just use skills like Hide," said Kaede. "Not all skills count as being in combat, but certain ones do."

"Really? Then you probably leveled up, Madoka," I said.

"Oh… Y-yes, I did! My license says I grew to level three!"

Everyone checked their licenses as well, and Melissa also gained a level, but the rest of the party would have to wait until the next battle to level up.

"All right, let's go back for a bit. We'll report to the Guild, then look over the loot we got…and maybe check in to see what's happening at the Beach of the Setting Sun," I suggested.

"Yes. I don't think anyone's opposed, including Four Seasons," replied Igarashi. It was such a tiny thing, but I noticed that Igarashi replied formally, with *yes* and not *yeah* or *sure*, as if *she* were the assistant manager here.

"…Really, it'd be fine either way. With Atobe, with me…"

"Hmm? …Did you say something just now?" I asked Igarashi.

"N-no, nothing! …All right, Cion, you're in charge of scouting for enemies. Theresia, you stay with Atobe and monitor our rear." Igarashi went on ahead with Cion to guide the way. If she was trying to tell me that her situation didn't matter, as long as she got to work with me… Well, thinking that might have been what she was trying to say made me feel like I was just being overly self-conscious. I blushed and had a hard time calming down.

"……"

Theresia seemed concerned about me or something, because she patted my back. I was touched by how much she cared, but it wasn't good for me to constantly act like I needed to be treated with kid gloves. I was too old to get this flustered. I decided to just tell Igarashi what I really felt, back when she was in Four Season's party—how important she was to my party.

CHAPTER 3

Assistance in District Seven

Part I: The Secret to Success

We exited the labyrinth and took a breather in the square outside the entrance. There hadn't been any monsters on our trip back, so we'd made it this far without a fight.

"Yo, check out this group. They just went in not long ago, and they've already come back out," someone said.

"What's with all the girls he's got with him? Makin' his own harem or something?" asked another.

"Coward. I could do 'em better—both the seeking and the fun at night, too," replied the first. The speakers were a middle-aged, male Seeker with a mohawk (apparently, those existed in the Labyrinth Country, too) and a long-haired man who looked like an archer or something. They saw us file out of the labyrinth, then started jeering audibly at us, making crude jokes followed by loud guffaws.

Typical senior Seekers... Figures there'd be some here.

There were some in District Eight who dragged new Seekers around under the pretense of showing them around, which I didn't really think was all that bad in the end. Then, there were those ones who tried to swoop in and steal our loot after we defeated Juggernaut for them... Thinking about it, we had run into our fair share of bad people and other less savory types.

"...Those guys looking to die?"

"Hey, Ellie, wait! They're not even worth getting worked up over," said Suzuna.

"I know, but they're bad-mouthing Arihito..."

"You'll give them quite a shock if you say something. Besides, they wouldn't last a minute against you. Though, I do kind of want to give them a piece of my mind..."

"It doesn't really bother me, honest. They just don't know what we went through in the labyrinth... Uh?" I then realized Theresia, who had been behind me a moment before, had vanished without a trace. *No way she'd actually—*

But that's when it happened.

"......"

"H-holy shit... What's with this chick? When did she...?!"

"Gah... Bitch, don't think the guards won't say nothin' if you try it here...!"

Theresia had vanished and reappeared by the men, holding one of her dirks to the throat of the mohawked man who called me a coward. "She's a damned demi-human... You half-wit—you dare defy a human?!"

I felt my blood begin to boil. They could say what they wanted about me, but I couldn't stand them talking bad about my friends. Theresia glanced at me for a brief moment. Even without words, she could tell me what she was thinking.

"You piece of shit!"

"......!"

The long-haired man went to punch Theresia. She immediately pulled her targe up to take the hit.

◆Current Status◆

> Arihito activated Attack Support 1, Defense Support 1 ⟶ Target: Theresia
> Welles attacked Theresia ⟶ No damage
> Welles's karma increased
> Theresia's attack hit Welles
11 support damage

"Gaaah...!!"

Theresia struck him with a simple kick, but the eleven support damage that impacted at the same time wasn't trivial, forcing him to stumble back and collapse to his knees. Because he wasn't a close-combat fighter, he must have a fairly weak defense.

Theresia's karma didn't increase. Her action was determined to be appropriate self-defense since he struck first. The man had worked his way up to District Seven, so he had to be at least level 3 or 4, meaning the attack wasn't fatal. That didn't mean he wasn't angry about it, though.

"B-bitch..."

"—That's enough!"

The rest of the party was about to intervene on Theresia's behalf when a woman's cold voice echoed across the square.

"Madam G-Guild Savior... W-we didn't do anything..."

The person who appeared was someone I didn't expect to see: Seraphina. I'd thought she'd returned to the Guild Savior headquarters, and we wouldn't be seeing her for a little while. She must have been working alone today, because she didn't have any of her subordinates with her. Even so, she was wearing her Guild Savior armband, and the square fell silent at her presence, tension running through the crowd.

"I'll just take a look at your license…," said Seraphina. "This man, Welles, attacked the girl first."

"N-no, that's wrong! This demi-human threatened me with a knife—"

"And you guys started it by talking trash about us. That's why you got your asses handed to you," retorted Kaede. "You've got no right to call us a harem or whatever just 'cause we all came out of that labyrinth together."

"Rrgh… You shut your mouth, girlie! Look at you flaunting that body in front of a bunch of men— Eep?!"

Seraphina looked at the man yelling at Kaede, getting visibly angrier. I was angry as well, but hers was a step up from mine. It was enough to make you instinctively flinch away.

"I will let that slide if you back down now. Otherwise, I'll beat that mettle right out of you however I see fit…," she growled, grabbing the man by his shirt collar.

"S-s-spare me… Uh, I mean, forgive me, please…!" he begged pathetically, his legs giving out from under him as he passed out. She looked at the two men and shrugged with a huff.

"Why cause all this trouble outside a labyrinth? That people like them—people who hardly ever enter the labyrinth—would

insult those who are constantly out on seeking expeditions... It's downright outrageous." True, we'd been seeking without a single break, and it had crossed my mind that maybe we spent too much time in the labyrinths—but apparently, that sort of thing wasn't considered normal, because the surrounding crowd was visibly surprised by the statement.

"I apologize, Mr. Atobe. I'm sure you dislike people resorting to such forceful methods..."

"No, not necessarily. I couldn't stand idly by even if I would end up in trouble for it... But I'm not very strong, so Theresia helped me out."

"......"

Theresia looked at me as if to ask if what she did was all right. I smiled to tell her she didn't need to worry. I was always grateful for everything she did.

"Sorry you have such a timid master. I really did want to punch that guy myself," I told her.

"......"

She shook her head slowly, then flexed her arm. It was like she was telling me she was stronger even if she didn't have bulging biceps.

"They managed to make you that angry, Mr. Atobe? Well then, I really should straighten them out..."

"N-no, I think they've gotten what they deserve. It'll be hard enough for him to come back from passing out like this, and I'm in a better mood now." I couldn't forgive them for bad-mouthing Theresia, but they'd shown themselves to be quite pathetic, then passed out. They'd both likely need healing. It would be hard on them. And their karma went up.

Seraphina pulled out her license and started using it. I guessed she might be looking something up, and when she saw it, she grimaced.

"These two have caused trouble before. They're banned from entering almost all the entertainment districts in District Seven... and this isn't really something I should be telling you, but their party broke down, and they've been unable to go into the labyrinth. It seems they're spending their days wasting their savings."

Losing a companion you'd worked with for a long time could destroy the party balance—sometimes, people couldn't recover from that. I had absolutely no desire to end up in that situation. Every single person in my party had an indispensable role, and it wasn't just that. There were no serious mismatches in the members' personalities; everyone got along well, and that was an incredibly hard thing to replicate.

"There's no need to look that upset, Mr. Atobe. As long as they're in District Seven, they have access to ways of becoming respectable Seekers again. The Guild offers training programs and works to rehabilitate any Seeker who needs it," said Seraphina.

"The Guild would do that? They really are involved in everything that happens in the Labyrinth Country."

"That is our duty. Ever since the former king fell out of power, the Guild has needed to act as the government of this country."

So the king had fallen out of power... Louisa had told me that there was a family that established the Labyrinth Country but they had been exiled from District One, and now the Guild administrators and the head of the church were the highest authority in the country.

"However, in the end, the Guild's primary duties involve ensuring the labyrinths are explored to their completion and developing Seekers capable of adventuring in the most difficult labyrinths," continued Seraphina. "It is quite unlike a more typical government that would extend its reach beyond the country's borders and not simply keep within the labyrinths."

"So then...does that mean there's countries other than the Labyrinth Country?"

"...I'm sorry. I'm sure a time will come when you will learn that. It's not something I can discuss as a Guild Savior." I was curious, but there was no point pressing the issue. There were still a lot of mysteries I didn't have the answers to. For now, I just needed to keep accomplishing things as a Seeker. "Right, I'll have my people take care of these two."

"Okay... Sorry to bother you, Seraphina—I thought the Guild Savior headquarters was in a higher district."

"That's correct. It's in District Five, but we received a request from the branch in District Seven and so ended up stopping here for a short while. The more populous districts are always shorthanded..." If she was doing rounds by herself because of the shortage of people...it'd be unlikely we could get her to join our party again.

Suddenly, she added, "Mr. Atobe, you were in Silvanus's Bedchamber, correct? When I was a new Seeker, I had a bit of a tough fight with a beetle-like monster that could fly." She must have guessed, considering we were near that labyrinth's entrance. She probably fought a Fake Beetle as well... She seemed to mean it when she said it was a tough fight, because she was smirking, which was uncharacteristic of her.

"Speaking of, our Suzu here shot a Named Monster that was waaay up in the air with her arrows. It was a huge mess," said Misaki. It was the kind of fight we'd be lucky to walk away from if we made even a single mistake, but Misaki's tone didn't express any of that concern. It was sure to make Seraphina chuckle, at least...or so I thought.

"A...Named Monster? One of those beetles that fly at such high altitudes...?" she asked.

"Uh, y-you know, it was just good luck, or maybe bad luck. I guess in the end it was a good thing. It was called a Paradox Beetle. We all worked together and managed to beat it somehow," said Misaki.

"...Are you saying...you defeated the creature that's killed so many people...? Mr. Atobe, the Paradox Beetle has a bounty on it. I'm sure your caseworker will be shocked when you report this to them."

"I think we shock her every time. Louisa probably mentally prepares herself whenever she sees Arihito's face," said Elitia with a smile. She was always so cool and reserved; this expression felt rare and valuable. Suzuna saw it and smiled as well.

"Thank you. I'll make sure to file a proper report," I said.

"That's good," replied Seraphina. "I'm quite surprised as well... I felt this way before, but it does seem like you are guided by some sort of fate." I wasn't quite sure it was right to call Misaki, our designated good luck charm, the fate that guided us—although, to be fair, she'd been a huge help to us so far.

"Fate, huuuh? It's got a nice ring to it. Real dramatic," mused Misaki. "Oh, that reminds me of a drama I recorded once...but then, my brother recorded over it, and I lost it."

"You'll make everyone sad talking about that kind of thing," I said.

"Ha-ha… You're so nice, Teacher. We've all had plenty of time to reminisce over our past lives. We can handle it," said Ibuki.

"Hey, weren't you just talking about how you'd love to have some okonomiyaki or takoyaki?" said Kaede.

"H-hey… Don't tell Arihito that—it's embarrassing."

The food here was nice enough, but I'd always miss Japanese cuisine in particular. Personally, I'd love some soba noodles. Nothing beats the first bite of a croquette dipped in the warm broth from one of those soba stalls near the train station.

"The Guild can suggest restaurants if there's any kind of food you want," mentioned Seraphina. "Obviously, District Seven will make food with the resources they find in the labyrinths here, but there are restaurants that serve French cuisine, Chinese, and many other options. You should try them if you like." I was shocked to hear names of foods I actually knew, but my companions were even more excited about it.

"F-French… Ooh, but Chinese is good, too…," said Misaki. "Ramen noodles, fried rice, shumai dumplings… Aw man, what should we eat…?"

"Which would you prefer, Arihito?" asked Suzuna, who patted Misaki's shoulder to comfort the girl as she struggled over the decision.

"I was just thinking about soba. I know it's completely different, but the Chinese place might have ramen-style noodles, so that would work for me."

"We've had pasta here before, but I'm happy to know we have different noodle options available," said Igarashi. She was completely right—whether it was soba or ramen, I felt like any flavor that was close to what I came to love in Japan would ease some of my homesickness.

"Madoka, Melissa, is that all right with you two? Or is there something else you want to eat?" I asked.

"That's fine with me," replied Madoka. "Pretty much the only thing I don't eat is tomatoes."

"Any place that has monster meat works for me," added Melissa. "I'd really like to get some of today's catch cooked...but that can wait." The materials from the monsters we'd defeated today were in Melissa's Repository, but I wasn't sure if there was anything edible on the beetle since it had been covered in armor. There were some crabs that you could eat whole with their shell, so it was possible beetles would be surprisingly tasty...but it would take some serious courage to bite into that.

We returned to the Upper Guild's Green Hall in the early afternoon. There weren't many Seekers present; perhaps most people didn't have business at the Guild at this time of day.

"Arihito, does your party normally report all together? Ryouko usually does it for us by herself," asked Kaede.

"So does Atobe, usually," answered Igarashi. "It might be a good idea for both our representatives to go, since we did a joint seeking expedition today."

"I agree. Would you mind waiting with everyone?" I asked Igarashi.

"Sure, we'll wait over there. Just let us know when you're done… and don't get too happy because you two are alone together."

"Uh… O-of course, I wholeheartedly agree. I will conduct myself with the utmost—"

"H-hey… I was just pointing it out! Don't act like we're back at work or anything. You're making it awkward!" Igarashi gently shoved my upper arm.

What was that for? It was the kind of frustrated shove you wouldn't even expect from a high schooler.

Everyone else followed Igarashi away, leaving Theresia as the last person. She pattered over to me—well, not exactly. Her footsteps didn't make any noise.

"……"

"…Wh-what's up, Theresia?" She seemed caught up on what Igarashi had done, because she touched me on the arm in the same place to see what it felt like. I had no idea what she was doing, and I felt very awkward.

"……"

"…Oh, Igarashi didn't mean anything by that. It was nothing, really… Theresia?"

Theresia suddenly dashed off to catch up with Igarashi and the others. She must have suddenly felt more embarrassed, because even from here, I could see she was turning slightly red.

"Wow… That was kinda bittersweet. Even I'm blushing a little," said Kaede.

"I feel like I can understand what she's trying to say even though she doesn't use words…," said Anna. "She seems pained."

"Oh… I-is that what she meant? Are you sure she didn't just

want to touch him because she respects him?" asked Ibuki. The three girls spoke in whispers. Ryouko stood nearby, apparently lost in her own thoughts, but then approached me after coming to some conclusion.

"We're both leaders, you and me. That's why I don't see the need for us to hold back when we work together... What do you think?" There was a lot of room for misunderstanding when a mature and sensual woman wearing a boa coat over a bikini said something like that to you. Her gently wavy hair brushed her shoulders, and her large eyes had something catlike about them—but this wasn't the time to be looking her up and down. I already knew she was beautiful; that much was apparent the first time I saw her.

"Y-you're right... We're both leaders. You're completely right," I said.

"Crap, Ryouko's totally got Arihito under her spell...," muttered Kaede. "He'd never look twice at a bunch of kids like us."

"Tanned skin and a bikini... Why do men *always* fall for that?" grumbled Ibuki.

"Anyone can wear a swimsuit," said Anna. "We could hold our own against her. I think there's stores in District Seven that sell them..." The remaining Four Seasons members chatted as they left the Guild. I heard them mention swimsuits. Did they think I particularly liked a woman in a swimsuit? I'll admit I'm not exactly used to seeing it, but I wouldn't say it makes me fantasize about anything...

...*Wait. If that was enough to make Kaede and the girls misunderstand things...what will Louisa think when I show up with Ryouko?*

"Um… Is something wrong? You look upset," asked Ryouko.

"Uh, uhhh, I just realized something… I've been wanting to ask you for a while now, but… Your boa coat—that's a pretty rare piece of equipment, isn't it?"

"Y-yes. I had to defeat some frog monsters in the Sleeping Marshes in District Eight in order to make it water-resistant… I barely managed that one. I used to be so grossed out by frogs that I couldn't even touch them. But it's a good piece of equipment, so I can't get rid of it now."

"Sounds like it was tough. Speaking of monsters that have water-resistant materials, we once fought something called a Gaze Hound. It looks like a dog, but it only has one eye, which can Stun you…"

"One eye… There's a monster like that? I'd like to hear more."

Ryouko's tanned skin gave off the impression that she'd be quite lively and energetic, but she was normally fairly quiet. Chatting with her was quite soothing. It might have helped that we were almost the same age, too—only one year apart.

"…Mr.…Ato…be?"

I froze in a moment of sheer shock, like they do in manga sometimes, now aware that reaction was possible in real life. Again, like in a manga, I turned around slowly, like a tin man whose joints hadn't been oiled, beads of sweat dripping from my forehead. There, behind me, I saw Louisa, who looked the same as always, holding a leather-bound folder filled with paperwork, a professional smile on her face.

"L-Louisa. Good, I was just about to come see you to give you today's report," I said.

"Oh... I s-see. Is that so. I was just thinking you really were getting friendly with a new woman...but a report is perfectly fine. We can begin immediately."

"Huh? ...Um, Atobe, you normally have to wait in line at this Guild, even hours at a time...," said Ryouko.

"Louisa arrived from District Eight with us. She's our exclusive caseworker."

"It is rare for a party to have an exclusive caseworker at this point in their career, but Mr. Atobe had such an incredible performance in District Eight that I received permission to do so," said Louisa. Ryouko was quite surprised by that but accepted it, since she had fought with us and understood our capabilities.

"I see... Thank you for the explanation. I would like to reintroduce myself properly to his *caseworker*. My name is Ryouko Natsume. Today, Atobe and I conducted a seeking expedition *together*. It's very nice to meet you."

"Y-yes, the pleasure is all mine... My name is Louisa Farmel. I have been Mr. Atobe's caseworker *from the moment he came to the Labyrinth Country*. I have been *alone with him* many times during his postexpedition reports."

I wondered what would happen if I told Louisa she didn't need to say it like that? I'd likely end up souring my relationship with one of them if I sided with the other. And that's precisely why I decided to sit this one out, even if that made me indecisive and wishy-washy.

"Ryouko and her party have the same goals as us, so we decided to work together. They were a great help today," I said.

"N-no, not at all... Your party did all the helping...," said Ryouko.

"Louisa, I'm sure you have plenty on your plate since we've

just come to District Seven, but I was hoping we could go over my report immediately. It's all positive, so I'd like to share it with you as soon as possible."

"Y-yes... Of course. I was waiting for you to return..."

Things seemed safer now. Nothing good would come out of the two of them turning antagonistic; it was better for me to mediate things as much as I could.

Louisa continued. "Okay, I'll show you to a meeting room. This way please, Mr. Atobe, Ms. Natsume." By now, her expression had returned to that of an upstanding Guild employee. She walked ahead with perfect posture. The Guild uniform really suited her, as always. It included a pencil skirt—that had to be a conscious decision on someone's part.

"Atobe, you started off at the Upper Guild here, right? I don't mean to pry, but I was wondering what your rank was...," said Ryouko.

"Two hundred and ninety-four. Things went well in District Eight, and I managed to earn a lot of contribution points..."

"What...?" said Ryouko, stopping in her tracks. I realized we hadn't discussed our ranking much yet. What rank was Four Seasons? They'd recently come to the Upper Guild, so they'd likely be in the two-thousands.

"...Um, L-Louisa, how did Atobe get such an incredible rank...? I wouldn't have realized it by looking at him, but he fights incredibly well..."

"That is strictly confidential between myself and Mr. Atobe. I have yet to determine whether you and your party will be privy to such information."

"O-okay... We'll do everything we can to prove he can trust us. I hope you can help us!"

Louisa shook her hand and, for some reason, removed her glasses before smiling at Ryouko, but I was confident they'd get along at some point. Igarashi and Louisa had gotten much closer after they had drinks together; Ryouko would surely open up as well in that sort of setting. Ever since getting reincarnated to the Labyrinth Country, my secret to success had become "if you can think it, you can do it"—nothing's gonna happen if you're too afraid to make anything happen.

"...Mr. Atobe, I was wondering if I could join you for dinner tonight once I've shown you your new lodging?" asked Louisa.

"Oh, um... If you're going to join them, could we as well? I'm so pleased to see the girls making new friends, and I'd love to chat with you and the others, Louisa," said Ryouko. Our numbers for dinner tonight were jumping through the roof. I vaguely wondered if the Chinese restaurant would be able to accommodate a reservation for that many people; I got flashbacks to that time I organized my company's New Year's party.

Part II: Nine Stars, New Equipment

Louisa led Ryouko and I into the first floor of Green Hall. Doors lined both sides of the hallway. The ones right in front of us were simple wooden doors, but farther down, there were three doors made of a different, blackish material. It could have been ebony, like my slingshot. A Novice Appraisal Scroll might have told me what the material was, but more interesting were the stones embedded into the doors. I felt like I'd seen the pattern before.

Is that...some sort of constellation? There's nine stones... Wonder what that means.

"This is a symbolic representation of a map of the Labyrinth Country, but I can't say I know any deeper meaning than that...," explained Louisa.

"Do you think that maybe...the higher-ups in the Guild might know something more?" I asked.

"Yes, most likely. I've been promoted to an employee of District Seven, but that doesn't mean I've received enough authority to be privy to those secrets. I was, however, given duties as a librarian of the data repository archive in District Seven that the Guild manages." That reminded me: Seraphina had said that the odd numbered districts had these data repositories.

"Louisa, if possible, I'd like to visit the archives sometime."

"Of course. It would have to be when I'm off duty... There aren't many people I'm in charge of helping at the moment, so I should be able to make time to show you around. How about you, Ms. Natsume?"

"If it's not too much trouble, I'd love to see it as well. There's so many things we'd like to know."

"The archives contain information specific to each person's job, and with your current rank, Mr. Atobe, I would be able to give you that information. You would also have access to the restricted materials," said Louisa with a small smile, but I just felt nervous, because the words *restricted materials* made me think of words like *proprietary information* and *company secrets.*

"Well then, please make yourselves comfortable in this room. I will bring some tea." Louisa held open a door and gestured for us to enter. She left me and Ryouko in the room. Ryouko looked at the antique-seeming table, her eyes sparkling with excitement, and didn't seem able to decide where to sit.

"Ryouko, are you interested in furniture like this?"

"Oh... How could you tell? Yes, I like this kind of antique furniture. When we were first rank in District Eight, we went through such an impressive room... I thought I'd love to have furniture like that when I got my own home."

"Really? I don't know much about this kind of furniture, but it is elegant."

She seemed quite happy to chatter away in response to my simple question. I realized that the fact that they had made their way up to District Seven did mean they'd been at the very top of District Eight at some point. A party as capable as them could still struggle in District Seven... Well, it was actually because that alliance was blocking their way. It's good we could start working with them before they got too stuck.

"Um, could I ask something? After this, are you—?" started Ryouko, but there was a knock on the door. I stood up to open it and let Louisa in, who then placed cups on the table and poured tea from a teapot.

"I'm sorry to keep you waiting. Let's get started right away with your report. May I please see your licenses?"

"Yes, of course."

"Go right ahead."

Ryouko and I both placed our licenses on the table. Louisa seemed quite nervous as she steadied herself and took a deep breath before using her monocle to look at the licenses.

```
◆Expedition Results◆
> Raided SILVANUS'S BEDCHAMBER 1F: 10 points
> MADOKA grew to level 3: 20 points
> MELISSA grew to level 4: 40 points
> Defeated 1 GRAND MOLE: 50 points
> Defeated 1 bounty ★PARADOX BEETLE: 1,800 points
> Subparty defeated 2 GRAND MOLES: 50 points
> Party members' Trust Levels increased: 140
  points
> Subparty members' Trust Levels increased: 200
  points
> Conducted a combined seeking expedition with
  a total of 13 people: 65 points
Seeker Contribution: 2,375 points
District Seven Contribution Ranking: 255
```

"...Oh, ah... I see we have that star again in the report...," noted Louisa. "So you encountered another Named Monster...?"

"Y-yes. It was a huge, beetle-like monster flying high in the distance. I thought it was a Fake Beetle at first, but...I didn't realize it was Named until it came closer," I replied.

"According to the record on your license, you attacked while it was out of detection range... I didn't know that was possible, though I suppose Seekers in the higher districts might be capable."

"Incredible, isn't it? ...We were just baffled. I'm ashamed to admit it, but we barely kept up with his party," said Ryouko.

"I can see that your main work was defeating two Grand Moles. Mr. Atobe's party led the fight against the Paradox Beetle... Meaning they will receive more contribution points. Each one of his members will increase in rank. First of all is Mr. Atobe, who may be able to reach rank two hundred quite quickly... There are so many Seekers who come to District Seven and never make it this high. You really are extraordinary..."

I'd jumped up again by thirty-nine ranks, but there were still a lot of Seekers between me and the leader of the Alliance, who was currently rank one.

"About how many contribution points would I need to gain in a single expedition in order to go up one rank from here on out?" I asked. "I'd like to know as it'll help me decide when we should leave the labyrinth."

"Well... The Seekers above you in the ranks will occasionally go into the labyrinth to maintain or increase their contribution points. I believe you will almost certainly gain a rank if you earn one thousand contribution points. Five hundred should maintain your current rank," answered Louisa. In other words, most parties would find it difficult enough just to maintain their rank.

"Our party took up four ranks in a row, starting with 2,548. But with your help, Atobe, we were able to defeat a Named Monster, and that alone gave me nine hundred contribution points. That brought me up to 1,983," said Ryouko.

"Congratulations. One thousand points in one seeking expedition is quite an accomplishment even in District Seven," said Louisa. I'd received around fifty thousand and one hundred contribution points from the stampede, but that was mostly because it was an emergency situation and we'd defeated a lot of enemies. Monsters wouldn't normally gather in such high concentrations, meaning it was difficult to make even a thousand points, like Louisa said.

A single Grand Mole is fifty points... Without a bonus from increased Trust Levels, but including any additional points from gaining levels, we'd have to beat just under twenty of them. That is a lot of work.

Even if we did try to take out a lot of weak monsters to gain points, they didn't live close enough together to make that feasible. People gathered in the best hunting grounds; some people took them over for themselves, and it turned into a fight among one another to earn anything. Having said that, there was still reason enough to avoid the less populated hunting grounds. There seemed to be quite a few labyrinths that people avoided in District Seven—the fact that there were so many people who moved up from District Eight yet still ended up getting stuck here meant there were likely risks that I wasn't yet aware of.

"...Louisa, I heard that the person currently ranked number one in District Seven created an alliance and is taking over the best hunting grounds for themselves. How does the Guild view situations like that?" I asked.

"You heard as well? The Guild has no rules against inviting others to join when you're in the first-floor lobby, but the guards do sometimes monitor those who continue to push others to do so. In particular, we've received complaints about a Seeker named

Gray who has been urging parties with many women in them to join."

This Gray was the gray-haired man who was trying to get Four Seasons to join him. Ryouko's face clouded over when she heard his name.

"...He and his group are at the top of District Seven, right? Which means if they move up a district, then they'll all go," she asked.

"I can't discuss other parties too much, but their actions have an impact on all Seekers who are aiming for rank one. I will explain as much as I can. First, their alliance's name is Beyond Liberty. Their captain is a man named Roland Vorn, and second-in-command is Daniella Vorn."

"They have the same family name... Are they related?" I asked.

"They're married. Roland is an Air Trooper, and Daniella is a Doctor."

When you came to the Labyrinth Country, you weren't automatically accepted for whatever job you wrote on your license, which meant these two had some sort of experience from their previous life or an aptitude for those jobs. As a former air force member, Roland would already have been fairly physically fit. Then, there was Daniella's Doctor job. Other than the Healers, I'd seen people who were Nurses, which just showed that people who came to the Labyrinth Country could have all sorts of different experiences.

"Roland didn't spend long in District Eight, but he had to take time off for medical treatment while he was rank one in District Seven," Louisa went on to explain. "His wife assisted him, but it took two years for him to recover, and he fell to the very bottom of the ranking. He's now worked his way back up to first and, despite his time off, has maintained his level of seven—and is therefore one of the most powerful people in this district."

"Getting to District Six isn't easy, even for someone as tough as him…," I said.

"It is not. Luck plays a significant part in the advancement exam as well… Some of the requirements include beating at least three level-six or higher Named Monsters in District Seven and the leader of the party earning over twenty thousand contribution points in a month. Those requirements are in place because there are so many labyrinths in District Seven and therefore many Named Monsters."

Ignoring the contribution points for a moment… Level-6 Named Monsters?

Both Ryouko and I seemed to realize it at the same time, because she looked at me in surprise, then asked Louisa for clarification.

"Louisa, the Named Monster we encountered today was level six… My party didn't contribute much to the fight, but would it still count toward the requirements?"

"Yes, it would. Congratulations. You will only need two more… Although, that will not be easy, considering how rare it is to encounter a Named Monster and how difficult it is to defeat one… But if anyone can do it, it's Mr. Atobe's party."

Louisa looked like she was trying to conceal her concern for us behind a tough exterior. I had no intention of rushing or doing anything reckless to get up to District Six. But if this Roland person was panicking because he hadn't found the Named Monsters necessary…that was a little concerning.

"I see… So Roland is getting everyone to help him so that he can earn the required twenty thousand contribution points," I said.

"I believe so, yes. Only Roland's party will move up to District Six, where they will switch focus and assist a different party in gathering the contribution points, then keep moving up party by party. That method seems to be working fairly well for them."

"That gives me a lot to think about. I imagine we'll end up doing something similar."

"…Are you sure it's all right, Atobe? We only just met. Just letting us seek with you has been incredibly helpful. I wouldn't want to impose further…," said Ryouko, clenching her hands together in uncertainty. The motion made the front of her coat open up to reveal a peek at her swimsuit-clad, competitive swimmer's body… which made it hard for me to keep my calm.

"Oh… I-I'm sorry. This doesn't have a zipper, so I just keep it closed with buttons… But it can be annoying when I button it up, so sometimes, I undo it… Perhaps this is too improper."

"N-no, it's not. I'm the one who should apologize."

Ryouko fastened her coat, doing up all the buttons. They looked like they were made of a material from a monster's horn. She had had it fastened while walking around town, but it was quite…bold of her to undo it once she was inside.

"So those are the kinds of swimsuits Mr. Atobe likes…," murmured Louisa. "Oh dear, I'm not sure there are any stores in town where I could buy one..." She then jotted something down in her notebook.

I had no idea what to say. I felt like all the women around me misunderstood every time I reacted to the swimsuit. I considered the possibility that this would all lead to something problematic but figured they wouldn't all put on swimsuits just to show me. We probably wouldn't have time to go swimming for fun since we were seeking every day, though there were some labyrinths like the Beach of the Setting Sun that sounded swimsuit-appropriate.

"In that case, I suppose I should get a swimsuit, too...," I said.

"Ah... M-Mr. Atobe, did you hear that? I'm sorry, I was just..."

"Atobe, have you swum before? I'd love to coach you, if you like..." Ryouko's proposal was incredibly tempting, but even if we found a place to swim in the labyrinths, I didn't have the spare time for it. I wouldn't say no to swimming if there was somewhere I could do it safely. It was important to take breaks between our adventures and to rest. The problem was that when it came to Louisa, Ryouko, and even Igarashi, I had a hard enough time finding a safe place to look when they were wearing normal clothes. I wouldn't be able to relax if they were all in swimsuits.

"Mr. Atobe... Is something the matter? Oh, that's right—it's a problem for a Guild employee like me to intrude on private affairs..."

"N-no, that's not an issue at all. I'd love for you to join us if we had the opportunity. Before I got reincarnated, I'd sometimes go swimming at the gym as a way to relax when I wasn't at work."

"Well then, you must already have the basics down... All right,

I'll teach you skills you can apply to the real world. I'll have to find something that can work as a kickboard... Hee-hee." Ryouko just seemed to be looking forward to it, so why did this seem weirdly erotic? I had no idea where Louisa and Ryouko's initial tension had gone. Now they were just smiling gently at each other. I was only being optimistic when I thought their relationship would improve if they just had a chat, but they'd started opening up to each other so quickly.

"Well, then... If the opportunity arises, I would be very happy to join you," said Louisa.

"Y-yeah. By the way, are there any labyrinths where you have to go in the water?"

"Yes, there are. Not many Seekers can go into the water, however, meaning many of those labyrinths have yet to be explored at all. There are a few Seekers who specialize in such expeditions, though."

Perhaps there were people with a job like "Diver" or something. I used to dream of going diving in Okinawa, so I'd be plenty interested in doing that here if we could just get the preparations in place.

Louisa would be joining us for food once she got off work. She told us about a Chest Cracker in District Seven, and we parted ways for the moment. We possessed three red chests and two wooden chests. I was, of course, excited to see what was inside the ones we obtained in District Eight, but I was even more interested in the chests from our new district. Considering how tough the Paradox Beetle was, I imagined there'd be at least one or two magic items in the chest we got from it.

"We've had almost no opportunities to open chests... And the one we did open was just a normal one, so they told us any Chest Cracker could open it," said Ryouko.

"Some chests are harder to open than others. We got help from an incredibly skilled Chest Cracker in District Eight."

"Really, so you've found chests before... Wow. We were jumping up and down with joy when we found ours...and it pretty much just had money in it. There was one magic stone, which we used to upgrade Kaede's boots."

"Oh, wow, her boots? So that must be part of why she's so fast."

I checked my license while we talked and started to head toward where everyone was waiting for us. It showed they were a short walk from Green Hall, on the corner of some streets that were lined with shops, one of which was called Boutique Corleone. Cion was sitting outside waiting, which implied everyone else was inside. She gave a small woof when she saw me and wagged her tail, so I gave her a good head rub.

"If they're all inside, then they're probably shopping," I said.

"Oh... Sorry, Atobe, there's actually something I'd like to buy. I'll be back in a moment. I'll find the girls, then we'll hurry up and finish shopping."

"Okay, see you... Hmm?" I'd intended to wait out in front of the store, but an androgynous-looking store worker who was in the shop behind the counter—who I assumed was probably a man, even though he was wearing makeup—came out of the store and started talking to me.

"Oh my, welcome! We have menswear as well—fancy a look? I'll put together an outfit that'll look great no matter where you wear it to."

"O-oh... Do you work here?"

"Yes, I'm Corleone, the owner. Don't worry, one of our shop ladies is taking care of the girls. I'm only interested in dressing men."

"Ha, ha-ha... I actually don't put much thought into my appearance, so... Whoa!" Corleone suddenly grabbed my shoulders firmly. He had short-cropped hair and a very manly physique, so getting jostled by him was a little scary.

"...So the man himself is the only one without a clue, hmm? Those girls have their work cut out for them."

"Uh... Wh-what do you mean?"

"Oh, nothing. You have money, right? I've got some suits for sale that are a similar make to what you're wearing now. I'm so happy to have found someone who can wear them. The Labyrinth Country is filled with people who only wear unsophisticated armor, but a capable man wears a suit. Don't you agree?" He was a real character, but I had gone this whole time without a change of clothes. I'd somehow managed to stumble upon a store that could make a spare for the suit I'd been doing everything in until now. Everyone else was probably buying things they needed, so I gave into Corleone's urgings and bought myself a new suit.

"Huh...? K-Kyouka, what's that? You could practically cover your entire head with it."

"Erk... D-don't talk so loud. It's not that different from yours, Ibuki."

"Th-that's not true at all. I'm no comparison to you, Kyouka. Ah-ha-ha..."

"You should stop talking about that—you'll get distracted. You won't be able to pick something if you don't calm down."

"You should go with something like Ellie's that doesn't restrict movement. And, Kaede, I don't think you should be picking something so flashy."

"Wha—?! ...I—I don't think it's over-the-top at all. And it's not like I'm gonna be showing it to anyone anyway... Seriously, I'm not!"

"...I personally don't really mind if it's a little restrictive. Anna, stop staring at me like that."

I could hear people talking somewhere inside the store when I went into a fitting room to try on the suit. It wasn't hard to over-hear the other party members' conversations.

"Hmm, it's cute, but... Ooh, this might be nice. What do you think, Suzu?"

"I don't know why, but I can't wear normal underwear... Oh, they have something I can use, too. Thank goodness..."

"Theresia, you're not going to try it on? No, no, it'll lose its shape if you do that! Although, it does suit you perfectly, so maybe it'll be fine..."

"......"

The equipment a person could use was different depending on their job. Just as I started to imagine those differences, I shook my head back and forth. I left the fitting room, praying I wouldn't run into the others, and put on my new tie.

Part III: The District Seven Chest Cracker

Corleone was from Italy. He used to work for a fashion brand before he was reincarnated. He seemed uncomfortable talking about his reincarnation, so I didn't press it. He was smoking a type of cigarette made with "respiration tobacco" that improved your lung function. He offered me one, but I politely declined because I didn't smoke. He shrugged and lit his cigarette, and a thin trail of smoke curled upward.

"Goodness, I suppose it's been five years already since I've come here. I did a bit of seeking when I first arrived, but some of my friends got married and moved to the support side of things, see. I just love all the various little shops and the people living their lives in this district, so I decided to start a business here. Thankfully, I had a skill I could rely on."

"Are people with the Tailor job rare in the Labyrinth Country?"

"There aren't that many people who choose jobs related to fashion. Since seeking in the labyrinths is the default, a lot of people go for the combat-related jobs. People coming from a society with guns might be able to choose 'Gunner,' but that's got its own pitfalls."

"By *pitfalls*, you mean...?"

"Guns weren't readily available here in the Labyrinth Country until fairly recently. Officially, they're still treated like they don't even exist. Then, a Gunsmith came along and started making some, but they could only create a few. People will find them in chests dropped by monsters and use them in secret... It happens sometimes." It would be really difficult if you chose a job and couldn't find a weapon you could use... Would the Guild warn people about choosing such jobs? "You're using a hunting slingshot, yes? I can tell it's not a normal weapon."

"I've had it modified a bit. I'll keep using it for the time being."

"And you have what looks like a katana on your back. Can you use that, too? You're not a Weapons Master, are you?"

"I'm not, but I can use the katana okay. I mostly stick to the slingshot, though."

"Hmm... An interesting job. Well, in that case..." Corleone stubbed out his cigarette in the ashtray on the counter and went into the back of the store, before returning with a case made of a gleaming silver metal.

"Corleone, is that—?"

"A magic gun I used as a Seeker. I got it from a chest dropped by a Named Monster. Guns are a general-purpose weapon that most jobs can use, so they're popular among people who do know they exist." I just started to wonder why he was showing me this when he stuck one finger up in the air. "The suit you just bought isn't my highest quality. If you come back with the high-quality fabric that I want to use and order a suit made of it, I'll give you this gun—and it's up to you who'll use it, of course."

"Are you...sure? I mean, this has to be important to you..."

"Of course I'm sure, deary. Making high-quality suits is my passion, and you bought one from me just now. I think this little gun here would be happy to be back in use again, too."

"...All right. High-quality fabric, right?"

"Yes. I'm sick of the run-of-the-mill fabric I get. I can't wait to have something better... By the way, deary, what's your name?"

"Sorry I didn't introduce myself sooner. My name's Arihito Atobe. It's a pleasure to meet you."

"Oh… And you can call me by my real name, not the name of the shop." The very last thing he did was tell me that Corleone, the name of the shop, was not in fact his real name. I got the impression that a lot of people made that assumption, so he normally just went with it. "My name's Luca Bernardi. Come talk to me about anything related to clothing. I'm not quite like a witch, though. I can't make a magic dress without the proper materials."

"I'll work hard to find materials that live up to your expectations. Thanks for today." Luca waved as I left. I exited the store and saw the others, who were done with their shopping, using the storage unit's key to put their clothes away.

"Welcome back, Arihito. Oh, you have a new suit!"

"That store had a lot of high-quality products. I see you bought a new suit so you can wash your other one. You have to be careful if you always wear the same thing or it'll get damaged faster," said Igarashi.

"The owner of the store said the same thing, so I bought two. I shouldn't be spending so much money, but we've got some extra right now." I'd also told everyone they could use a hundred gold pieces as they saw fit, but they must have been aware that they only had limited spending money, because the transaction history on my license showed that they all only used around ten gold pieces—other than Igarashi, who'd used a little more.

That must be why she was struggling with picking out underwear, I started to think, but it was probably just that different people liked to buy different things.

"You only really change equipment when getting something stronger. Spending money any other time is super expensive. Arihitooo, can I have some more money?" asked Misaki.

"Your puppy-dog eyes won't work on me... Why don't you try gambling for more money since you're so good at it?"

"But what if it goes so well because of my skills and everyone finds out...? Are you okay with something terrible happening to me? You saboteur!"

"I'm not sure you're using that word correctly... Did all that shopping get you worked up, Misaki?"

"Yeah, about that—honestly, shopping with Kyouka is like going on a roller coaster of emotions! Not that I can tell you what caused those emotions, though." I definitely could not let Igarashi realize I'd actually heard them.

"Good thing that was before Atobe came. Misaki normally just says whatever pops into her mind," said Igarashi.

"Heeey, I do not! I've got loooots of deep thoughts! Right, Suzu?"

"Uh... Um, d-do you...?"

"I do!"

"Stop trying to force Suzuna to back you up," interrupted Elitia, finally getting Misaki to calm down. The three of them had some sort of strange balance that worked.

"...So rowdy," noted Melissa.

"Melissa, did you find what you wanted to buy?" I asked. She turned her large, catlike eyes toward me and nodded.

"Nice store. Not many sell denim overalls."

"I'm so glad they have turbans!" said Madoka. "Um, Arihito, is it all right that we didn't buy any clothes for Theresia? The rest of us got what we needed."

"She can wear things over what she has, but she doesn't seem to like that kind of equipment. I think that's probably because she can't take off her lizardman-specific gear and she's not good with the heat." Although, that didn't mean she always had to wear all of her equipment. Her cute, frilled, lizard-like hat didn't come off, but she easily removed her skintight leather armor when she took a bath... Come to think of it, I wonder if maybe she'd need underwear, but Theresia herself didn't seem to think it was necessary. Guess she was fine as long as she had that equipment. "...Oh, right— Melissa, I asked you to make some armor with that camouflage stone from before. How's that going?"

"I made a prototype, but it didn't go well. There's a problem when I use the stone to use the active camouflage function."

"A problem...?"

"It'll be ready for use once I solve the issue. I'm making a suit crafted from Death from Above hide and imbued with the camouflage stone's abilities." I was surprised Melissa had thought that far ahead and chose to use materials she hadn't started working on yet. I'd only told her to save it until we needed it. I had to make sure I thought about how to use materials most effectively. "If I had to name it, I would call it a stealth suit. The outside is finished. I need a special material to finish the lining."

"I see... It just needs the lining, and then it'll be finished." Theresia learned the skill Sneak Attack, which doubled the damage of her attack if the enemy wasn't aware of her, but we couldn't use it effectively since she hadn't yet taken Hide. But if she could use active camouflage with this suit and its camouflage stone, she'd be able to save the skill points.

Theresia came pattering over when she heard her name. She was carrying the clothes the girls had bought for her. Seeing her with it made me as happy as if it were my own.

"That's nice, Theresia. Whether or not you wear it, clothes are... Huh?" Theresia pulled something out of the cloth bag she'd received from the boutique. I looked away the moment I realized what it was.

"D-don't do that, Theresia. You can't show that in public—wait until we get back home," said Igarashi.

"......"

There was a good reason why Igarashi rushed to stop her. Theresia had pulled a striped swimsuit out of the bag. I didn't even need to wonder why she'd buy a swimsuit of all things.

"There was only one of these left in stock...and it looked like it'd fit Theresia, so we decided she should get first choice for it," explained Igarashi.

"And it should help you feel more comfortable, Arihito. Since you're always going together...," said Suzuna.

"By going together...do you mean going to take a bath?" They meant I wouldn't have to feel embarrassed when Theresia came to wash my back. I couldn't keep my face from turning red from the fact that they'd be that considerate.

"......"

"Men looove a stripy aqua number like this! But we were just talking about how we're not quite ready to wear a swimsuit, right, Kyouka?" said Misaki.

"...Wh-what? I'll wear one if I need to, but I don't need one right now, obviously," replied Igarashi.

"Hey, I didn't say anything... Erk, wh-why are you glaring at me like that?" I asked.

"Hmm, I wonder why. Ever-so-serious Atobe, shall we head to the Chest Cracker next?"

"Wh-why is Igarashi angry...?"

"I better keep quiet for now. You know what they say; the early bird gets the worm!"

"Um... Misaki, I think it's actually *silence is golden* in this situation," pointed out Madoka. Misaki responded by sticking her tongue out. It was probably one of those habits where people stick their tongue out when they've been caught making a mistake. It was a silly gesture that made me and Madoka laugh.

To get to the District Seven Chest Cracker, we had to walk for a while, following an alley near the clothes shop. Outside the Chest Cracker was a sign with the name SHICHIMUAN, written in Japanese, along with a drawing of a chest. That probably meant the owner of the shop was Japanese.

"Excuse me, is anyone in?" I rang the doorbell, then called, and the door opened a few moments later. We were lost for words when we saw who came out of the store.

A demi-human... And by the looks of it...

They were wearing a helmet in the shape of a rhinoceros bee-tle's head, and their whole body was clad in a metallic carapace. I couldn't tell if they were a man or a woman from their height and build, but the fact that they were a demi-human meant there was another person who was the shop owner.

The beetle demi-human opened the door and gestured for us to come in. The decor inside had a traditional Japanese aes-thetic. There were paper lanterns that emitted a soft light, giving the whole scene a dreamy feeling. They were on the edges of an area the size of a small bedroom. A woman wearing a kimono and smoking a pipe sat on the tatami mats.

"Welcome. I apologize for my appearance. I didn't expect any more customers today."

"It's all right. Thank you for seeing us," I replied.

"E-excuse me... May I ask one question? Is that person...?"

The beetle demi-human stood there without a single word, almost like they were guarding the woman. They looked so strange, so different from any demi-human we'd seen so far, and it put everyone in the party on edge.

"This is my younger brother, though he may not look it. His name is Takuma... Takuma Asakura. And I am Shiori Asakura."

"I see..."

"It was quite a long time ago, so you don't need to let it bother you. I'm just happy that we can live together like this as brother and sister... But enough talk about us—let's discuss what it is I can do for you." Shiori tugged on her kimono's sleeve and stood up. Choosing that kind of clothing even though she was in the

Labyrinth Country meant it must really suit her aesthetics. "My job is Pawnbroker... I only wear this because I like kimonos. I imagine it's the same reason that you wear suits. Life is boring if we don't indulge our preferences."

"A kimono... They have sushi and tempura here, meaning you can find someone who can make kimonos if you look hard enough..."

"Suzu, didn't someone like that make your Shrine Maiden clothing?"

"In that case, I'd be able to have them make new equipment for me."

"Eventually, we'll get to a point where strengthening your current equipment won't be enough. We also might find a chest, though." The equipment that came out of chests was equipment that Seekers had dropped in the labyrinth. In other words, if there were Shrine Maidens other than Suzuna, there was a chance we could find some Shrine Maiden clothing.

That's when I realized something. If that demi-human, Takuma, became a demi-human after fighting with the Paradox Beetle, there was a chance some of his belongings were in our red chest.

"Excuse me, Shiori, may I ask one important question? Takuma is the way he is now because he was killed by a monster in the labyrinth, correct?" I asked.

"Yes... I believe so. I wasn't seeking with him, though, so I didn't see the monster his party fought."

"Oh... Atobe, do you think...?" Igarashi suddenly realized the same thing I was thinking. Everyone else realized it as well and looked at Takuma, who was standing there quietly. From our storage, I took out the chests we'd brought with us. I showed the red one, which we had retrieved from the Paradox Beetle—we had also put a mark on it so we'd know which one it was—to Shiori. Takuma turned toward me and looked at the chest. His reaction turned my guess into a certainty.

"I believe this chest is likely from the monster that killed Takuma. If there's anything inside that belonged to him, we will return it. I think that's the best course of action," I said.

"…That's…that's…"

I wasn't certain there would be anything. However, the monster flew high in the sky where no one could reach it, meaning Seekers would only end up fighting it when it came after them. I couldn't deny there was a possibility other Seekers had fought it before us.

"…I wanted to one day get my revenge, but I wasn't strong enough, and I gave up…," said Shiori. "I can't believe this chest would find its way to me even so. I'm sure he'd yell at me if he could…"

"I'm…not sure about that. But it's not like demi-humans are doomed to never speak again," I replied. "We continue to seek with that hope in mind."

"A lizardman… I see, so she…" Shiori looked at Theresia. I couldn't tell what she was thinking, but she didn't continue to berate herself after my clumsy attempt at persuading her. "As a Pawnbroker, I handle the sales of any unwanted items within my clients' chests. That is where my chest-opening skills come from. I may not be able to open a Black Box, but I can safely open a red chest. This one will be on the house—"

"No, please let us pay. Besides, we won't know until we see inside if we really did defeat Takuma's attacker."

"…I've been watching him this whole time. I know. There's some fateful connection between this chest and my brother." Shiori directed Takuma to carry the three red chests and two wooden chests that I had. She pulled a cord that dangled from the ceiling, which pulled up a scroll hanging on the wall, revealing a hidden set of stairs. That likely led to the door that would teleport us to the rooms used for opening chests.

"This way, please. There, you will witness as I, Shiori Asakura, the founder of the Asakura House of Chest Crackers, perform a five-chest opening."

Even among Chest Crackers, there were all sorts of individuals. I hadn't thought there would really be any more unique than Falma, but I realized now that was naive of me.

Part IV: Fireworks of Treasure

Falma's shop was the same in that the teleportation door was below ground. It must be standard practice.

We descended the stairs that had appeared from behind the hanging scroll, when we came upon a door. There was a blue stone embedded in it, which showed the number twenty-seven when Shiori touched it with her hand. When she saw the digits, Shiori pulled a folding fan from inside the right sleeve of her kimono, opened it, and used it to cover her mouth as she looked at me.

"…That's not my age."

"O-oh, no, that's not what I was thinking…and you suddenly sounded like you were speaking in a Kyoto accent."

"Ha-ha, I apologize. I actually consider speaking like that all the time. Don't you think it's important for everything to match the part?"

"Ooh, I know exactly what you mean! I was thinking I should look like a Gambler since I am one," said Misaki.

What would a "rearguard" look like? At the moment, I just wore a suit since I was used to it and put my armor on over it. People might start talking about the Seeker who looked like a businessman, but that wasn't a problem since I didn't want people talking about my rearguard job anyway.

Shiori opened the door, and we entered. The room we found ourselves in was equally large as the previous times we had chests opened, with its ceiling so high that I couldn't see it. It was quite simply a massive space. Shiori spread a large cloth on the floor, and Takuma lined the chests up on it: three red, two wood. Shiori stood behind them, gesturing toward them with her fan.

"I'm sure you're in a hurry, but I'd like a quick word first. Are you all aware of what opening a chest involves?"

"It's like getting through a barrier to get the treasure inside… Basically, we can't let our guard down even though we've finished the battle itself. It's a final step that we still need to be careful of," I said.

"Exactly. Opening a chest comes with its own dangers. But what will happen if you can open it safely…? As you can imagine, the more difficult a chest is to open, the greater the rewards inside. A bit like fireworks, wouldn't you say?"

I remembered the moment the Black Box opened—before I knew it, the area around me had been filled with magic weapons and coins. She was calling that moment when the treasure spills out of the chest *fireworks*. I would understand the reason she was telling us this when I saw how she opened the chests.

"Pawnbrokers differ from other Chest Crackers. We actually have skills that allow us to use chests to attack our enemies. Even the most ordinary chest can act as a receptacle for explosions… Related to those skills are ones that allow us to safely extract the treasure from the chests." Shiori pulled another folding fan from her other sleeve as she spoke. Those fans were most likely equipment that improved the success rate of her skills. "My dear customers, I hope you enjoy the special show I am about to perform for you."

```
◆Current Status◆
> SHIORI activated ASSESS 3
> Detected RED CHEST A's traps —→ Success
Traps: Monster Summoning          Level 3 Trap
> Detected RED CHEST B's traps —→ Success
Traps: Sleep Fog                  Level 2 Trap
> Detected RED CHEST C's traps —→ Success
Traps: Explosive                  Level 2 Trap
> Detected WOODEN CHEST A's traps —→ Success
Traps: Poison Dart                Level 1 Trap
> Detected WOODEN CHEST B's traps —→ Success
Traps: None
```

Various different traps suddenly appeared on my license display. Each one of them sounded dangerous, but the explosive trap seemed most likely to kill us if we were hit directly by it. That was only level 2, though, so I couldn't help wondering how dangerous the level-3 monster-summoning trap was. Falma had told me how there were times when failing to properly open a Black Box ended up destroying entire sections of the city. These traps seemed measly in comparison.

I looked up to watch how Shiori would remove the traps. She opened both fans at the same time and crossed her arms. When she did, different-colored lights started coming from each box, starting with the red chest on the far left and flowing down the line. Then—

◆Current Status◆
> Shiori activated Fireworks of Treasure
> Traps level 3 and below on targeted chests were removed

—glowing patterns appeared on the surfaces of the chests, which then peeled off them and floated into the air in response to Shiori's rhythmic motions.

"…So pretty…," I heard Igarashi say. The patterns were like fireworks painting the night sky. Reds, blues, yellows—they danced about and were sucked one by one into Shiori's fans. Once the traps were removed, she bowed her head in front of the chests, indicating they were ready to be opened.

"Is this when we'd normally toss tips for the performance?"

"No, we don't have to toss anything. We can just hand it over normally—wait, hang on, she's not a geisha!"

"I am fine with however you wish to give a tip, but I'll have to charge extra if you'd like to put it *here*," said Shiori.

"Uh… N-no thank you, I think any risqué fun is more than I can handle," I said.

"I know, I just thought I'd say it. It's been so long since any customers have enjoyed my performance so much." Most of her clients were probably too excited about the treasure in the chests that they didn't bother to appreciate her dance. I thought that was a real shame.

"That was such a wonderful dance—so elegant and personal. I wonder if other Pawnbrokers have skills with such a Japanese flair."

"Kyouka, have you seen something like that before?" asked Elitia. "So that's what a geisha is like… I'd seen pictures and videos but never in real life." Elitia seemed quite moved by the unexpected Japanese dance. I'd also been so entranced by it that I wanted to give her a tip or, at the very least, some small token of my gratitude.

"Hey, Arihito, Suzu used to dance at the shrine since she's a Shrine Maiden," said Misaki. "She'd have a bell and go like *jing-a-ling-a-ling*!"

"Wow, that's really cool… Was it kagura dance, then?"

"Yes, I'd dedicate dances to the gods a few times a year. It's not nearly as exciting as Shiori's dance, though. It's slow and gentle."

"My... I wasn't certain, but you really are a Shrine Maiden, aren't you?" asked Shiori. "I'm interested in kagura dancing as well. I'd love to see it if you have a skill like that."

"S-sure... I don't know yet if I'll learn a skill like that, though. If I do, I will let you know."

Shiori did seem to quite like traditional Japanese arts and styles, so she stared at Suzuna and her Shrine Maiden outfit again with great interest. It would be good if we could build a friendly relationship with her—something that was more than just the relationship between a Chest Cracker and Seekers.

"Well then, please feel free to view the contents of the chests. Please let me know if you will need any appraisal scrolls."

"Thank you very much. Let's go with this red one first... It's been quite a while since we got this one," I said.

"We need to open chests we get faster from now on. This first chest we got...is it the one that Misaki found and ended up being captured?" asked Igarashi.

"Yeaaah, I don't like thinking about it even now...hmm? After the trap went off and I was teleported, there was some gold scattered around the chest. I assumed that was what was inside," said Misaki when the topic was brought up. Elitia went to recover the bag that should have contained the treasure from the chest that teleported Misaki...but if that was the case, where did we actually get this first chest?

"From my experience in opening chests...there are times when the trap on a chest can go off but not be removed. Even so, every time the trap is activated, some of the contents of the chest are released," said Elitia.

"Ohhh, is that what happened? So does that mean this is the red chest we got from the giant orc?"

"If that's the case, you did a really good job... Elitia, what's wrong?" I said.

"Nothing... I just realized that's probably the case now that you said it. I missed it before. I never really went with my party before to open chests, even when we did find them." Elitia still didn't know everything there was to know about chests and traps. That wasn't a problem, really. As long as she was in our party, we could learn together.

"I actually feel better knowing there's things you're not sure of. It means you'll be even more dependable than you are now."

"D-dependable... I'm the one who's always learning things..." Elitia fidgeted with her ponytails, seemingly uncomfortable. I wasn't surprised that Misaki looked at her like she wanted to crack a joke, but she seemed aware it would stop the conversation in its tracks and managed to hold herself back.

"Oh... Arihito, I looked at the mover's records for when they transported Juggernaut to the Dissection Center, and it mentions the chest. Misaki was the one to get it, so it was sent to your party's storage unit," said Madoka.

"Oh, I see. Then it *is* a chest from the Field of Dawn..."

"It appeared when we were fighting some Cotton Balls and Poison Spear Bees. Chests almost never appear if you're not fighting a Named Monster, so I was really surprised," said Elitia.

Now that we'd confirmed where we got it, it was time to finally look inside the chests. The first one we opened was the one that Misaki found.

◆Chest Opened◆

RED CHEST A: Acquired from POISON SPEAR BEE

> ?ANKLET

> POISON HONEY

> RICOCHET STONE

> ELMINA IRON

> 10 COTTON WADS

"Whoooa... Oh, um, there was some gold in it before, but now that I think about it, it's still in my bag. Yeah. Um, I'll be sure to put it back," said Misaki.

"Huh, I get it now. The fact that there's no money in it must mean it came out when you failed to undo the trap," I said.

"Almost like the chests are alive... They give you money as a consolation prize."

"Teleportation traps are dangerous, but...it was good there were no other traps on it, like the explosive or poison dart ones. I would feel so sorry for your family if something happened to you," said Suzuna.

"Sorry I made you worry, Suzu. But I'm all right now. I'll be super-duper careful from now on."

I didn't expect anything to change about her risky behavior, but I did want her to always be on guard. Even I'd seen her teleported off, right in front of my eyes. I couldn't let that happen again.

"...Poison honey—honey from Poison Spear Bees gathered into a bottle. You can smear it on your weapons," said Melissa. She'd seen plenty of materials as a Dissector and therefore had quite a bit of knowledge about them. The vaguely purple-colored honey didn't look all that poisonous, but there was no denying that it was.

"Poison honey pancakes are really popular. They're made using an antidote to neutralize the poison before cooking. I'd only tried them once when I was in District Eight, though," said Shiori.

"I'm sure it's quite the delicacy... You're pretty brave to try it," I said.

"You think? It's actually possible to build a slight tolerance for poison if you get used to it. Seekers going to fight in areas with a lot of poisonous monsters will sometimes undergo poison-resistance training overseen by a Pharmacist or Doctor... I've even heard there are some who can withstand poison that would kill even the most ferocious monster."

Equipment wasn't the only option for improving resistances to status ailments; apparently, you could use food as well. It was informative, but I'd still need a lot of nerve to put anything with *poison* in the name into my mouth. If possible, I wanted to stick to using equipment for that, like we had been doing.

We decided to gather the unidentified items and appraise them all together later. The other item from the chest that caught my attention was this ricochet stone. It was clearly a magic stone, but what exactly did it do? I asked Madoka to look it up on her license through the Catalog function that only merchants could use.

"When a ricochet stone is attached to a ranged weapon, it allows you to attack by bouncing shots off walls and other objects. If you put it into equipment—boots, for example—it allows you to jump very high."

"An attack that bounces... So I'd be able to ricochet my shots, huh? I'd really love to try that out. Not sure when I could really use it, though."

"Look at you, acting like a kid in a candy store... Atobe, you are excited by the strangest things sometimes."

"Would it be rude to say he's rather...innocent?"

"Ricocheting shots! That's sooo cool. I don't think a magic stone would fit on my dice, though." Misaki was also excited by the idea, but she was right that a magic stone probably wouldn't fit on her weapon. She wasn't primarily an attacker in the party, though, so there wasn't any immediate need to modify her weapons.

"Okay, next up. This is the chest we got from Death from Above," I said, placing my hand on the chest and opening it. When I did, there was a flash of brilliant light that momentarily blinded us, though it wasn't quite as bright as when we opened the Black Boxes. A moment later, piles of treasure appeared around us. The amount and quality of this treasure was definitely far better than what came out of the red chest from the Poison Spear Bee.

◆Chest Opened◆
RED CHEST B: Acquired from ★DEATH FROM ABOVE
> ?BOOTS
> ★FORBIDDEN SCYTHE
> FIRE GARNET
> ?CHARM
> ?CLOTH STRIP
> 138 GOLD COINS

> **655** SILVER COINS

> **130** COPPER COINS

> **35** UNUSABLE COINS

This was what you'd expect from a chest that a Named Monster had dropped. There were a few different pieces of equipment and quite a bit of money, though I couldn't help feeling it wasn't that much, considering I'd seen what could come out of a Black Box.

"Is this...a scythe? Looks almost like what the grim reaper carries..." Igarashi was looking at the most peculiar item that came out of the chest: a weapon called a "Forbidden Scythe." There was a star next to the name, which implied it was a special weapon. I suppose it was almost like a "Named" weapon.

"Wait, you should appraise it before you touch it. If it's cursed, you might not be able to put it down again," warned Elitia, and Igarashi pulled back from the scythe. First, Madoka tried to use her skill Appraise 1, but she was only able to glean a small amount of information from that. We bought a Mid-grade Appraisal Scroll from Shiori.

"I'm sorry I couldn't be more helpful, Arihito...," apologized Madoka.

"No, you've done great. You still get us a discount on scrolls and opening the chest itself. Your Negotiate Price skill has helped us many times," I said.

"The market price for a Mid-grade Appraisal Scroll is five gold, but I just can't say no to this girl. You'll make a wonderful merchant," said Shiori.

"Th-thank you..."

"When we were shopping for clothes earlier, we got a discount simply because Madoka was there. I couldn't get a discount even if I tried," said Misaki.

Corleone ended up helping me himself while I was there, but maybe I did get a discount thanks to Madoka's skill. She also helped make it so we could sell items at a price that was at least 10 percent higher than normal. Her Negotiate Price skill was only level 1 right now; I couldn't imagine going shopping without her once she got to level 2 or higher.

"Arihito, I'll appraise the item." Suzuna opened the appraisal scroll and read it. My license displayed the item's description after Suzuna successfully identified it.

```
◆★Forbidden Scythe◆
> Absorbs some of the enemy's vitality when
  attacking.
> Chance of one-hit KO on critical hits.
> Must be wielded with two hands.
> Breaks easily.
> Only one in existence.
```

"This...could be a really valuable weapon depending on its critical hit ratio. There's only one, but it breaks easily. I wonder if there's something we can do about that," I said.

"Right now, the only people who can equip it are you or Melissa," said Suzuna.

"...I am interested, but my butcher's knife improves the likelihood of Partial Destruction of my target. I think I'm okay if I don't change right now," said Melissa.

"Okay, how about we put it in storage until a time comes when we can use it?" I suggested. Another issue was its weight; testing it by walking around with it wouldn't be easy. Furthermore, it'd be a waste if it broke after only a few attacks.

I lifted the leather boots while I thought. I'd seen that metallic shine before. I'd had Suzuna's and Misaki's armor strengthened with elmina iron at Ceres's forge, which was done by adding a thin layer of metal to the inside of the garments to avoid ruining the appearance. These boots were modified in the same way.

"Madoka, I think you could manage with Appraise 1 on these boots."

"O-okay, I'll try..."

I passed her the boots, and she tried to appraise them, with perfect success. I smiled as she held the boots out happily. The size looked about right for me, and I was happy for the update in equipment. That's about all I expected, but I looked at the appraisal report and was lost for words.

◆Elluminate Mountaineering Boots◆
> Small chance of nullifying enemies' status
  ailment attacks.
> Slightly reduces physical attack damage
  received.
> Slightly increases effectiveness of skills
  that strengthen allies.

"These..."

"Arihito, are they that good?" asked Elitia.

"Yeah. It improves skills that strengthen everyone. I've been wanting to collect more equipment of this type."

"Judging by the design, they're clearly men's boots. I bet they'll suit you," said Igarashi.

"Th-thanks. I've never worn something like this before." I had no idea why these boots were made or how they got this ability, but I assumed they'd once been used by a man in a support class like me.

Other things from the chest included the fire garnet, which added the Heat attribute to weapons. The charm looked like some sort of protective amulet, and the cloth strip just looked like a ribbon to me, but my license showed that both were unappraised. There was money, too. I was happy to get something to supplement what we had to spend on living costs. We gathered the scattered coins into a pouch and decided to open the last chest. Before we did, though, I looked at Shiori and then Takuma, the beetle demi-human who was standing by her.

"...Please, go on."

If Takuma really had been killed by the Paradox Beetle, there would likely be something to indicate that in this chest. Everyone locked their eyes on the chest as I opened it, and—

◆Chest Opened◆
RED CHEST C: Acquired from ★PARADOX BEETLE
> ★AMBIVALENZ
> ★DEXTERITY GAUNTLETS
> ?NETTED RAGS
> ?RING
> ?RING

—out of the box came a particularly shaped spear-like weapon that had blades on either end, along with a piece of armor that looked like a pair of gauntlets.

And there was more.

Without another word, I bent down to pick up one of the small, metal rings. Theresia picked up the other. We didn't need to appraise them; they were clearly meant for a person's fingers. There were characters of the Labyrinth Country language engraved on the insides of the bands. I handed the one I picked up to Shiori. It rested on the palm of her hand, and she lovingly stroked it with her other hand, tears gathering in her eyes.

"He'd never said a word about it to me, but... It wasn't until my little brother turned into a demi-human and returned home when I heard he'd been engaged..." The engraving was probably either Takuma's name or his fiancée's. The party they were in had been attacked by the Paradox Beetle, and their belongings had ended up in this chest.

"Please let us give the rings back to your brother," I said.

"...Thank you. I couldn't do anything for them..."

People who lost their lives in the labyrinth could come back as demi-humans, but it wasn't common. Some part of me had always believed that as long as I didn't give up, I'd never lose one of my party members. This showed me that I was naive to think that, and it shook me to my core.

Why were there so many Seekers in District Seven who'd stagnated? It was because they feared death. I couldn't blame anyone who'd given up advancing because of that.

"Arihito..." I didn't want to make anyone worry about me, but Elitia was looking at me with concern. I told myself to get it together...told myself I just needed to not show how upset I was.

The moment I decided that, though, Takuma walked over to stand next to me. He silently held out his hand. I placed the two rings in his palm, and he simply stood there, staring at them. I couldn't think of anything to say. He'd come back home as a demi-human, but his fiancée had not. Right then, I didn't have it in me to even try and console him or express how absolutely tragic the whole thing was.

"...We'll send the items from the chest to our storage and finish looking them over later," I said. "Shiori, Takuma—thank you both so much."

"I should be the one expressing my gratitude...but... I'm so sorry—could you please leave me alone with my brother...?" Shiori tried to keep it together, but she was at her limit.

Igarashi stepped forward to wrap her in her arms. Shiori seemed about to burst into tears.

"I can only imagine what happened...but please, let me at least do this much. I can't just leave you like this without doing anything," said Igarashi.

I wanted to give the two some space, so the other party members and I respected Shiori's wishes and headed toward the teleportation door to leave. Just before walking through the door, I looked back to see Takuma standing there, squeezing the rings in his hand as he stared into the nothingness above him—perhaps, saying a prayer for the person he lost.

We got incredible things from the chests, but it was an experience that tested our resolve. Igarashi came out after Shiori had settled down a little. We started walking to the Chinese restaurant we'd planned to meet Four Seasons at. I brought up the rear, but Igarashi came to join me. Theresia walked quietly on my other side. She seemed to be concerned for me after our visit to Shiori.

"...Losing someone important to you can make you lose your reason for seeking. I suppose that's true for pretty much anyone," I said. Georg from Polaris had said something similar once—that losing Sophie would spell the end of his party.

Misaki and Madoka were walking ahead, chatting about something. Melissa and Cion were a little farther up; Suzuna and Elitia were walking together, exchanging the occasional word. Everyone must have a lot on their minds. They might even have some reservations—which was all the more reason I needed to speak up.

"This might be naive of me to say, but—I swear I'll protect each and every one of you." I absolutely needed to say it. I would never forgive myself if I let the situation get to a point where they gave up. I knew it would be hard. Even if I prepared for everything I could, I could end up shooting myself in the foot with my guesses. An action I thought would be beneficial could end up forcing us into a difficult situation. I knew that was just how the labyrinths were, but I did not want to let anyone die.

"Shiori said they would help us if there was anything they could do. I don't think it's right to use large numbers of people to take over hunting grounds, or force people to join us, but I do think we'll need the help of as many people as we can get," said Igarashi.

"Yeah…I agree. You're really dependable, Igarashi. You know that, right?"

"Wh-what are you talking about…? Did you lose your cool? Where's the Atobe that stays ridiculously calm no matter what happens?" She tried to cheer me up, and it worked a little. My deep dark mood started to lift. "I'm happy to hear you say you'll protect everyone… But you know, I intend to protect you with my own body if it comes down to it. Don't get too upset if that happens. I want to protect you as well."

To think that my manager, Igarashi, would protect me with her own life… I wasn't actually that surprised. It seemed natural now. It wasn't like she'd wanted to make me suffer just because we didn't get along. She meant it when she said she wanted to protect me. The fact that I could believe that was, in itself, quite incredible.

"…I'm not going to let you say that I shouldn't be sad if you're not around anymore," I said.

"…Well, if it did end up happening, I'd be happy just knowing you were safe…"

Part of me wanted to be angry and ask how she could say something like that. Part of me was grateful. I didn't know what to say about the fact that I thought this, but now I could look back on the fact that I used to be her subordinate, be proud of it, and remember it fondly. That was only possible in the present, though, after all we'd gone through.

"……"

"…You can't do anything too reckless, though, for Theresia's sake. Are you all right from when the monster got you before?" asked Igarashi.

"Yeah, I'm fine. That's right... I should do what I can to prepare and make sure we don't end up in a bad situation. Or at least, make it so we can run away if we do end up in one."

"That'd be good. And you should do your best to keep everyone from worrying."

I reflected on how concerned my party was for me, and everyone walking ahead turned back to look at us. They must have heard parts of our conversation. I raised my hand, trying to say I was sorry for worrying them. Everyone smiled in response, and then I saw the restaurant we were heading for. Four Seasons was waiting outside for us since there was still some time until our reservation.

CHAPTER 4

The Long and Busy Night

Part I: Refreshing Heaven

There were quite a few popular restaurants in the area around the Upper Guild in District Seven. But as far as I could see, there was only one Chinese restaurant, and it had a line out front for people who hadn't made a reservation. REFRESHING HEAVEN—that was the restaurant's name on the sign. Four Seasons was waiting outside just below that sign, and they started walking our way when they saw us.

"Ah, Teacher! You made it in time—we've still got a bit longer until our reservation." They must have gone back home for a bit, because they'd all changed. Ibuki was wearing denim shorts and a weird shirt with kanji on it. Misaki cracked up at the sight of it and turned the other way, her shoulders shaking with suppressed laughter.

"See, they're all laughing at it... You're embarrassing us," said Kaede.

"Th-that's not true—Arihito isn't laughing," said Ibuki. "Besides, you're the one who didn't even bother spending enough time putting on makeup."

"Wh-what are you talking about? We're just eating. This is a perfectly normal amount to wear for that."

"...I feel like Ryouko was rushed, too, but it's best not to talk about that," said Anna. Ryouko had been wearing her bathing suit before, so maybe she needed to hurry more than the other members. Her usual outfit of a boa coat over a bikini really did stand out too much. Now she was wearing a cardigan over a camisole with a skirt. It was actually quite normal. Even so, not many people in the Labyrinth Country dressed like that, so it was quite refreshing to see. People usually wore their regular gear when walking around.

"I see you put on the clothes you bought from the boutique before. That store did have a lot of nice things," said Igarashi.

"Yeah, it's one of the more popular shops in this area. It has more variety than the stores in District Eight. We were all amazed the first time we went," said Ryouko.

"Sooo... Ibuki, where did you get that T-shirt with the kanji for *sincerity* on it? Just for my own reference," chimed in Misaki. Anna was wearing one that said *genuine* in kanji. The store must have been selling those designs because they looked so cool. Ibuki and Anna had pretty good taste for buying them. I wasn't against an odd T-shirt. My friends probably wouldn't even look at me funny if I just wore it to sleep.

"There's a stall that sells clothes near the Middle Guild. Anna and I bought them because we thought they were cute. Are you going to buy one, too, Misaki?"

"Uh, hmmm. Well, I do like a retro look like that, but I personally think, based on what's in fashion this season, that a simple, casual look is better."

"I'd love to buy something like that if any place sold it…," said Elitia.

"As long as you have the materials, you can have something custom-made. You'd be able to have a look like the one Misaki described," said Igarashi. They both had their own preferences for clothing. I wasn't too worried about what I wore, but when I considered how the others must feel, I realized they'd probably be happy to wear clothes they liked.

"Kaede isn't into rough appearances like this," explained Anna. "She likes soft and cute things. She might be really tough while she's fighting, but she's actually a bit of a girlie girl."

"Urgh… I-it's not girlie—just normal! It's not like I wore something I wouldn't normally just 'cause Arihito is here."

"Sorry about all these chatty girls, Atobe… No point standing around here talking. Should we go into the restaurant now? You first," said Ryouko.

"Yes, let's go. Thank you."

The rest of the party continued to talk with Four Seasons while we went in. We weaved our way through the outdoor seating and entered the restaurant. As we did—

"Ugh, it's *them* again: Beyond Liberty. Going around acting all important."

"They probably rented out the big room. Must be nice getting to be one of their big bad leaders, getting to drink while surrounded by women."

—some of the people waiting in line to get in—a young man who looked like some sort of warrior-type job and his companions—were standing by the entrance slinging insults. Apparently, we would be sharing the restaurant with the alliance that Gray was a member of. They probably wouldn't pick a fight since their karma would go up, but I did prepare myself for the possibility.

"Their leader, Roland, wasn't always like that, you know. People change a lot when they fall in rank."

"And that's probably why he got so greedy. If Beyond Liberty keeps increasing their membership like this, they'll have control over everyone in District Seven for a long time to come."

"Um, Daniella treated me in the labyrinth once, so I'd rather not say anything bad about them."

"C'mon, Kasha… So you're sayin' an invite from the leaders of the Alliance wouldn't be all that bad—"

"Don't be stupid. I wouldn't accept an invitation from a womanizer like that even if hell froze over. I'd punch him in the face if my karma wouldn't go up." What had Gray done to try and entice this woman named Kasha to join the Alliance? Four Seasons's members all looked unhappy.

It was about that time when one of the restaurant staff noticed we'd come in. She rushed over to us, looking apologetic.

"I am very sorry—we are currently booked full. We won't have any more tables for another hour…"

"Oh, actually… I'm Atobe; I have a reservation for a guard-dog-friendly room."

"My apologies for the misunderstanding. Atobe, was it? One pet-friendly room for thirteen. This way, please." She was wearing a uniform that resembled a cheongsam, perhaps to match the atmosphere of the restaurant. She led us to one of the private rooms with a single, large, round table inside, and we took our seats.

"Can I get you any drinks to start with?"

"That would be great. By the way… The room next door seems to be having quite the time."

"Yes, a large number of customers have booked up two of our rooms." Of all places, we had to be in the room next to them, though it was most likely because we were also a large party. It made sense that the large rooms were next to one another.

"Are you guys okay with this restaurant?" I asked Four Seasons.

"Thank you for your concern, Atobe…but we're fine," replied Ryouko.

"Yeah, we don't come to fancy restaurants like this too often," said Kaede. "It'd be a waste to let them get to us and leave now. Thanks for booking us a private room, Madoka."

"This was apparently the only room that could fit more than ten people. I only managed to get the reservation because Arihito suggested I book ahead of time."

"Atobe, you were always so busy at work but still managed to organize work parties…," said Igarashi.

"…Arihito, you're surprisingly social. I've never made a reservation like this even once…"

"No, it's not a big deal. We can easily contact any restaurants that are members of the Merchants Guild."

Despite my explanation, they all seemed impressed for some reason that I'd organized work parties in the past. People usually ended up doing that just because they were the kind of employee whose bosses could get them to do it… That was who I was as Igarashi's assistant, so it was really just my job.

"Arihito, they have this 'Refreshing Heaven House Shaoxing

Wine.' It says you can order it on the rocks or mixed with water. What's *on the rocks* mean?" asked Misaki.

"That's for people who can handle their liquor. It's probably strong enough to make your throat burn... I'm fine with an oolong tea."

"This *wheat alcohol* here is beer, right? I wonder if 'Cool Breeze Beer' is the name of the brand," said Igarashi.

"It says here that it increases your resistance to attacks with the Wind attribute for a set period of time. I guess that's why it's a little more expensive than normal beer." We noticed the note at the bottom of the menu when Suzuna pointed it out. It said a number of their drinks had additional effects. It didn't seem like they'd make a massive difference when it came to seeking, since it was just a beverage; it was only a bonus.

"Arihito, you sure you wanna drink? You don't have to worry about us. Go on, driiink!" Igarashi and Ryouko started fidgeting in response to Misaki's urgings. They must've wanted to order something.

"You two don't have to hold back for me. I'm going to make sure everyone gets home safe, so I'll just have tea...," I said. "Eh, actually, just one drink shouldn't be a problem. All right, I'll have one of these Cool Breeze Beers."

"S-sorry, looks like we forced you into it. Can I have the same thing?" asked Igarashi.

"All right, I'll also have a Cool Breeze Beer. I've had one once before. It was so refreshing. I'm pretty sure there's nothing better to have after a hard day in the labyrinths..." Ryouko seemed quite fond of alcohol, because she put her hands to her cheeks in excitement. I wouldn't say I loved beer, but I would have one every once in a while after getting home from work.

Another interesting thing on the menu was the "Treant Apple Juice." Everyone ordered the drinks they wanted, along with some "Armored Goat's Milk" for Cion, which most likely came from some sort of goat monster.

We chatted among ourselves for a little while, but then we heard some boisterous voices from the hallway. We might not have been on friendly terms with Beyond Liberty to begin with, but I still couldn't help getting annoyed by them.

"I'm sorry I'm late!" Louisa had finally arrived.

"It's all right, Louisa. You made it just in time. Would you like to order a drink?" I asked.

"Atobe said he'd have one drink with us, so we each got a beer," said Igarashi. "Will you have one, too?"

"Oh, if you insist… May I place an order, please?" Louisa called over the waitress, who then listed the drinks they had available. Both Igarashi and I were wide-eyed with shock when Louisa didn't hesitate a moment before ordering a Refreshing Heaven House Shaoxing Wine, on the rocks.

We clinked our glasses together in a toast and continued to talk for a bit while we drank and chose our food.

"Whoa… 'Hellfire Noodles'? Sounds dangerous," I said.

"…I like spicy food. I'll order some," said Melissa.

"A-are you sure? I think this 'Noodles with Tender Dairy Cow Brisket' is a better choice…"

"Were you thinking of ordering that, too? The food descriptions make everything sound nice," said Igarashi, before ordering what Madoka had just suggested—not that it meant anything for her to order breast meat. If Ryouko and Louisa ordered that dish and I'd reacted the same way, they'd have all thought I was totally worthless.

"It's written with the Chinese characters for *supple* and *milk*… So milk that makes the body supple?"

"O-oh, I see… So it's tender. That's what I thought," I stammered.

"What's wrong, Atobe?" asked Igarashi. "Your face is turning all red—are you hot? There's no way the alcohol's getting to you already. Do you want some water to drink?"

"S-sorry, I don't get this drunk normally."

"Alcohol can affect you differently depending on your condition. You just need to be careful," cautioned Elitia. I wasn't actually drunk, but I took the water Elitia offered me. It had some sort of herb in it, because it was quite refreshing. My mouth felt cleansed. Must've been something like lemongrass.

"…Wh-what's up? Why are you both staring at me?" I asked Kaede and Ibuki.

"O-oh… I was just thinking how this all felt really comfortable. It's so natural how Kyouka takes care of you."

"So… You and Kyouka really are dating, aren't you…?"

"Uh… N-no, we're not. We worked at the same company before we reincarnated, so we've known each other for a long time…"

"So you were able to build a good, trusting relationship at your company before you reincarnated," said Anna.

"Uh... Th-the thing is...I wasn't exactly the best manager...," murmured Igarashi. Everyone else would start to suspect me if I tried to help her now, and it'd just turn into an infinite loop. I instead decided to just change the subject.

"Have you guys decided what you're ordering?"

"Oh, y-yes. I'm going to have this 'Sea Hummingbird's Nest Soup.' And this 'Drunken Mud Shrimp'...is that like normal drunken shrimp? I'd like to try that as well."

"Me too. About this 'Rising Dragon's Treasure'... You read the kanji as *xiaolongbao*, right?"

"The description says they're dumplings filled with meat and soup, so that must be what they are. I'll have that and..."

Four Seasons went about ordering their food. Elitia also seemed interested in the *xiaolongbao* buns, so she asked Suzuna and Misaki if they'd like to split an order.

I let Theresia, who was sitting next to me, look at the menu and had her choose what she wanted.

"......"

"You're gonna get the same thing as me? I'm not sure that'll be enough for you. I think you should get two more small dishes."

Theresia nodded. She chose salted fried noodles with vegetables and rib meat, and roast Sweet Bird. The latter seemed to be eaten a lot like Peking duck based on the menu's illustration.

There was a rice-based menu as well, so everyone was able to pick something they wanted. Next was just to wait and see what it all would taste like.

Originally, soy sauce and other seasonings we were familiar with practically didn't exist in the Labyrinth Country, but they'd been replicated to a certain degree after a lot of research from the reincarnates who came before us. When I said *to a certain degree*, what I meant was there were problems with perfectly replicating it. The soy sauce in District Seven didn't match the flavor and intensity of the soy sauce in our memories. The ingredients in the food were slightly different in their flavors and aroma, but we all still enjoyed the food a lot.

Melissa was swallowing her Hellfire Noodles like they weren't spicy at all, leaving the rest of us dumbfounded. Misaki took one bite and almost passed out in agony, so it definitely was spicy. I ordered some mixed fried rice and "mala power noodles," a dish that was similar to ramen. The broth tasted like it was made with pork bone, but the stock was made from monster bones and meat, which was why it had the additional effect of slightly increasing your strength.

Theresia sat next to me eating quietly, her appetite making me smile like always. She'd occasionally stop to wipe her mouth and take a drink. She was like a competitive eater, bringing more food to her mouth even after she'd eaten more than anyone else in the party could manage.

"…Mm…"

It wasn't proper manners to watch people while they ate, but eating was the only time that Theresia made a sound that wasn't quite a voice. I found myself fascinated by it.

"Theresia, you are in top eating form…," said Misaki.

"It's all turned into energy. She must have a great metabolism," said Elitia.

"I'm so jealous! It's so nice being young… My girls here are still growing, so they can eat all the sweets they want."

"Ryouko, you're making it hard for me to order anything when you say that…," said Kaede.

"So you're not gonna order dessert? They have fried red-bean-stuffed sesame mochi," said Ibuki.

"I can't eat any more… My tum-tum's gonna burst."

"Uh, Anna…? What did you just say? *Tum-tum*?"

"…I'm full."

I'd definitely heard Anna as well. She always seemed so cool and reserved, but she had her playful side. Though, she blushed slightly in embarrassment when her choice of words was pointed out. Actually, Anna wasn't the only one with a red face. The air in here seemed to be affecting everyone except Melissa. The most delicate way I could put it was that it smelled like alcohol. There was some alcohol used in the cooking, but that wasn't enough to account for it.

"…Mr. Atobe… Can I jusht have…one more?"

"L-Louisa, are you all right? I think you're pretty tipsy."

"I'm fiiiine, I jusht…love alcohol, ish so nice. I'm n-not drunk."

I'm pretty sure you'd actually call this *smashed*. Louisa had been drinking the strong stuff, and apparently, too many too quickly.

"…I'm hot… Aren't you hot? Ish so hot in here…"

"Uh… D-don't do that, Louisa. Calm down—you can't take that off in here… Ah, Atobe, do you mind going out in the hall for a minute? We'll call you back when it's safe."

"S-sure...!"

This did happen sometimes when people went out drinking...maybe. It'd never actually happened to me before I got reincarnated. It might be best to serve Louisa only an appropriate amount of alcohol in the future.

Part II: The Alliance's Internal Affairs

Someone once said you can drink, but you shouldn't let the drink swallow you up. It was a good adage. Things would go downhill very fast if Louisa took off even some of the clothes that already barely managed to contain her large breasts, so it was a good call on Igarashi's part to have me leave and let her handle it. I wasn't upset by it, but I did feel a little sad to be away from the fun of the party. I guess I was adapting pretty well to the situation.

I wouldn't say I hated the company parties we had, but there was more I needed to be careful about... I still need to be aware of things here, but it's easier now.

I didn't want to just stand outside the door and decided it'd be nice to get a bit of fresh air. I walked down the hallway and found an entrance to a courtyard. Apparently, you could eat out there and enjoy the scenery. I wandered that way and noticed something. There were some people just outside in the garden talking. It sounded like two men.

"How much longer until Roland can take the advancement test?"

"He should make the required total contribution points after his next expedition. There's no other Seeker who's made this much just by hunting crabs."

It wasn't right to stand and eavesdrop, but it was a valuable opportunity to get some inside information on Beyond Liberty. I paid attention to my surroundings so I could get out of there anytime I needed to and bated my breath in an attempt to make as little noise as possible.

"It's not actually a bad strategy... Doesn't matter how many crabs come at us—as long as our three parties are looking out for one another, we can hunt safely."

"Even so, will they help us out even when Roland's party moves up to District Six? It's more efficient for them to seek there."

"Originally, it was just Roland and Daniella in the party, so they call all the shots. I can't stand how *he's* always trying to have a word in what they do, though."

"You mean Gray? He's good at bringing other people in just because of his job. He was swapped into the main party just like that, with no explanation given to us. The hell is he up to?"

The man with the deep voice sounded like some thug—the kind who shaved their head bald and covered their back with tattoos. From what I could hear, they were one of the lower-ranked parties that made up the Beyond Liberty alliance.

"I mean, there's always people better at making their way in the world. He's just particularly good at it... I guess."

"Well, the man's a Suit, after all. It's the kind of job that lets him climb the ranks with such ease. You need a little bit of muscle, you know."

A Suit—I imagined a terrifying man in all black. Did that sort of thing even count as a job in the Labyrinth Country?

"Seriously, though, the ladies he talks to always end up acting really compliant to him. What's with that? Even today, he's just sitting around with a ton of women, and no one seems to object."

"Saying *It's just the job he has* ain't gonna cut it... Men'll get more and more jealous of him. All we can do, though, is keep an eye out and see what he does..."

I didn't know if Gray had a particular skill or if he simply had a way with words. It'd be particularly bad if it was, for example, a skill that gave him advantages when trying to win women over. I couldn't rule it out based on what these men were saying. I had no intention of letting my members get stolen away, but that meant I needed to be cautious of any interaction with him.

Apart from that, I wanted to hear more about the status of the Alliance. They had taken over the Beach of the Setting Sun—a three-star labyrinth. That meant we still didn't have enough contribution points to seek there, but there was a chance we would someday, and I wanted information on it.

"Whether we like it or not, we'll be reaching our goal the day after tomorrow. Roland will have twenty thousand contribution points... Then he'll just have to hunt the required number of Named Monsters, and he'll get into District Six."

"He's done it so carefully that it's practically safe, but it's taken a long time since each crab is only worth sixty contribution points."

"And if you take out fifty of 'em, you have to wait a couple of days until more show up. There's the fish, but we have to stay in position and not go to the beach... This strategy has both its ups and its downs."

"Even with the crabs, if you let your guard down, you'll lose a finger...and we can't even compete against the spiders and mantises. Even the moles and beetles will get you sent to a Healer clinic for a ten-day treatment if you're not careful."

The moles, which burrowed below the earth, and the beetles, which flew high in the sky. Even though we'd managed to beat them by working together, all that fighting took quite a lot out of the party. Four Seasons had told me before, but these men confirmed that the spiders and mantises were fairly dangerous opponents. It'd be worth trying to beat them if there was a lot to gain from doing so, but considering how much easier this crab hunting sounded, I wanted to give that a try first.

There was one thing bothering me, though—were any of the labyrinths I'd seen before easy places where a strategy like that would fly? It sounded like these guys might have considered the same thing.

"But...is there any guarantee he'll be able to beat the number of Named Monsters he needs to?"

"Nah, there isn't. But with all the labyrinths in District Seven, there's a chance he'll get lucky and run into one he can defeat. Only those lucky enough or those strong enough to make it happen can move up. As long as we happen to be in the same place, it'll count toward the number of Named Monsters we need to beat. It won't be worth anything if we run."

"Yeah, that's the truth... Hey, I get it. Don't make that face. I have no intention of going down here. We'd have no chance of moving up to District Six on our own strength alone. We've already taken a share of the contribution points and... Hmm?"

"It's about time to wrap it up. Gray's got his guy Basel running errands for him..."

Ah... Crap, I'm gonna be trapped!

The two men were about to come into the hallway from the courtyard, and this Basel guy was calling them from the room where Beyond Liberty was partying. I was so focused on listening to the conversation that I couldn't find somewhere to hide right away. I started to wonder if I could play it off like I had just been passing by, when something unexpected happened.

◆Current Status◆
> Melissa activated Cat's Call ⟶ Rodney's and Chen's actions were canceled

"Meeooow!"

"Mm? ...Was that a cat?"

"The restaurant allows guard pets. Maybe it's with one of the other parties?"

The two men were distracted as they were about to enter the hallway from the courtyard. I checked my license, saw that Melissa was somewhere nearby, and remembered I had a skill that could be used when I needed to make an emergency escape.

What the heck is "Cat's Call"? ...No, not the time to worry about that!

After a brief moment of blindness, I suddenly saw the back of a girl with pale hair. Looked like Rear Stance worked.

"Ack... You scared me. You're suddenly behind me," said Melissa in a low voice as she turned around. She and Anna had come looking for me, before realizing I was in a tight spot.

"I gained a level earlier and acquired a skill called Assess Battle," explained Anna. "I was able to use it to figure out you were in trouble."

"I...guess a skill like that would help you as a Tennis Player, like you were gauging the flow of a match."

Anna nodded. We watched from a distance as the Alliance's members met up and headed into their own private room.

"Sorry it took so long, Atobe... What happened? You're covered in sweat," said Igarashi.

"How should I put this... I may have pushed my luck a little too far. There were some members of that alliance standing around chatting, and I wanted to gather some information if I could."

"......"

Theresia stood up from her seat at the table after having finished all her food and came over to wipe the sweat from my brow. I felt relieved, but also, I realized that I was not suited to spying.

"......"

"Hmm? ...Theresia, what's wrong?"

"...She says don't hesitate to take her along, anywhere," said Melissa.

"R-really...?"

Melissa seemed better at understanding what Theresia was thinking than anyone else in the party. Perhaps that was because she had the blood of her demi-human mother in her veins.

"...Do you mean we're always together, and you're like my bodyguard anyway, so I don't need to hesitate to take you along?"

Theresia nodded. Everyone smiled at the clear and emphatic answer.

"Mr. Atobe... It might be, nosy of me, but ish frushtrating to watch... You should let everyone...take care of you more..."

"Louisa, drink a little more water...," pleaded Igarashi. "She's calmed down a lot, but it was a real problem when she was trying to take her clothes off earlier."

"It might be best to wrap this up soon and let her get some rest. Louisa, are you staying in the dorms for Guild employees?" I asked.

"...No... I'm your excluuusive caseworker... I'll be staying with you..."

"So a room has been prepared for you in our lodging. Could you show me on my license where it's located? Sorry to ask—I know you're still in bad shape."

Louisa was seated on her stool, leaning her upper body on Igarashi, who was next to her. She took my license and somehow managed to show me the location on the map there.

"...It's this address... Your rank when you came to Dishtrict Seven was two hundred...ninety-four...so you are assigned a terrace suite..."

"A terrace suite?"

"It might be like a terrace house? We won't know until we go," said Misaki. If she was right, it could be a walled-off plot with a row of similar, attached houses.

"District Seven's lodgings feel a bit small once you've experienced the Lady Ollerus Mansion in District Eight, but you should have plenty of room in a terrace suite," said Ryouko.

"Aw man, sounds nice. We just have apartments. Each one can only have two people, so we use two. Everyone could live together if we had a terrace suite," said Kaede.

"We need to work hard so we can move up to better lodging. We should be able to advance now that we're working with Arihito and his party," said Ibuki.

"...I'd like to visit you when we have time," said Anna.

It appeared that while Four Seasons used the Upper Guild, their lodging was not the same level as ours. I thought back to when the party was just Theresia, Igarashi, and me. Even then, our lodging was almost too big for us.

"All right... Atobe, I know you just came back to the party, but...," started Igarashi.

"No... I'm fiiiiine... I can...walk..."

Even Louisa's speech was affected by the alcohol. She was definitely not fine.

"Okay, I'll carry her. Is that all right, Louisa?" I offered.

"...Suuuuure..."

"Oooh, do you think Louisa planned this in advance so she could get him to carry her?" asked Misaki.

"A-as far as I can tell...she really is drunk. I think the drink was just stronger than she expected," replied Suzuna. Igarashi seemed conflicted. Louisa was completely listless and mumbling something I couldn't hear. She was very clearly wasted.

"Here we go... All right, this should work."

"...Sorry...mmm..."

I slid Louisa onto my back so I could carry her piggyback, and everyone stared enviously. She wasn't that heavy. My movements felt a little restricted from the way I had to hold my arms under her legs and support her against my back, but I was fine otherwise.

"...I knew it. She must have planned this so she could get that close."

"R-Ryouko... Keep that to yourself," chided Kaede.

"Arihito really is a man... He lifted her so easily," marveled Ibuki.

"He's so dependable," agreed Anna. "Kaede, I see why you say he's like an older brother."

"Is everyone ready to go?" I asked. "Make sure you don't forget anything... Madoka, would you mind paying since I've got my hands a little full?"

"Sure, no problem."

I held Louisa firmly and left the restaurant. The members of Beyond Liberty had said their meal was wrapping up soon, but that must have been put off, because they were still quite boisterous. I should acknowledge how lucky we'd been, since we'd managed to avoid running into them.

Part III: Terrace Suite

We left Refreshing Heaven, and Four Seasons returned to their own lodgings. We agreed to meet in front of the labyrinth the next day to go seeking again. Our target would once more be Silvanus's Bedchamber. We headed west from the Upper Guild's Green Hall and found ourselves walking up a tall hill. Like District Eight, the fringes of the city seemed to have more space available, so there were more mansion-like buildings with gardens attached. The most extravagant one was even decked out with security guards. That would probably be where Roland lived.

A little farther down from that building was the row of terraces, with two-story homes of the same type set in a tight line and sectioned off with a fence. There was a small garden in the front and a hut for guard animals, which was where Cion would be staying.

"Personally, Cion, I'd be fine having you stay inside with us...," said Igarashi. "I'm sorry. But you can come in if you get lonely."

"Woof!"

"Kyouka, you and Cion have grown so close. You're like sisters!"

"Oh... Y-you think so? Suzuna, you always say the sweetest things... I practically swooned just now."

"Noooo, Kyouka! Arihito will be jealous! Besides, Suzu is miiine!"

I decided I wouldn't be rude and point out that Misaki was the one who abandoned Suzuna in the first place. Plus, I'd been so hung up on my time as a corporate slave that I didn't even think to form a party with Igarashi in the beginning.

"The most important thing is for everyone to get along. Madoka and Melissa seem to have opened up quite a bit, which is good," I said.

"Yes, it's been going so well with everyone. I find myself thinking like ten times a day how lucky I am that you invited me to join the party," said Madoka.

"...Me too. I got to dissect a Named Monster. I got to destroy parts, and I gained a level. You can't do new things if you don't go seeking." Melissa didn't change her expression at all while she spoke, but if she claimed she was happy, then I'd just take her word for it.

Right then, a thought crossed my mind—I'd noticed that Melissa's mannerisms seemed somewhat catlike. Everyone else except me and Melissa went into the lodging, so I decided to ask her about it.

"Melissa, you used an interesting skill to help me earlier..."

"...I meant to tell you about my skills at some point today. But I'll mention this first: My mom's a werecat—a demi-human."

"By *werecat*, you mean...she has cat abilities?"

"Yes. But I can't use everything my mom can. Only a little bit."

It was likely thanks to her demi-human heritage that allowed her to swing that huge butcher's knife around, despite her slender arms. Theresia was like that, too. Her physical abilities were significantly better than those of other girls her age. Elitia was quicker than either of them, so a person's physical strength must go up as they gained levels. I'd noticed I could move more easily after I'd just come to the Labyrinth Country, but since I was a rearguard, my physical abilities weren't that impressive unless certain conditions were met. When I'd used Rearguard General to its fullest potential, it had almost been like it wasn't my own body that was moving.

"You really saved my neck back there. And you sounded just like a real cat, too."

"It's a skill that makes the target drop their guard. They believe a cat is somewhere nearby, which distracts them. It works on any monster that can hear, but it's more likely to fail if their level is higher."

"Good thing it worked, then. If you hadn't come, my only choice would have been to play dumb."

"...You'd be bad at that. You can't lie; it's not in you."

"Ha-ha-ha... I mean, I've been told I'm honest to a fault."

And that I wear my heart on my sleeve. I sort of wanted that skill Poker Face that Misaki's job could learn.

Just then, Misaki's voice came from inside the lodging. "Arihito, it's pretty nice in here! If you don't hurry, we're gonna choose rooms without you!"

"...Mr. Atobe... Where...will I stay...?"

"Sorry, Louisa, I've just been standing here talking this entire time," I replied. "Um, are you all right with staying at our place?"

"...Please don't say I should go somewhere else... I'm not used to it—it'll be lonely..."

"Uh... O-of course. I'll ask everyone else about assigning you to a room."

"...Thank goooodness..."

I had no idea what a drunk Louisa would do. I still had her on my back, but she was tightening her grip around me. She seemed to be getting impatient.

We went inside. The decor was quite rustic, with rugs over hardwood floors. Unlike a Japanese home, you didn't have to take your shoes off inside. The entrance hallway extended back into the building. The first room on the right was the living room, which was where I heard everyone's voices coming from. It also included the kitchen, which was delineated from the living room by a breakfast bar counter. A menu was placed on the counter. There was a service we could request where they would come to our kitchen and make food for us. We could, of course, make our own food as well, but I had a feeling we'd end up eating out a lot anyway.

"Atobe, you must be tired. Why don't you lay her on the couch for now?" suggested Igarashi.

"All right. What should we do about a bath for her?"

"She should be able to do it herself once she sobers up a bit. She could even have one in the morning."

I laid Louisa on the couch, and Igarashi covered her with a blanket she had been holding. Louisa didn't seem likely to wake up for the time being, and she didn't look uncomfortable. It was probably fine to leave her there to rest for now.

"Louisa must have drunk so much because she was as nervous about coming to a new district as we were."

"I think we'd be better off treating her as a member of the party if she's going to be with us every time we move to a new district...," said Elitia. "What do you think, Arihito?"

"True... It'd be nice to find a way to help her unwind if she's worried about coming to a new district. I want her to feel like she can completely relax around us." Everyone else was as worried about Louisa as I was, so we were on the same page. We'd had so much happen up to that point; everyone was probably completely worn out. I wanted to have a nice, relaxing evening.

"Arihito, there are three bedrooms on the second floor, and ten beds in total," said Suzuna.

"So there are extra beds? Maybe that's so there's enough if you have any subparty members. How are they divided among the rooms?"

"One room has four beds, and two rooms have three beds."

We were up to nine people with Louisa, so we should just do three to a room. It'd be best if there were a smaller room that I could use, since I was the only man, but you couldn't have everything.

"Should we do a lottery? Or draw straws?" asked Misaki.

"You're awfully perky all of a sudden... Are you up to something?"

"No waaay! I wouldn't cheat with room assignments. I'm totally fair and square about that sorta thing."

"R-right... Sorry I doubted you. Let's go with a lottery, then."

"Yeaaaah! Okay, I'll find something to write with." Misaki went off to find a pen.

In the end, I wound up in a room with Louisa and Theresia.

"......"

"Haaah..."

"Guess it's the three of us. Theresia, I'll take Louisa into the room later."

"Ooh, Arihito's trying to take Louisa into the room alooone!"

"Don't make it sound weird. Atobe just wants Louisa to be able to rest easily," chided Igarashi.

"Um… Kyouka, it looks like I'm in your room."

"…Me too."

Igarashi was sharing a room with Madoka and Melissa, and the last room was for Misaki, Suzuna, and Elitia.

"By the way, Madoka and Melissa, you both gained a level, right?" I asked.

"Yes. Um, I actually wanted to ask you what skills I should take…," said Madoka.

"I'd like to help with that as well. I still don't quite know what skills either of you have."

"…All right. I'll take whatever skills you think I should," said Melissa.

The other members were going to take a bath before us, so we could use that time to discuss skills. We'd put everything we got from the chests into the storage, so I'd have to ask Madoka to retrieve anything we would need for the following day's seeking expedition. It looked like there were still things I needed to do; my day was not yet over.

Part IV: Battle Skills and Crafting Skills

The water for the bathtub was heated using something called a "magic kettle," which needed a certain amount of magic put into the magic stone that acted as its source of power. We recovered a certain amount with a night's rest, so we decided to spread the burden across the party. I could make an infinite magic-charging loop with Charge

Assist and Ariadne's Energy Sync, but that would require Suzuna to act as Ariadne's medium. I chose not to use that method right now.

"...Atobe, I'm going to take a bath now," said Igarashi. "Make sure you tell Theresia she has to wear her bathing suit when you two take a bath later."

"H-hey, Theresia might want to bathe alone from time to time, you know."

"......"

Theresia immediately shook her head. I had assumed as much, but I couldn't help smiling at how clear she was in her response.

"Guess she really prefers joining you...," said Elitia. "I wonder what Four Seasons would say if we asked them for help on this."

"I'd prefer if you didn't tell them...," I replied. "Theresia's just, like... Uh... How should I put this?"

"I think Theresia's always grateful toward you. As am I... And Misaki, too," said Suzuna.

"Y-yeah... Way to drag me into this, Suzu! But anyway, I just want to say I'd never take a bath with Arihito unless we had bathing suits on. No way Jose!" Misaki was joking, but she did seem quite embarrassed by the idea. She was pressing her hands to her red cheeks. I had a feeling she had to trust me a decent amount to even say she'd do it if we wore bathing suits.

"Anyway, she needs to wear the bathing suit. Right now, we only have one for Theresia. If everyone gets one... Um, we could look after Atobe with Theresia if we go in wearing bathing suits. I'd do it."

"I-Igarashi, that's a little..."

"I-it's just... Y-you're always, um, always taking care of us, A-Arihito...," said Madoka.

"…I hate baths. I take them but want to leave right away," said Melissa.

They were all practically saying they'd be happy to take a bath with me if they got bathing suits. It might be better to clearly decline that, or at least, that would be the normal thing to do.

"You two don't have to do anything you don't want to," I assured everyone. "Depending on the situation, I'm sure it's more efficient to have multiple people take a bath at one time, but I think it'd be best if I just take a bath by myself after everyone else… W-wait, Theresia, I didn't say we couldn't—"

"It makes me uncomfortable that you two always go together. I think it would be better if another person went with you both," suggested Elitia.

"Don't you think you're being a little overprotective of him? You're acting more like an older sister than Kyouka," said Suzuna.

"Hmph…it's not being o-overprotective or anything. There's only one man in the party. Shouldn't someone just watch to make sure nothing strange is going on…? N-not that I don't trust Arihito—it's just, normal men aren't so relaxed about this kind of thing…" Elitia was saying everyone should take turns going with me, which seemed to have everyone convinced.

"…We could consider the bathing clothes again. If I could get a bathing suit, then I guess I can…w-wash his back… He's always working so hard…"

"I-Igarashi, I appreciate the thought, but there's other things you can do," I softly protested.

"Uh…I—I suppose…"

I was really happy she felt that way, but I honestly wasn't sure there was a bathing suit that could easily cover what her knit sweater emphasized even more. It did seem that everyone wanted a bathing suit, though, so we'd have to see if we could find and buy them, or perhaps even have them made. Hopefully, while we continued to be successful Seekers. We're talking long term.

"We could try asking Ryouko. She should know where we could buy a bathing suit. Arihito, what do you think about competition-style swimsuits?" asked Misaki.

"Wh-what do I think...? Let's just set this conversation aside. You go take your baths."

"Hmph, you could tell us that much at least. Suzu's suuuper curious, too."

"...Arihito, do you like the kind of bathing suit that Ryouko wears?"

"I-if I had to say...ugh, don't make me answer that."

The answer I did give made it sound like I wasn't against competition swimsuits, either, and sure enough, everyone clearly had their own ideas about what I liked. I'd never be able to say this out loud, but I thought it would be best if everyone got a bathing suit that suited them the most.

Igarashi returned to her room for a bit, while Suzuna and the others went into the bath first.

"Arihito, could you please help me with my skill selection?" asked Madoka. "I'd really appreciate it."

"Of course, I'd be happy to. Could you pull up your skills page?"

She swiped on her license, then showed it to me. It was the same every time someone showed me their skills: I always felt a combination of excitement and nervousness.

◆Acquired Skills◆

Inventory 1:	Expands inventory to hold up to 50 items.
Negotiate Price 1:	Slightly reduces prices of items during purchase and slightly increases them when selling.
Appraise 1:	Appraises an unknown item. Can only appraise certain items.
Unpack Goods:	Selects and fetches items from inventory or in storage.
Hide:	Renders you undetectable to prevent the enemy from targeting you.

◆Available Skills◆

Take Inventory:	Controls and manages goods in your storage.
Abacus Calculation:	Completes calculations at high speeds when equipped with an abacus.
Document Creation 1:	Transfers any necessary documentation from your mind onto paper.
Sales Skills 1:	Improves business negotiation skills.

> Purchase 1: Gives someone money or valuables to make them agree to any terms and conditions you offer.

> Remaining Skill Points: 2

"You have five skills already... Does that mean you've received seven skill points so far?"

"Certain jobs are given a skill at the beginning. Since I chose Merchant, I was given Inventory 1 without spending any points."

"Really? I didn't know about that. Thanks for the info. All right, what skills are you interested in? We'll discuss a bit before choosing."

"Oh... I've always wanted Take Inventory. The people in the Merchants Guild always said it's a really important skill and that I should take it."

"It does sound great... Whether or not you have it could really change how useful the storage unit is. I think it's important to have."

"Thank goodness... I'm glad you think so, too. You were so nice to let me into the party, but I haven't been very helpful so far."

Madoka was relieved. Merchant was definitely a support-oriented job, but there was no doubt that she'd proven helpful to the party ever since she joined.

"All right, so how about you learn Take Inventory? All the other skills look good, too..."

Document Creation seemed like it could have its uses, although I wasn't really sure what those would be. I asked Madoka, but she shook her head.

"I can make my paperwork fast enough right now. It'd be a useful skill, but I think there's others that would be better."

That was one skill ruled out. Abacus Calculation and whatnot didn't seem necessary at the moment. Purchase 1 could also be necessary, but again, I wasn't certain. Perhaps it was best to hold on to one skill point.

"All right, so what if you learn Take Inventory and then hold on to the other point for now?"

"Okay... It's been so long since I've learned a new skill. It feels nice."

She had a lot of great skills, but I thought her ability to carry many items at once was perhaps the best. In the end, each person should decide what skills to take for themselves.

"...Congratulations."

"Thank you, Melissa."

Our group's Dissector had been waiting her turn and came over once Madoka learned her new skill. She sat in the chair next to me, swiped through her license, and set it on the table for me to see.

"...Look."

"Okay... Oh, I see. This is what you have..."

```
◆Acquired Skills◆
   Knife Artistry: Increases attack damage
                   for bladed weapons.
   Helm Splitter: An attack that aims for
                  the opponent's head.
                  Increases chance of
                  Partial Destruction.
      Lop Off: On success, cuts off parts
               such as horns or tails.
```

Dissection Mastery 1: Dissects the target and divides it into parts.

Magic Item Creation 1: Modifies a piece of equipment by fitting it with a magic stone.

Cat's Call: Produces a call that distracts the opponent. Cancels the target's action when successful.

Repository: Teleports monster materials to a predetermined storage location.

◆Available Skills◆

Level 2 Skills

Scale Removal: Increases chance of reducing the target's defense on attack. (Prerequisite: Lop Off)

Hang and Cut: Hangs the target up and then attacks. Increases chance of Partial Destruction. (Prerequisite: Dissection Mastery 1)

Frenzied Scratch: A barehanded attack consisting of up to 8 consecutive strikes. Inflicts Bleed status. (Prerequisite: Scratch)

Magic Item Creation 2: Conducts a Compound modification by using 2 or more different magic stones. (Prerequisite: Magic Item Creation 1)

```
Level 1 Skills
      Assess 1:  Ascertains the quality
                 of monster materials.
     Cooking 1:  Adds additional effects
                 to food when cooking a
                 meal.
      Scratch:   A barehanded attack
                 consisting of 2
                 consecutive strikes.
                 Inflicts Bleed status.
       Ambush:   Conducts a surprise
                 attack when the enemy
                 is unaware of your
                 presence. Increases
                 critical hit rate.
 Cat's Landing:  User takes no damage
                 even when falling from
                 a significant height.
        Groom:   Nullifies systemic status
                 ailments affecting the
                 target's body.


Remaining Skill Points: 4
```

Melissa also had more skills than normal for her level. That could be because she was in a support job, or it could be because of her demi-human mother.

She's got skills for battle, monster dissection, and installing equipment with magic stones... She can take level-2 skills now that she's level 4. I see some skills that must be specific to werecats, too.

"...What do you think?"

"They're all interesting, both the ones for fighting and the ones for dissecting. It looks like you've been very careful about your choices so far."

"...It's best to assume you can't redo where you put skill points. I chose things I wanted to use or things that are necessary. I want to be better with my knife."

Right now, she had plenty of skills to make the best use of her butcher's knife, but she'd probably get even more that made it stronger in battle. The skill I was most interested in based on its description was Magic Item Creation 2. Because she could combine two or more magic stones, she'd be able to make powerful magic stones as long as we had a lot of them and all the necessary recipes.

"...Hmm? This Cooking skill..."

"I help with cooking at home, so I can cook a little already."

One potential labyrinth-seeking issue was having food during long expeditions. Portable food just didn't have much flavor to it nor any of the additional benefits you got when you ate at a restaurant.

"...I like cooking. I want to try out Cooking 1."

"In that case, I feel like Assess 1 would be good, too. I imagine determining whether a monster's meat is edible would fall under ascertaining quality."

"It's important for a Dissector to be able to tell the quality of materials."

I didn't know if that was something Rikerton had taught her—she looked like she was thinking about something for a moment, but then, she looked at me and gave me a small nod.

"So those two... Frenzied Scratch seems good, too, but I think it's better to have you use your knife and aim to destroy parts for the time being."

"That's what I want to do. I want to take Magic Item Creation 2. Dad said he wanted me to."

"All right. Let's just put off any battle skills, then. You can take those when you get more skill points."

Melissa used her license to take Magic Item Creation 2, Assess 1, and Cooking 1. However, she hesitated a tiny bit. She was looking at Groom. She seemed drawn to what was probably a special werecat skill, like she wanted to take it.

"…I don't like taking baths. If I had this skill, I could groom Cion. Like a pet groomer."

"Ah, I see… That's a tough decision, then."

"I can learn it after the next level I gain. I think Madoka might get there before me, since we don't always work together. I'll make it to level five sometime, as long as I'm in your party."

As she spoke, I realized again that even those charged with support roles wanted to learn new skills. Examining potential new abilities, picking the ones you wanted—those moments made you all the happier when you considered how hard it was to gain a level. Even though I wasn't the one learning the skills, watching people take them made my heart sing.

"Melissa—and you too, Madoka—let's try to make sure your levels aren't too behind the rest of the party. There's got to be plenty of ways to boost you up, even if you don't have battle-oriented skills."

"Arihito…"

"…I want to groom Madoka, too. I think I can use the skill on humans."

"Uh…I-I'm not really fluffy or anything, though… My hair's just a little unruly…"

That sort of explained why she liked to wear turbans so much. She called it unruly, but to me, it just looked like it had a tendency to curl outward at the bottom.

"You don't only have to take skills that are good in combat or that benefit the party. But that said, sometimes, I might literally get on my hands and knees and beg you to take a certain skill. If that happens, you can just laugh at me and let it slide."

"Hee-hee… I'll just bow even lower, then!" replied Madoka.

"…Me too. I can get very low." Melissa must have the physical abilities of a werecat, meaning she's likely very flexible. I thought of when cats crouch down then spring off after their prey—this could be very promising. If she equipped the Forbidden Scythe, then used Ambush to get a critical hit… Obviously, its instant kill ability wouldn't work 100 percent of the time, but it could be an auto-kill combo if we combined it with Misaki's Morale Discharge.

I wanted to have her take Ambush and Groom when she next leveled up. For that, it would be best to have her come with us and not sit on standby. But at the same time, she was capable of doing so much while she was on standby, making the decision incredibly difficult.

"Right… Everyone's going to be finishing their baths soon; you two can go next," I said.

"Okay. Thank you very much, Arihito!"

"…Thanks."

The two thanked me, then went to their room to change. I decided to go check on Louisa, who was still asleep, and Theresia, who was with her.

Part V: The Receptionist's Past

I knocked on the door, and Theresia opened it from the inside. I'd checked out the room a little when I'd brought Louisa in here, but there were three beds with just enough space to put a chest of drawers between each of them. The warm light of a magic-powered lantern filled the room.

I still wasn't sure it was all right for us to share a place with Louisa. It must've been hard for her to live alone in a terrace suite like this, but I hadn't asked if sharing housing with some of the other Guild employees was an option. She was normally so proper and put together. The fact that she'd gotten so completely wasted must've meant she was really stressed. With that in mind, I really just wanted to let her get plenty of rest—

"……"

Theresia was already ready to take a bath. On top of her bed was a large towel for drying herself, as well as a cloth bag. Her bathing suit was probably in there.

"So if I wear a bathing suit, there won't be any problems… Hmm?" I asked for confirmation.

She vigorously shook her head. I tried to think about what she meant by that but, without many clues, could only make a guess.

"...Are you saying it's better if I don't wear one because I can't get totally clean that way?"

"......"

"B-but it's the same for you— I'm sorry, Theresia. Normally, you wouldn't be able to take a bath with a man my age. I've only allowed it as an exception so far..."

There was no point arguing with her; she had no intention of listening. Instead, she handed me my towel, then went behind me and pushed me forward, trying to guide me to the baths.

"I—I understand. Louisa's still sleeping, but I'm sure she'll take a bath with you when she wakes up."

"......"

"Uh... Theresia, s-sorry, it's not that I don't want to take a bath with you. It's that I'm an adult, and people would say it's wrong..."

Theresia started pushing harder and harder. It must be because she's a lizardman or something, because she was quite strong despite her small frame, and I couldn't resist. Even in a situation like this, I was reminded of the shortcomings of being a rearguard.

"Mmmm..."

"Ah... T-Theresia, wait a moment. Louisa seems uncomfortable."

Theresia stopped pushing and waited for me. I was grateful she let up as I went over to Louisa's bedside to see up close how she was sleeping.

"...Uuugh..."

Her face was flushed red; that alcohol must have been rough. She'd had two refills of the same stuff she first ordered, but she was normally good at holding her liquor. I'd thought she'd be fine, which was why

I'd decided to let her go at her own pace. But more importantly, the greatest problem right now was that Louisa, who was lying on her back and had thrown off her blanket, was very exposed.

Th-this thought's crossed my mind before, but... If someone doesn't cover her chest more, any sudden movements could be really dangerous...

Right now was exactly one of those dangerous moments. I cleared my mind of all inappropriate thoughts and tried to put the blanket back on her, but she just pulled it off again. She must have been hot. She squirmed in bed, until she rolled over onto her side, her bare back to me. Again, she pulled off the blanket when I tried to put it on her. If I left her like this, though, she'd be chilly and could catch a cold. Potions generally had a lot of demand in the higher districts, so they were traded at very high prices, which made it difficult to even get medicine to help someone sober up. It probably wasn't very realistic to hope I could get a Healer to come to the house and treat her this late. That left one option.

"Theresia, do you mind waiting a little bit? I'll worry too much if we leave Louisa like this."

"......"

She nodded, sat on her own bed, and watched, curious what I was doing.

I decided it was safe to assume that if someone was so drunk that they were unconscious, they likely had taken some damage to their vitality. My skill couldn't sober Louisa up, but maybe it could help her get there on her own by healing her vitality. I could even target her with my skills despite the fact she wasn't a member of my party through Outside Assist.

```
◆Current Status◆
> ARIHITO activated OUTSIDE ASSIST
> ARIHITO activated RECOVERY SUPPORT 1 ──➤ Target:
                                              LOUISA
```

It activated once every thirty seconds, so I had to wait a bit upon activating the skill. If her vitality was full, my license would display that she hadn't recovered any. This was my chance to verify whether or not being drunk reduced someone's vitality.

When exactly thirty seconds had passed, Louisa, still asleep with her back to me, was bathed in a faint, green light.

```
◆Current Status◆
> LOUISA recovered vitality
```

...She should've recovered five points—was that not enough to fully restore her vitality? W-was she really in that bad of shape...?

"...Zzz... Zzz..."

Her breathing became steadier as I watched. When I first got hired by my company, I'd gone out with some of my new coworkers, who coerced me into taking part in a drinking contest. I had a really rough time of it, and that experience really showed how drinking too much too fast could actually risk your life.

"...Louisa, next time, let's make sure you drink slower and order something not as strong."

I knew she wouldn't reply. I sat there and had Theresia wait until I could use Recovery Support to completely fill Louisa's vitality. One great thing about my healing skill was that it didn't take much magic—only time.

Everyone who'd taken a bath before us was in good spirits, but they did blush a little at Theresia coming to take a bath with me. I was uncomfortable, too, but for some reason, this was one thing that Theresia never turned red over. I asked her to wait in the changing room for a moment while I went in ahead. I used a wooden pail to scoop out some water and test it; you could never be too careful.

"...A little tepid, but that's perfect."

I was so concerned about the water because Theresia over-heating and getting dizzy was the one thing I needed to avoid. I personally didn't really care much about the water temperature, which made it easier to accommodate her.

I always imagined lizardmen would live by the water or in wetlands...

We still hadn't run into the lizard monster that Theresia had fought before. I assumed it was in one of the labyrinths that we hadn't explored.

Sometimes, I thought about this monster that still had all of Theresia's belongings—that is, if it was still alive. But then, I thought about how Theresia would feel if we ran into the monster that took her life, and I realized it might actually be better that we hadn't yet encountered it. Or perhaps, she wanted to be the one to defeat the monster that killed her. I felt like I'd come to understand her to a degree, but there's no way I could guess everything she thought.

I saw her spirit or whatever you wanted to call it when we fought the Vine Puppeteer. Even then, she'd had a lizard's tail, meaning that becoming a demi-human even affected your spirit... When I saw that, I decided I need to hurry even more to bring her back.

That's when the door to the bathroom opened. I realized my expression had gone quite dark, so I patted my cheeks to get rid of it.

"Theresia, did you put your bathing suit—?"

"……"

The reason I stopped midsentence was that I saw her and was lost for words. Her face was, as usual, covered by the lizard mask and hood, and she wore a string bikini with light blue stripes—a type of bathing suit I hadn't seen much of in my previous life. Parts of her body were covered in reptilian scales, but I could see far more pale skin than I was expecting. She was wearing a bikini, but I was having a very hard time finding somewhere safe to look. The first time she came to have a bath with me, she hadn't been wearing anything, though. This was a huge step forward.

"……"

"Hmm? Oh, yeah... Will you wash my back? Thanks for always helping."

Theresia took the washcloth and soap from me, worked up a lather, and cleaned my back. She used just the right amount of force without me having to say anything. It wasn't a problem to let her handle it. She was only in charge of washing my back and arms; the rest was for me to do on my own. Theresia understood that, too, so she began washing herself. For some reason, she didn't use the small stools to sit and do it, instead choosing to kneel on the bathroom floor. Her knees were covered in scales, so it must not have hurt.

It wasn't appropriate for me to watch her, so I turned my attention to washing my hair. I usually lathered up my body first, but I wasn't dead set on sticking to a routine. As I was lost in my thoughts—

"...Hmm? Theresia, did the door just...?"

Before I could finish my sentence, I realized there was some-one else in the bathroom other than the two of us.

"...Mr. Atobe. I'm sorry you had to see me like that earlier."

"—?!"

All the words in my head flew away, leaving me unable to form a sentence. I could sort of understand why Theresia wanted to come take a bath with me, but Louisa and I weren't yet at a point in our relationship where... Actually, it's normal for a relationship to never make it that far and for a person to spend their entire life bathing alone.

"Well... Everyone else has already finished their baths and gone to their rooms...and I was wondering if you and Ms. Theresia wouldn't mind if you added one more person..."

I kind of started to understand what was going on as Louisa explained. It was the same as when Igarashi and Elitia said they wanted to keep an eye on what I did because it bothered them.

N-no, even if that were the case, would she do this...?

"...Would you prefer it be just the two of you? If so, I'll..."

"N-no, you don't have to... I just, I'm not sure what to say... I-I'm happy you're feeling better..."

"Yes, I think it's because you took such good care of me, Mr. Atobe... I'm really quite the lost cause. I can't believe I got so sloppy and drunk. I do remember you speaking to me so gently, though, and I felt so much better when I woke up..."

That's when I finally understood her completely. The reason she'd been bold enough to do something like this was because of what I'd done earlier.

Is it because...I used Recovery Support on her while she slept? It only took about a minute to get her back to full vitality...

"Oh... I—I...I'm sorry, you're in the middle of washing your hair."

"N-no, it's okay. Actually, I can't open my eyes now, so this is probably the best time for this..."

Theresia was there, too, but I couldn't just sit there, losing my cool. I started trying to convince myself that Louisa and I were sharing a room and it would be all right to allow us to bathe together today as long as I was just really, really careful about not looking at her.

I could sense Louisa moving closer and closer, until she was right behind me. I couldn't stop what was happening—my only choice was to give in.

"Mr. Atobe, may I just do a little something? What you did for me earlier made me so happy..."

Louisa took over washing my hair, but then, something happened that I never could have expected. She used her fingers to massage my scalp, and the tension drained from me; all of my fatigue and stress drifted away.

"Louisa, this..."

"It's my skill Pressure Point Massage. I use it to help myself relax... How is it?"

"...It feels really nice. A-actually...it makes me want to fall asleep..."

Louisa giggled.

Before I got reincarnated, I once saw a show where someone went to Bali, visited a spa, and had a full-head massage treatment like this. I imagined this was what it must have felt like... That's how good she was.

"Uh...this is out of the blue, but what's your job...?"

"I am currently retired from it, so I'm going to keep it a secret for now. It's not *Masseuse*, though."

Her teasing whisper sounded nice. I was only sitting, but I felt like my mind was going to slip off somewhere... No, it'd already gone. I was going to be so relaxed when I finally finished my bath. While entranced, I felt like I could sense Theresia coming closer as well. For some reason, she was always fine when it was just the two of us, but now, I could sense her lizard mask had turned red.

Part VI: The Innocent Merchant and the Storage Unit

Louisa had a different job before she was a receptionist for the Guild. Her Pressure Point Massage skill sped up her party members' self-healing processes, improving their physical condition and allowing them to sleep better. It could heal the Anxious status as well as the Paralyzed status, allowing her to administer emergency first aid while in the labyrinth. Even so, it seemed most useful for when the party had returned to their base.

I had a vague memory of Louisa telling me these things while she was massaging my scalp. Apparently, it wasn't uncommon for people to fall asleep during the process. Like them, I hadn't been entirely able to maintain consciousness, not really being fully aware of anything until I'd left the bathroom and gone into the living room. Louisa stood in the entrance to the living room, wearing a bathrobe and bowing profusely. Her hair was gathered up in a scrunchie; it seemed like she normally did that after taking a bath. This was my first time seeing a woman wear one, but this wasn't the time to lose my cool.

"I—I am so very sorry... I must have been a little drunk still when I woke up, and I stepped over my bounds... I may be staying in the same housing as you, but it's absolutely not acceptable for me to go into the bath while you're inside, much less give you a massage while you're bathing..."

"L-Louisa, please, lift your head. You've done nothing wrong. In fact, I should really be thanking you..."

I couldn't heal myself with my own skills, and I had used some magic when I'd used Rear Stance earlier. Thanks to Louisa, I was fully healed, and I felt great. She must have been still coming to her senses throughout the massage. Since we'd left the bath, she had done nothing but apologize. As far as I could remember, she had never dropped her steel-wall-like guard in there with me anyway, which made me feel better about the whole thing. I thought of what would have happened if she hadn't been wearing a robe and almost lost consciousness again.

And even when that robe got wet... I swear I'll never mention that. I'll just have to hope she'll forgive me, considering I wasn't even entirely conscious the whole time...

"......"

Theresia was still red even after we finished our bath. My best guess was that for some reason, she felt uncomfortable when Louisa had given me the massage. That was the general feeling she was giving off.

"...You just have so much promise, Mr. Atobe... It's all so moving, and I find myself lost for words... You must think I'm taking advantage of you."

"N-no, not at all... I'm so grateful that you're our exclusive caseworker, and I'm happy that you can relax and recover here in our lodging. Our relationship is one where we help each other out when we need it. You don't have to worry about taking advantage of me. And I'm really just happy that you think I have a promising future. Nobody ever thought that of me before I got reincarnated. Please stop bowing."

I felt awkward sitting while she was bowing like that, so I stood and urged her to lift her head. They must have used different herbs in the soap in District Eight, because she smelled nice, although everyone else was probably using the same stuff. But that's how close I was when she finally lifted her face and looked at me. She was normally so capable, but now she was showing me a much more vulnerable side. As a man several years her senior, I realized I should be careful not to give her the wrong impression.

"...Mr. Atobe..."

That's when I realized it—how close we were, this mood... This was what most people would call an "opportunity." It wasn't simply heat remaining from the bath. Her eyes shone, and I couldn't miss the glances she gave me as her lips tried to form her next words.

"Ugh... M-Misaki, didn't I tell you this was a bad idea?"

"Here you go again, Ellie. You're the one who said we should go see what they're doing 'cause you were so curious."

"Haaah... I—I don't see what the big deal is, honestly. It's not like there's anything between Atobe and Louisa. You guys are just worrying too much."

"G-goodness, everyone's here...," stammered Louisa. "How long have you been watching?"

It seemed the other three—Elitia, Misaki, and Igarashi—had been spying on us. It would be suspicious if we panicked and jumped away from each other, so instead, I cleared my throat and calmly placed an appropriate distance between me and Louisa.

"H-how should I explain this...? Since we're in the same room, we decided that it would be all right to take a bath together as long as we were careful. Or something like that."

"Y-yes... It's exactly as Mr. Atobe says. This is my first time being anyone's exclusive caseworker, so I'd never had an opportunity to use my skills. I was thinking that I would like to start using them again. Today. Would any of you like a Pressure Point Massage?"

"Wha—? You did *that* in the bathroom? ...A-A-Atobe, are you sure you were okay with that?"

"Whoooa, I've never seen Kyouka this flustered! Suzu's gotten really attached to him lately, too. You guys oughta realize how lucky you are that it was just the three of them in there."

Misaki was just messing around, but I sort of wanted to tell her not to stir up trouble. It wasn't really in me, though, to upset a girl who was young enough to be my little sister. The orphanage where I was raised had other kids there who were younger than me and called me their big brother. Remembering it always brought a lump to my throat. It wasn't something I'd ever forget.

"...Sheesh, you look like you've just had an epiphany or something. I guess I have no choice but to trust you when you make a face like that."

"No, not an epiphany—I was just remembering something from a long time ago. Anyway, Louisa was clothed the whole time. Nothing scandalous."

"I—I apologize... It's good I had that much sense left in me, at least...but it was still plenty embarrassing even though I was wearing a robe." Louisa pressed her hands to her blushing cheeks. Even Theresia was red. Something really had bothered her, and with how things were now, there was a possibility the two were only going to aggravate each other more. Thankfully, Madoka came down the stairs from the second floor and broke up the situation.

"Um... Arihito, why are Theresia and Louisa so red?" asked Madoka. "Oh, was the bath hot, maybe...? It really is hard to get the temperature right in Labyrinth Country bathtubs."

It wasn't the most convincing explanation even though we'd just come out of the bath, but Madoka believed it right away. Considering her age, she might be reluctant to jump to conclusions regarding relations between a man and a woman. I hoped she would hold on to her innocence as she grew up.

It was shortly before bedtime, but everyone still had plenty of energy. Each residential area of the district was equipped with a teleportation door that you could use to go to your storage unit, so we decided to head there and allocate equipment. The hut with the teleportation door was monitored by guards, though they did give us a little space. Elitia explained that it was to keep people from trying to break into other people's storage units.

"Sometimes, people will have someone else move the goods so their karma doesn't go up… And you ought to know that by now, Misaki."

"Oh man… D-don't remind me. I won't get any sleep tonight if I think about it too much."

Monsters weren't the only threats in the labyrinth—you also needed to be careful of other Seekers. It was a difficult topic, but you needed at least a little caution to make sure you could protect your friends.

"Arihito, I placed the items we got from the chests earlier in this section," said Madoka.

The storage unit was smaller than the rooms used to open chests, but it had plenty of space to hold what we'd picked up so far. The room was actually about the size of a high school classroom, though the ceiling was ten feet high. The items Madoka had put in there had been organized onto shelves that lined the walls, and all our goods were stored safely. We decided to start with the items we got from the red chest that the Poison Spear Bee had dropped. First, we appraised the anklet. Madoka's skill was easily able to ascertain all the information necessary.

```
◆Insect-Repelling Anklet +1◆
> Effective against insect-type monsters.
> Protects against Poison up to Poison 1.
```

"I see... I'm not sure how exactly it's 'effective' against insects, but Poison is strong enough that we can't take it lightly, so defense against that would be good," I said.

"Poison 1 can be fatal if your vitality is low, and anything above Poison 2 requires treatment within a certain amount of time—or to extend that time with a recovery item... Basically, it's best to treat Poison as quickly as possible."

Based on Elitia's advice, there were likely to be labyrinths in the future that absolutely required some sort of countermeasure for Poison. She had something called a Blackcurrant Charm, which protected her from Poison 2 and below as long as she was carrying it with her.

"We should probably have someone who's more likely to take hits equip this, don't you think?" said Suzuna.

"How about we put it on Cion's paw? There's so little she can equip anyway," suggested Igarashi.

"Oh, that's a good idea. And she uses Covering to protect us... I'd prefer if she just never took damage, but I doubt things will go that well in the future."

After listening to everyone's opinions, we decided to equip

Cion with the anklet. We hadn't brought her to the storage unit with us—she was back at the house with Louisa. We needed to hurry back; I didn't want them getting lonely.

"This Poison Honey...it'd have to be used every time, but it could be used to make poison arrows," I said.

"I think so, yes. You can apply it by brushing it onto the blade of a weapon. One bottle should probably be able to make five poison arrows," said Elitia.

"All right, I'll take that, then." Suzuna placed the vial of Poison Honey in her pouch. I did consider having Theresia use it on her dirks, but it would be hard for her to get it on the dirks in the middle of battle and then throw them. I assumed we'd use it for a battle we could prepare for.

"Next is the ricochet stone. It's applied to projectiles of ranged weapons to improve their ability to ricochet..."

"Don't you think we ought to use it on your weapon, Atobe? It's the one I can most imagine ricocheting."

"I have a feeling it'll be hard to use it right... If we put it into Theresia's shield, I imagine she'd have an easier time deflecting enemies' ranged attacks."

"Since we don't really know how to use it right now, I think it's best to use it for a weapon. You can choose whether or not to use any special attacks from magic stones when it's in a weapon. If it doesn't seem like it'll work, we can take it back and think of another use."

Listening to Professor Elitia's class on how to do things, I realized I'd be better off following all her seeking advice. Everyone was looking at her in admiration, and she started to blush in embarrassment.

"D-don't look at me like that… I'm just saying this stuff for your own information—that's all."

"You really do teach us a lot, though. I even like your advice on what skills to take," I said.

"But that's the leader's job. I'm the vanguard; my job is only to protect you and attack things… We need someone to give commands so that we use tactics effectively in a real battle. Arihito's the one who's been doing that for us—and he's good at it."

"Yeah…you're right. I'm in the rear, so I should be more aware of my role as a sort of controller in the back."

"You go to the front every once in a while. You're super brave even when we're in a really tough spot. Even if I had your skills, I wouldn't be able to use them," said Misaki.

"And you're pretty good at telling when we have a chance of winning," Igarashi continued. "Back when we worked together, if there was no way we'd meet a deadline, you'd just tell me we weren't going to. If it was close, you'd tell me you'd *'manage somehow'*…"

If you did a job enough, you started to understand your own capacity. Monsters, on the other hand—even if it seemed like the monster was going to go down with one more hit and I tried to get that attack in, it wasn't because I'd properly analyzed the situation. I attacked because that was the only thing I could do. These decisions I had to make when the situation was so unclear could make the decision between life or death. I used Rear Stance as an ace in the hole, but I couldn't forget that it had its risks.

"Let's go ahead and put the ricochet stone on my weapon. Melissa, can you remove the poison crystal and put that on instead?" I asked.

"I can do two or three stones before bed. Four or more will

have reduced effectiveness." She was at her limit just with the requests the party had for her. The stones I wanted to prioritize trying were the heat stone, the explosion stone, the mole stone, and the fire garnet.

"...There's so many. There aren't many parties who hold on to them without putting them into their equipment. We need to take advantage of them," said Elitia.

"You're right. I'd sometimes get a weapon with a magic stone in stock, and it'd sell immediately," said Madoka.

"From now on, I want to start using anything we get as quickly as possible. If we increase what we can do by even one ability, it'll also mean we're prepared for more situations," I said, and everyone nodded. I felt that discussing everything like this increased the party's knowledge as a whole, improving our capabilities. We discussed what to do with the rest of the stones, deciding to put the heat stone into Theresia's shield, which would allow her to use a mirage-type skill to confuse the enemy. Then, we decided to put the explosion stone into Suzuna's bow, giving her a blast-type area-of-effect attack.

Part VII: Trump Cards and Their Risks

Madoka researched the mole stone's uses, and after some consideration, we decided to put it into Misaki's armor.

"Huuuh, are you sure it's okay if I get a stone, too...?"

"You're an asset to this party. It'll let you hide when things get dangerous, so make sure you use it well," I said.

When attached to a weapon, the mole stone gave the user a "drill-type" attack, which was especially effective against enemies with heavy armor. When attached to armor, it had a special effect called "Mud Dig," which we decided Misaki would likely be able to use for an emergency escape.

"If that's what you want, I'll do my best to use it as effectively as possible! By the way, what exactly does this *Mud Dig* mean?"

"You'll see later. It works in only some situations, but it's very effective during those times," Elitia explained.

"We'll attach the confusion stone to my armor so I can resist that status. Then, we can put the fire garnet on Cion's anklet so she can have an attack with an attribute...," said Igarashi.

"Good plan. Then she'll be able to attack enemies that are immune to claw and bite attacks."

Next was the charm that came out of the chest we got from Death from Above. It was a small charm with writing on it in the Labyrinth Country's language. Madoka appraised that and the long, thin piece of fabric.

◆Ghost-Warding Grand Charm +1◆
> Protects against Energy Drain.
> Allows user to attack ghost-type monsters.

◆Unicorn Ribbon +1◆
> Reduces damage from magical attacks.
> A portion of your attack pierces the target's defense on a critical hit.
> Can only be equipped by women who meet the requirements.

"Elitia, what's this 'Energy Drain' thing do in the Labyrinth Country?" I asked.

"It's an attack that absorbs your life force. Ghost-type monsters use it a lot, with skills like Cold Hand. Sometimes, they also steal your experience points..."

"...I-I'm not afraid of some silly little ghosts. Besides, I have Mist of Bravery if we need it." The fact that Igarashi was insisting she wasn't afraid of them, even though we hadn't asked her anything, implied that she was, in fact, afraid of them. We could see her fear all too well even though she tried to hide it.

Considering the charm's effects, it seemed best to give it to Suzuna since her job could be effective against ghosts. I looked at her, and she responded with a nod, accepting the charm.

"This ribbon's color is a bit like the ones you're always wearing, Elitia," said Suzuna.

"Yeah...and it has great effects. I don't prioritize critical hits, but I bet this would've been useful to have back when we fought the Paradox Beetle. But it says it has requirements, so I wonder if I'd even be able to equip it..."

"Ellie, can I try tying your hair up with it?" Suzuna tied the Unicorn Ribbon into Elitia's hair, and she seemed to be able to equip it without any issues. I then realized what the *unicorn* part might mean.

Maybe, just maybe, it only trusts female virgins...? I mean, it says it can only be equipped by women, so... Uh, a-anyway, as long as she can equip it, that's all that matters.

"Arihito, I'm sorry—I can't fully appraise the next few items with Appraise 1," said Madoka.

"Oh, really...I see. Can you try using a Mid-grade Appraisal Scroll?"

"Yes, I'll try... Oh, that worked! Learning Appraise 2 will be so useful."

The remaining nonappraised items were the Ambivalenz, the Dexterity Gauntlets, and the Netted Rags. For some reason, I felt like I'd seen something like these rags somewhere before. Madoka showed me her license, which displayed the appraisal results, and this was what it said:

```
◆Black Spider Tights +3◆
> Increases speed.
> Increases maximum magic.
> Reduces damage from enemies' attacks.
> Effects are boosted if combined with other
  equipment.
> Currently damaged. Effects cannot be used.
```

"Oh... Atobe, th-this, um... It'd be really, *ahem*, age-inappropriate to make someone wear this. You catch my drift, yes?"

"R-right, yes, I understand. They're damaged anyway, so no one can wear them."

"Yeah, but the effects are so good that I sort of wanna try 'em on myself. They're definitely for mature ladies, though, like Kyouka or maybe even Louisa," said Misaki.

"There's no way you can wear tights with this many runs in them," countered Igarashi. "Besides, it came from the chest we got from the Paradox Beetle, which means..."

I agreed it was almost certain that it used to belong to someone else, but if we had a problem with that, we'd never be able to equip anything that came out of a chest. I did want to double-check that it didn't belong to anyone in Takuma's party...but I felt it was somewhat inappropriate to show the tights to Shiori and ask her if she recognized them.

"...We only found these items because we defeated the monster that killed their former owners," explained Elitia. "Once I realized that, I thought it would be better to put the items to good use. Those people died before they could accomplish their goals. I think they'd rest better if they knew their equipment was helping others." No one responded. It was very likely that the items in the chests belonged to Seekers who died before accomplishing what they wanted to do. Not every piece of treasure was, but those rings showed that some definitely were.

"If you put it that way, we need to try and use these tights even though they're broken..."

"No, not exactly... I think we can use them after we have them repaired. We can't make Igarashi wear them as they are," I said.

"Wha—? Why are you just going with what Misaki says? It's not like adults are the only ones who can wear tights," said Igarashi.

"Tights are pretty difficult to repair... But an expert should be able to do it with the right materials," said Suzuna as she carefully inspected the torn tights. I realized that the *spider* part of the name might be a hint.

"*Spider*... What if that means it was made from materials that come from a spider-type monster?"

"...I think you're right. This Unicorn Ribbon was probably

made out of materials from a one-horned monster. It's quite common for a piece of equipment to be made of materials from that specific monster if it's in the name," replied Elitia. Thinking of it, my Hardened Ox Leather Armor was made from Marsh Oxen materials. That meant it was fairly safe to assume that the *spider tights* were made of materials gained from the spider monsters we'd already heard about.

"Atobe, we can make Anna's racket and your new suit with materials from the sheep monster, then we can repair the tights with materials from the spider... Looks like we've got a few goals to accomplish now."

"Yes, good work, Igarashi. Let's knock each one out."

We would go as deep as we could into Silvanus's Bedchamber. Once we gained enough contribution points, we would head into the Beach of the Setting Sun. We'd be able to obtain all the materials we needed on the way. I'd be all the more powerful in battle if I could get that magic gun from Corleone.

"We just have the gauntlets and this...strange spear thing left," said Madoka as she started to appraise them with Mid-grade Appraisal Scrolls. Most unnerving of all was that even a Mid-grade Appraisal Scroll wasn't enough to fully reveal the details of Ambivalenz.

◆★Dexterity Gauntlets◆
> Number of regular attacks and attacks from
  skills increase along with speed.
> Damage taken from enemies increases slightly.
> Regular attacks drain a small amount of magic.

◆★Ambivalenz◆
> User also takes damage when attacking with
  this weapon.
> Damage taken from enemies decreases.
> Damage to target increases as the user's
  vitality becomes lower.
> Possesses hidden powers.

Both of them would be very powerful without their inherent risks. Ambivalenz in particular was a big gamble, making it difficult to use in actual battle.

"It has its risks, but I think Elitia is the one who can best put these gauntlets to use. You already have good gauntlets, though, so I'll leave it up to you to decide if you want to change or not," I said.

"Oh... A-are you sure...?" Elitia sounded surprised to hear her own name come up. She was very clearly interested in the item.

"Only people with a lot of magic can make good use of them without much difficulty," agreed Igarashi. "Since you're level nine, I think the advantages gained from increasing the number of your attacks will outweigh the drawbacks."

"...But I think the party would get stronger if we increase the number of Theresia's or even Suzuna's attacks..."

"We can think about changing who equips them once everyone gains levels and has more available magic. At the moment, though, you are our primary attacker. I think having more attacks in your Blossom Blade will help us in some difficult battles," I said.

"...All right. I want to make sure everyone else gets good equipment, but...for now, I'll use these and do my best to contribute to the party." Elitia held the gauntlets to her chest tenderly, like they were something precious. Thankfully, they weren't too big, and she was still able to wear them despite her small frame.

"I think it's too dangerous to use this Ambivalenz right now. We can leave it in storage until a time comes—," I started.

Igarashi cut in. "Atobe, would it be all right if I take it? It's spear-shaped, so I think I'm the only one who can equip it right now."

"Uh... B-but it's dangerous. We don't know how much damage you take when you attack."

"It looks like it'll have some effect even if I'm only carrying it. Just strapping it to my back should reduce the damage I take. Plus, I'm also curious about these *hidden powers*. Don't worry! I'll make sure to listen to your orders when I do use it." Sounded pretty much like she wasn't really open to discussing it. But it was like her to consider the party and decide to take it along with her, even though she was aware of the risks.

"...As long as you don't do what you did before. Don't do anything ridiculous just to protect us."

"I wouldn't even think of it. The pain was so bad that I thought I would die. I won't do anything ridiculous."

Since she said that, I couldn't be overprotective and a worry-wart. Ambivalenz wasn't lightweight, but Igarashi lifted it, spinning it around like it was lighter than her current cross spear.

"It doesn't weigh much, but I can see how formidable it'd be in battle... What an incredible spear."

"Kyouka, it may not be cursed, but please be careful with it. There's no guarantee these 'hidden powers' are anything positive," cautioned Elitia.

"Yeah... But my vitality and magic aren't going down just because I'm carrying it. I'll use my cross spear most of the time. This will just be my backup weapon."

"All right, that sounds good. It's getting late—let's go back home," I said.

"""Okay!"""

I wasn't expecting everyone to respond in unison, but it made me smile since they all seemed so relaxed and at peace. Surprisingly, even Melissa gave a normal response, although it lacked the energy of everyone else's. I thought about how I'd like to hear Theresia's voice someday. But first, I needed to be patient and explain to her that she had to actually rest in bed instead of trying to guard me and falling asleep standing.

CHAPTER 5

Between Life and Death

Part I: The Morning Scenery

Yet again, Theresia didn't let me see her sleep at all. I assume she eventually dozed off and then woke up, which was when she roused me awake as well.

"Good morning, Mr. Atobe. I'm sorry—we have a morning meeting at the Guild, so I have to hurry out of here," said Louisa.

"Oh... G-good morning, Louisa. You don't have a bad hangover, do you?"

"No, thanks to you... Um, Mr. Atobe. Since I'm not an official member of your party, technically speaking, I shouldn't be living with you..."

I guessed what Louisa was trying to say, and my sleep-clouded mind suddenly cleared. To put it bluntly, I was already sort of addicted to her Pressure Point Massage skill. Every once in a while in my past life, I'd go get an osteopathic massage to work out the stiffness of my body that had built up from sitting at a desk all day every day. It was a form of self-care. Louisa's skills rivaled those of the professionals I used to go to. My vitality and magic were now full, and I'd even slept perfectly well despite being in an unfamiliar bed. That was one of many reasons I was happy to have her living in the same house, but perhaps it was just a little too convenient. I was plenty lucky simply to end up sharing a room with her.

"...I knew it—I'm just causing trouble by being here. I appreciate you allowing me to stay here last night as a special case, but I will put in a request to move..."

"No, you're not causing trouble at all. Actually, if you're going to stay our exclusive caseworker and move up to higher districts with us...I'd feel better if..." It took a lot of courage to come out and say *Let's live together*. She was acting like she wanted to stay, though. No one in that situation would be happy if I hesitated to speak up. "If you like, please stay here with us. I doubt it's my place to offer it, though, since I'm only renting the house from the Guild..."

"A-actually, your name is on the records as the primary lessee...and in general, it is that person who must give permission for someone to live in the lodging."

"In that case... You have my permission. Will you please live here, Louisa?"

"Ah... Y-yes... Mr. Atobe, I don't deserve such kind words from you... I will do everything in my power to be more useful to you as a caseworker." Tears brimmed in Louisa's eyes as she clenched her hand to her chest. It'd felt nice like this almost every time I'd spoken to her lately...but we couldn't forget Theresia was there with us. "O-oh... Ms. Theresia, what's wrong? You're buried in your bed."

The only thing showing from beneath the blanket was Theresia's tail. I wondered if she was trying not to interrupt us. I had been far too insensitive just now.

"Theresia, how about we go downstairs?" I suggested. "Our food should be ready right around now. Could you just wait outside until I get changed?"

"……"

Her tail moved a little at the word *food*.

Louisa smiled. "Mr. Atobe, you really do understand how Ms. Theresia feels, don't you?"

"I've always hoped so… Theresia, did you sleep well? You can't always wait to go to bed until I've fallen asleep, you know."

"……"

Theresia wriggled around under the blanket, turning over and poking just her face out. I didn't know if she had slept or not, but at that moment, she was quite cute, and I lost all will to make any dumb comments.

Come to think of it, I had a vague feeling that someone had come into my bed in the middle of the night. Louisa wasn't drunk by that point, so I didn't think it was her, and I couldn't imagine anyone else doing something like that. Must've been a dream.

Louisa promised to eat breakfast with us the next day and rushed off to work like she said she had to.

There was a morning food market on one of the streets near our house, so Melissa, who had the skill Cooking 1, and the other members who felt awake enough went to pick up some ingredients for breakfast. The smell of food cooking in a hot frying pan wafted from the kitchen by the time Theresia and I went downstairs.

"Good morning, Arihito."

"Morning. We bought some freshly baked rolls. How many do you want, Arihito? About three?"

We were greeted by Suzuna, wearing an apron and carrying a pot with soup to the table, and Melissa, who was in the kitchen. She looked at me, loaded the bread rolls onto a tray, and carried it out toward us.

"Wow… Those are incredible," I said.

"They look hard, but if you cut them open, the white part inside is soft."

"Melissa brought a bread knife for cutting them as well." Suzuna seemed like a morning person given how energetic she was. She, Melissa, and Madoka were chipper early in the day. Igarashi, on the other hand, had low blood pressure, and it took her awhile to fully join us in the morning.

"*Sniff, sniff…* Is that freshly baked bread I smell—? Aaaaah! Suzu's wearing an apron!"

"Good morning, Misaki."

"Oh my gosh, Suzu, you scared me! Seeing Arihito and then you there in an apron, you looked EXACTLY like a newlywed! I was, like, totally squeeing, y'know?"

"I just wanted to ask… What are you even saying?" I replied.

Misaki smiled and brushed me off, then took a peek into the kitchen to see if she could be of any help. She seemed to have come to some sort of realization and instead just came back and sat in her seat.

"Arihito, you'll get in everyone's way if you just stand there. Why don't you come sit next to me?" she suggested.

"What, are you bad at housework? ...I mean, no surprise there."

"I'll prove I'm capable when it's my turn! I'm gonna slice those veggies into the prettiest ribbons you've ever seen!"

"Misaki, the market didn't have any vegetables that can be cut like that," said Suzuna.

"Oh reaaally? Shucks, that's too bad. All right, instead, I'll just show how awesome I am at removing air from hamburger patties! If you don't do that, they'll just explode when you cook 'em."

It was starting to sound like it'd be better to not have Misaki cook, but I decided I shouldn't say that out loud. We needed to spread the load of housework out among the whole party. If someone didn't know how to do something, we'd just teach them.

"If you end up on kitchen duty with me, the first thing you'll be in charge of is keeping an eye on the food to make sure it doesn't burn," I said.

"Hands-on cooking practice with Arihito... I bet you'd just wanna eat Suzu right up, huh?" Misaki teased.

"Uh... A-Arihito...would never...say something like that... right?" Suzuna stammered.

"W-well, uh... I don't think it's something I'd say at this point in time, yeah."

Before I got reincarnated, I never really had a chance like this to joke around with and talk to kids this much younger than me, other than with the children at the orphanage. I wasn't quite sure how far I should be pushing the jokes. I could laugh it off and say I wouldn't say something like that, but I had a feeling it was a bad idea to completely shoot down girls their age. Maybe I was worrying too much.

"Arihito always looks so cool and suave, like he's ready for a photo op whenever. Suzu's the same. Kyouka would probably need a moment to get herself together, I think."

"What kind of guy do you think I am? ...Hey, stop messing around and help set the table."

"Okaaaay."

I sort of just cut off the conversation like that, but Misaki actually listened to me. That was enough to make me think she really was a good girl. I was impressed. I tried to go into the kitchen to help out and saw Melissa there cutting up what looked like roast chicken. It seemed she'd topped it with the fruit-based sauce that Madoka had made.

"It also tastes nice if you sandwich it in a roll. I prepared some of these Rolly Leaves and other vegetables you can add to the sandwich," explained Madoka.

"I see... What's this drink?" I asked.

"I grated some parts off an Ice Carrot and mixed it with other juices. It tastes really good, kind of like a smoothie."

I quenched my thirst with some of the juice Madoka gave me, then looked at my license to notice that my Frost attribute had increased slightly. A drink like this would even help reduce a fever when you're sick.

I wonder if there's a Frost type of magic stone. These numbers might have an effect on Igarashi's Ether Ice skill... There seems to be quite a few situations in which defending against attributes will be just as important as defending against status ailments.

"Oh... By the way, Arihito, Ice Carrot is a kind of monster. That doesn't bother you, does it?"

"Hmm... Really? This just tastes like very refreshing carrot juice. It's good. I don't mind at all."

"You don't seem to have any strong preferences for food. My dad hates vegetables. I wish he could learn from you."

"Just to let you know, the one thing I don't really like is celery. Although, I don't mind it in soups for some extra flavor."

"Can you cook by yourself? That's rare for a grown man."

I wondered what percentage of adults living alone actually cooked for themselves. I felt like most people had to every once in a while.

As I pondered, another message appeared on my license. I knew whenever a new message appeared just by carrying my license around. Must be some sort of magic effect.

◆Current Status◆
> Melissa activated Cooking 1 ⟶ Arihito's maximum vitality was temporarily increased

"Wow... Incredible. Looks like our abilities get a temporary boost when Melissa's in charge of cooking," I said.

"...Okay. I like cooking. I'll help with it every day if I can," replied Melissa.

"Thank you. We can stick to a rotation normally. It's not your turn today, either, Madoka, but you're doing a great job helping out."

"Ah... I-it's nothing; um, I'm just used to getting up early like Melissa... I'm not useful in battle, so I want to help out as much as I can in other ways..."

I'd known this already, but Madoka was really something. In

District Eight, she'd worked so hard at her Merchant business, but it never made her cynical.

"Some lame excuse about me not being good at waking up probably isn't going to cut it when you're all up early and working hard... Guess I'll have to come up with something else."

"Oh, good morning, Igarashi. You were always on point in the morning back at the office, though."

"Um, well, that was just... You can't show your weaknesses as an adult. Now it looks like Ellie's the heaviest sleeper. She always looks worn out, so I'm glad she's getting the rest."

I felt nothing but happiness at the possibility that Elitia was starting to relax since she'd joined our party. The last to wake up, she looked a little embarrassed, but we smiled, and she joined in. We couldn't let our guard down when we were out on seeking expeditions, so I wanted everyone to at least be able to take it easy while we were at home.

Part II: The Ricocheting Bullet

We took a little break after finishing breakfast, then headed off to the entrance of Silvanus's Bedchamber. On the way, we passed some men who were members of Beyond Liberty, though they weren't the ones I'd seen the previous day. I'd heard them say the leader of the Alliance would reach his required contribution points the following day, but they were probably going into the Beach of the Setting Sun today as well.

"Those look like some members of that alliance. I saw a sign saying that way was to the Beach of the Setting Sun... I'm a bit curious," I said.

"Arihito, did you spy on the competition while you were out of the room last night? That's bold of you...," said Elitia.

"That's what ended up happening, but it's generally not a good idea to eavesdrop. They said they're going to get the contribution points they need—not today, but tomorrow. Going into the labyrinth every day seemed to be weighing their members down."

"We go seeking every day, too, and you're the one who always seems the most tired, Arihito," added Misaki. "But today, your skin looks all fresh and dewy for some reason... Ah!"

"It's because of Louisa's Pressure Point Massage. You should all ask her for one sometime, since she's going to be living in the same house as us." I'd thought this when I looked in the mirror this morning, but my complexion was looking a lot better. Igarashi looked like she wanted to say something, but she seemed hung up on how to ask, *Under what circumstances did you actually get the massage?*

Instead, she said, "W-well, you look a lot less tired, which is good. Louisa also seemed to be in a good mood. Looks like there were no problems with you two sharing a room."

"It's fiiine—Theresia was there, too. She's our party's con-science!" said Misaki. Theresia didn't react to her name and just continued to walk quietly on my left. The rest of the party was starting to trust that Theresia and I could share a room together without issue. Actually, Theresia was the one starting to take on the role of supervising me.

"Kyouka, your shoulders look really stiff. Maybe you should ask Louisa for a massage today."

"Now that you mention it, I did use to have stiff shoulders all the time, but not quite so much since coming here. Sitting at a desk all day working really isn't good for your health. Swinging a spear around seems much healthier."

"I feel like fighting monsters makes me use muscles I never would normally. My body even feels lighter; I can move more easily now," I said.

"Your complexion looks so much better now than the first time I met you. I felt like even your soul was tired," said Suzuna.

How many of these ladies could have ever imagined they'd join the party of a tired salaryman? To be honest, though, I was more surprised than anyone how things turned out.

"Tired down to his very soul, wow... But everything's okay now, right?"

"Yes, Arihito is full of energy now. He's the liveliest of us all."

I felt a little embarrassed for some reason when Suzuna said that, but it was true that I had more energy now. I had to keep pulling everyone forward—actually, since I was in the back, it was more like I was following them. But as the leader, I needed to be the most motivated out of everyone.

"A-Arihito! Good morning!"

"Teacher, should we get ready to make a simple camp today? We're hunting the sheep monster on the second floor, but we're not sure how long it'll take to find it."

We were greeted by Kaede and Ibuki, who both looked like they slept well and were full of energy. Anna, on the other hand, covered her mouth with a hand to hide a yawn, and Ryouko still seemed half-asleep.

"...Oh. I'm sorry. I'm a little tired because I woke up early to make some packed lunches," said Ryouko.

"Ryouko's like our mom," said Anna.

"P-please, I'm not nearly old enough to be your mother... Look, you made Atobe laugh."

"I'm surprised to see so many parties making their own food to take on expeditions. Must be because all the portable meals are so bland," I said.

"We sometimes buy food from the stalls, but in general, we make our own breakfast and lunch. Then, we treat ourselves by goin' out to eat almost every evening after we get back from seeking," said Kaede.

Packed lunches were all well and good, but you'd need food that kept for a long time if you were going camping. We also purchased some fuel for bonfires at night in case we needed to spend a long time in the labyrinth. We filled Madoka's Inventory up as much as we could. Despite carrying an even larger number of items, she didn't seem weighed down in the slightest.

When we entered the labyrinth, the first floor was as pastoral and idyllic as before. We had no problems passing by the area where we defeated the monsters the previous day, and we didn't see any Fake Beetles flying in the sky, either. After a short while, we arrived at the entrance to the second floor without having battled any monsters.

Our current party setup had Madoka in Four Seasons. Even when Igarashi and Cion were in the other party, there were still quite a few situations where I could assist them with Attack

Support. It took a decent amount of magic, though, to keep using Outside Assist. Something I learned in previous battles was that there came critical points in combat where I needed to support the other party—and constantly using Outside Assist meant risking running out of magic in those moments.

After strolling through the rolling plains for a little while, we came to a hill that had two stone pillars placed on its crest. We passed between the pillars and were teleported to the second floor. The scenery wasn't all that different; the biggest change was that the clouds moved through the sky slightly faster, but then, I felt on edge for some reason the moment we teleported.

"...Well, that was quick. Those are—," I started.

"Ah... They're the sheep's friends!" cried Anna in excitement. They'd shown up the moment we'd entered the second floor. These monsters were balls of fluff, much like the Cotton Balls we'd fought in the past but significantly larger. The only major difference was that these Stray Sheep had something like horns sprouting from them.

◆Monsters Encountered◆
STRAY SHEEP A
Level 1
On Guard
Dropped Loot: ???
STRAY SHEEP B
Level 1
On Guard
Dropped Loot: ???

```
Stray Sheep C
Level 1
On Guard
Dropped Loot: ???
```

"Stray" Sheep... Are they lost? And why are they all level 1...?

"Arihito, there's more over there...," said Elitia.

"D-don't you think it'd be hard to fight those things? I mean, they're kinda cute," said Misaki.

"Y-yeah... I'm not sure I can shoot those cute little sheep with my bow..." Suzuna was as hesitant as Misaki. But Four Seasons needed materials dropped by those sheep to make Anna's weapon.

I was still hung up on the fact that we'd come all this way and the monsters were level 1. On top of that, the Cotton Balls had these evil little faces, and I could see by using Hawk Eyes that these Stray Sheep had big round eyes that made them look like cute stuffed animals.

"Anna, are those the sheep that you need materials from in order to make your racket?" I asked.

"No, the Stray Sheep will immediately run if we try to fight them. I heard there's a monster in the same family as them that I need... I looked into how to capture it, and I came prepared with one of the methods that was suggested."

"Oh... They ran away. Those li'l guys are harmless, but we'll probably have problems with whatever other monsters come out before we find the one we're looking for," said Ibuki, apparently fond of cute things. She was showing a side of her that was so different from her usual image of a stoic Karate Master.

"Other monsters might eat those Stray Sheep... That's so sad, but I guess that's just the circle of life in the labyrinth," said Igarashi. She had always liked fluffy things, so she was relieved that we didn't have to fight them.

Considering their low level, they'd give very few contribution points even if we did fight them, and if we didn't set traps to capture them, hunting them would be inefficient anyway. Despite those drawbacks, I saw another party in the distance chasing the sheep, which implied there was some value in doing so.

With that in mind, we needed to look for a place to set our traps where the other party wouldn't run into them. I wanted to focus on looking for the best location, but it wasn't going to be that simple: Another monster had appeared within Theresia's scouting range. It was a wolf-type monster that did indeed seem to be hunting the sheep. It growled menacingly at Cion, who was at the front of the party.

```
◆Monsters Encountered◆
AERO WOLF A
Level 1
In Combat
Dropped Loot: ???
AERO WOLF B
Level 1
In Combat
Dropped Loot: ???
AERO WOLF C
Level 1
In Combat
Dropped Loot: ???
```

"Sheep and wolves, both monsters that travel in groups...," I said.

"There's the one that's pulling our attention, but there's two more going around the hill and coming this way. I think we should go take care of those two," suggested Elitia. We split up into our two parties to go and fight the beasts. We got ready to intercept the two coming around the hill, while the other one let out a howl and dashed toward Kaede, Four Seasons's vanguard.

"—Cion, use Covering!"

"Woof!"

Cion shot out at the same time that the Aero Wolf started dashing. Cion and Igarashi were in my party, but we could balance our offensive power if they assisted Four Seasons. One of the benefits of doing it that way was that I wouldn't have to drain my magic using Outside Assist, so I could make sure Cion was covered with Defense Support.

◆Current Status◆
> Arihito activated Defense Support 1 ⟶ Target:
                                         Cion
> Cion activated Covering ⟶ Target: Kaede
> Aero Wolf A activated Aero Charge ⟶ Target:
                                         Cion

No damage

"Thank you, Cion!"

"Woof!"

The defensive barrier that appeared before Cion completely

negated the damage. Cion covered Kaede, then Igarashi followed behind in joining the two of them for a counterattack.

"—Cion! Test out your fire garnet!" I ordered.

"Kaede, let's match our counters with Cion's!" called Igarashi.

"All right!"

The Aero Wolf had bounced back from its attack, and I could see with Hawk Eyes that it was wrapped in wind. It reminded me that Cion was also capable of attribute attacks like that now, and so I instantly ordered her to use it. The anklet on her front paw glowed with red light that streaked behind her following claw attack.

"—GRAAAAAH!!"

```
◆Current Status◆
> Arihito activated Attack Support 1
> Cion activated Heat Claw ⟶ Canceled out Aero
  Wolf A's Aero Shield
12 support damage
> Kyouka activated Double Attack
> Stage 1 hit Aero Wolf A
12 support damage
> Stage 2 hit Aero Wolf A
12 support damage
```

The effects of my support skills were slightly greater thanks to the Elluminate Mountaineering Boots I had equipped. Even so, the three attacks between Cion and Igarashi along with the support damage wasn't enough to finish off the wolf.

"One more push!"

"—Kaede, wait!"

Ibuki called out a warning from behind Kaede. The Aero Wolf hadn't gone down from the series of attacks from before, and its eyes now glinted with a beastly hunger. However, Kaede must have anticipated that, because she moved in to intercept the wolf as it tried to get off a final counter.

"—Haaaah!"

```
◆Current Status◆
> Arihito activated Outside Assist, Attack Support 1
> Aero Wolf A activated Traveler's Fang
> Kaede activated Counter Slice ⟶ Countered Aero
  Wolf A
12 support damage
> 1 Aero Wolf defeated
```

The wolf started to attack, but before it struck, Kaede managed to respond with a counter. It was so fast that you could have missed it by simply blinking. It was nothing short of spectacular.

The other two wolves that had been the other half of a pincer attack didn't fall back when their strategy fell apart. They lashed out with attacks at Theresia, who'd stepped boldly forward. There's no way she should have been able to avoid those attacks, but the strikes hit nothing but air.

```
◆Current Status◆
> Theresia activated Mirage
> Aero Wolf B's attack failed
> Aero Wolf C's attack failed
> Theresia's Mirage ended
```

Theresia used the heat stone in her targe to create a mirage that confused the enemy. It disappeared after taking only two attacks, but Elitia wasn't going to miss the opening it created while the two Aero Wolves were shaken over their strikes failing. I put an Attack Support 2 onto her assault. I decided to try out one of the magic stones I'd just had added to my weapon.

A magical bullet with the effects of the ricochet stone... I wanna see how this is gonna pan out!

"Go dance with the dead!"

◆Current Status◆
> ARIHITO activated ATTACK SUPPORT 2 ⟶ Support Type: FORCE SHOT (BOUNCE)
> ELITIA activated BLADE RONDE
> 2 stages hit AERO WOLF B
> 2 stages hit AERO WOLF C
> FORCE SHOT launched by ATTACK SUPPORT 2
> FORCE SHOT bounced between AERO WOLF B and AERO WOLF C 3 times
> 2 AERO WOLVES defeated

"GRAAAAWOOOW!"

Elitia's dance of swords sent the wolves flying back as they tried to rush toward her. The magical bullet from my Attack Support struck one, then bounced between the two multiple times. Everyone widened their eyes in shock as they looked at the defeated wolves—Elitia and I included.

"...Wh-what... Arihito, what did you just...?"

"Whoa... Th-that was awesome! You totally beat those scary wolves to a pulp!" yelled Misaki. That might have been what she thought had happened, but I was just about able to see what actually occurred. The Dexterity Gauntlets increased the number of Elitia's attacks. My magical bullet only applied to the additional attack because of Attack Support, but it bounced between that monster and a nearby monster, racking up a lot of damage in one go.

"Urgh... That Bounce effect took more magic than I thought it would," I said.

"Arihito... Are you all right? That was an amazing skill, but you should be more careful when you use something like that for the first time." Suzuna came over and helped stabilize me as I teetered on my feet. I pulled myself together a bit, but Suzuna was right. I should really consider the risks of using new magic stones a little more.

"Arihito, I'll fetch you a potion!"

"Those are valuable, so I'd rather we save them, but... Actually, would it be okay if I had one?"

Madoka had deactivated her Hide skill and pulled a potion from her backpack before handing it to me. I was completely recovered after about two gulps and gave the bottle back to her.

"...Oh, that's right. Sorry, I only recovered myself. I'm sure everyone else has drained some magic, too."

"It's fine... Actually, potions lose their potency once opened, so it's usually best not to leave any left over," said Elitia. In other words, anyone who'd used magic in this past battle should finish off the potion I'd just drunk from.

"Um… G-go on, Elitia," offered Madoka.

"No, I—I didn't mean *I* needed any… Kyouka, you can have some first."

"Um, uh, well… Double Attack doesn't really take that much magic. Ellie, you're the one who used the most powerful skill, so you should go first."

"C'mon, guys, don't be shy," said Misaki. "It's already open, so you should just drink some. We'll probably run into more monsters later."

"…Can I have some? Potions are hard to come by, so I wanna taste one," said Kaede. Everyone argued about who should drink in what order, but finally, they decided, and each drank a mouthful. I knew that sharing potions like this would be necessary to make sure everyone recovered, but I couldn't stop feeling uncomfortable as I watched them.

"And last is Cion… Hee-hee, so cute!" Igarashi poured the last bit of the potion into her hand and let Cion lap it up. That finished off a single potion. We would take the bottle back with us and reuse it, since the bottles themselves were fairly valuable.

"Right, now that we've had a chance to see Arihito's sweet and innocent reaction to us sharing drinks, should we find somewhere to set up camp? I've aaalways wanted to say something like, *Let's camp here!*" said Misaki.

"What are you looking at? …Hey, Anna, do you want to find a place to set the traps, then camp near them so we can keep an eye on them?" I asked.

"Yes. I'd like to look for a few different places, then split up and watch them... Would you be able to help with that?"

"If this labyrinth hasn't been completely explored, we could probably learn necessary strategic information or something if we catch some of those Stray Sheep...or I might just be reading too much into it." Igarashi threw in her own idea, which I felt was a good possibility. If that was the case, I wanted to avoid wasting time in the event some Aero Wolves accidentally got caught in the traps. The problem was, could we even trap this sheep-type monster if we set the traps somewhere? I began to think we might have to explore the entire second floor, but Theresia started walking off.

"......"

"...Theresia, what's up?"

Theresia didn't respond, but she waited for us to start following her. Maybe she'd used her senses to find someplace where we should set the traps, even if we didn't really understand. She led, and we followed. We reached the top of a hill and, on the other side, saw what looked like a spring. There hadn't been many trees in this labyrinth so far, but the water was surrounded by lush, verdant leaves. There did appear to be something about that water. The Stray Sheep frolicking in the fields near the spring disappeared when they noticed us. They were as cute as always, but that didn't mean we could let our guard down.

Why were there level-1 monsters in this labyrinth? Would something happen when we solved that riddle? I shivered suddenly for no reason and warned myself that they were just trembles from excitement.

Part III: Survival of the Fittest

The spring looked fairly large from far away, and when we drew nearer, we could tell that it was large enough for someone to swim in. It was just about as big as an Olympic-size swimming pool at around 150 feet across, and as deep as a diving pool. The hills leading down to the other side of the spring declined sharply, to the point where they practically became cliffs. You could get to the cliffs by going around to the left or right, so it would be best to check later and make sure there were no monsters there.

"The water is so clear... I assumed there'd be monsters in this spring, but it doesn't look like there's anything living in it."

"You're right... I could swim in and check it out."

Igarashi and Ryouko approached the spring as they chatted about its contents. There had been three or four Stray Sheep near the spring a moment earlier, but they must have run away because they didn't come out again. Theresia and Cion moved closer to the small woods near the spring, but they didn't seem to find anything there, either.

The spring itself was surrounded by a beach of pure-white sand and had clear, blue water. It was the kind of place you'd only see in the pictures of some resort. I'd thought this labyrinth was filled with nothing but fields. Unexpectedly coming across this scenery made me relax.

"Arihito, you shouldn't let your guard down... Although, I know it's hard in a place like this." Elitia scanned the area, but she must have decided that it was fairly safe, because she also eased up a little. Suzuna grinned when she noticed Elitia relaxing.

"I'm surprised there are labyrinths with such gorgeous views," said Suzuna. "I always thought I'd have to grow up and save money before I could ever go see something like this."

"I know. It's almost too beautiful. Kinda makes me think there's got to be some sort of trap...but everything seems fine right now," I replied.

"Right now, we just have some cute little sheep. Oh, there's some wolves going after them, actually."

The Aero Wolves weren't going to cause us too many problems as long as we didn't let our guard down, and I couldn't see any other monsters. The fact that this floor only had wolves and sheep must be another feature of this particular labyrinth. But where were the strong versions of the Stray Sheep? Were they simply that rare? I hadn't seen a single one even though I had a wider field of vision.

"Anna, do you think this is a good area to set the traps?" I asked.

"According to my sources, setting the traps around this spring will capture a monster called a 'Thunder Head' sometime during the night."

"Based on the name, I think we can assume it uses lightning...," said Kaede.

"It could make your hair all frizzy if it hits you... T-Teacher, do you have anything to help against lightning?" asked Ibuki. She and Kaede seemed really anxious just imagining what fighting one would be like. Igarashi could use lightning, but I was concerned how powerful it could be if an enemy could use it.

"Maybe we should take off equipment that's conductive... Actually, I have a better idea. We can set up lightning rods to try and draw the lightning away from us. Anna, could I see one of your traps?" I asked, and she pulled one out of her bag. It was a simple cage trap that you put bait inside, and the creature would be caught when they went in.

"They were originally made to capture Stray Sheep. Sometimes, they'd trap other monsters, and that's how people learned about this Thunder Head."

"Really…"

Maybe Falma could make a trap like this, since she was a Trap Master. I'd never considered the possibility that there were monsters you couldn't find unless you set a trap for them. I was happy to have this experience.

"Would it be healed if I used Thunderbolt on it?" asked Igarashi.

"Possibly," answered Anna. "It's generally best to avoid using any skills that share an elemental attribute with the enemy."

"Um, Arihito, could I talk to you for a second?"

"Hmm…? What's up?"

Misaki lowered her voice as if she had a secret to tell me. We separated from the others for a bit so I could hear what she had to say.

"It's rare to see you so serious…," I said.

"How rude! I think about serious stuff all the time. I feel bad keeping this from Four Seasons, but it's about my Morale Discharge, and I don't think I should really let people know about that. I wanted to get your advice."

Still, if we had a secret conversation for too long, the rest of the party would get suspicious. I waved a hand to the others to try and show them we were just having a brief chat. They had been staring at us in curiosity, wondering what we were talking about, but then, they appeared to ease up.

"Ummm, we're not totally certain setting the traps will succeed, right? But if I use Fortune Roll, they'll definitely work."

"Oh yeah, we can do that. Good idea."

"Hee-hee, thanks for the compliment! I gotta make a strong enough impression or else people will start forgetting I exist. Lately, I've just been like one of those people on talk shows who doesn't actually say much—they only throw in the random word here or there."

"I'm pretty sure if you were on a talk show, you'd have something good to say about everything. I rely on you all the time to set the mood anyway."

"Oh, good! I'll make sure I'm ready to strike up a conversation at any time!"

Misaki was happier than I'd expected she would be. Perhaps she'd been worried she was talking too much.

"Well, you do need to be careful about taking the conversation off track, though... But I do think it's a good idea to let everyone know we can make the trap succeed for sure with Fortune Roll. Knowing it will definitely succeed means they can mentally prepare themselves."

"I'll leave that decision to you. We all talked about how you'd never tell anyone our secrets, so I trust you."

"Uh... Y-you did? When was that...?"

Misaki put her finger to her lips as if to say *it's a secret*. Once she did that, I couldn't really ask anything else—not that I had any further concerns.

Theresia and Cion came back from patrolling the area for enemies while we were talking. Theresia pointed to the tops of the cliffs with a finger, and Cion sat down and looked at me.

"Are you saying there's monsters there? We should take them out now."

"......"

"We should defeat them if we're gonna be setting up camp in this area," suggested Igarashi. "Also... Atobe, could you come here?"

"What is it?"

I turned around when Igarashi called me, and I saw the other party members watching Ryouko, who was about to walk into the water.

"...Ah. I'm sorry, Atobe," apologized Ryouko. "The water really is beautiful, but it probably is too dangerous to go swimming. We are in a labyrinth, so we don't know if there's anything in there."

"Y-yeah... I don't think it'd be too big of an issue for you to swim a little bit as long as the water quality itself is safe, though."

If Ryouko had become a Swimming Instructor because she loved swimming, then I could see how this spring would be quite enticing. As long as everything was safe, then there was no point in stopping her. I even thought we might make some new discoveries from examining the spring. But I had one other thought as well—this was pretty daring of Ryouko, who was normally so rational and acted as the mental strength that held up Four Seasons.

...If I had her show me her license, I might be able to see what's got her so keyed up... No, I'm just worrying too much.

"Here's what you can do if you want to test the water quality," said Ryouko as she slipped a hand into her boa coat and pulled out a bottle. It was used for carrying drinking water. She had the party drink it, took a few steps into the spring's shallows, and scooped up some water.

```
◆?Bottle◆
> A bottle containing water taken from
  Silvanus's Bedchamber.
```

"Oh... So we can do this and then use an appraisal scroll on the water, too," I said.

"Exactly. It is possible to appraise water if you scoop it with your hands, but this makes sure there's no mistakes."

"Um, may I please try to appraise it? If I can do it with my skill, then we don't need to use a scroll," offered Madoka.

"Yes, please do," said Ryouko. "As long as Atobe agrees."

"Go ahead, Madoka. Just be careful."

She took the bottle, slightly nervous as everyone focused on her, but activated her Appraise 1 skill.

```
◆Bottle of Clean Water◆
> A bottle containing clean water taken from
  Silvanus's Bedchamber.
> Has no negative health effects.
```

"Um, it looks safe to swim in. And we can drink it, too."

"Okay, can I try some? Ibuki, do you want any?" asked Kaede.

"I just drank the water that was in the bottle. I'll have a little, but not enough that I'll get all sloshy...," replied Ibuki. "Mm, it's nice..."

It was almost like we'd come here to have a picnic and a campout.

I used to do that a bit when I was a kid but didn't really have the chance when I got older... I didn't even have any outdoorsy friends who'd want to go camping with me anyway.

"Atobe, Anna said she wants to check out the areas where we're going to set the traps. You'll show her where you wrote them down on your license's map, right?" said Igarashi.

"Yes, I'll show her. I thought we'd have to wait quite a while until night falls, but time seems to flow differently on this floor."

"It looks like it'll be evening soon... If we're going to set up tents, we should do it before it gets dark," said Suzuna as she watched the passing clouds. Time passed more quickly inside the labyrinth—well, not really, it was more that it just changed more quickly between morning and night. Either way, our goal was dangerous to work toward after dark.

We started setting up the traps while staying on the lookout for an attack that might come in the night. We were going to divide the parties into a few different tents, but I still needed to be behind my other party members. I took out my license and looked at Anna's hand-drawn map of the spring and its surrounding area. My current plan for the traps was to set one in the woods that were west of the spring, one to the south, and the last to the east. Tent locations were something else we'd have to think about before we could begin setting up.

After that, I can summon the Demi-Harpies and have them scout from the sky... We'll also need to keep an eye on other parties in the area.

There weren't many groups on this floor, but some people saw us come near the spring and seemed curious. That didn't mean they were hostile toward us, but I wanted to avoid any competition over the monster we needed to hunt. I would imagine we'd have dibs on it if it got caught in our trap, though.

"Mr. Arihito, could I ask for your opinion? Where do you think the best location is?" asked Anna.

"I think the first should go in the woods by the spring, then here, where you think is good; and the last here, where we think is good."

"Okay. I think it would be best if we are facing out to look over the spring. It's so hard to decide where to set up camp because the monster will be on guard if it realizes we're there…"

"The woods to the west can act as a screen. If we take advantage of that… Oh, there's these hills to the east. They look like just enough to hide the tent from view if you're at the trap."

"If we're in an elevated position, we can have a good view over the area. Perhaps we should set one tent on the top of the cliffs."

From our discussion, we determined that Four Seasons would go in a tent to the east; Igarashi, Cion, Suzuna, Misaki, and Melissa would be near the woods; and Theresia, Elitia, Madoka, and I would be at the top of the cliffs. The party at the top was strong overall because we had Elitia as the main attacker and me to support and defend. I also felt better about Madoka being with us because then Elitia could protect her. There was always the possibility that one hit would take Madoka out, making it better if we could eliminate the enemy before they could attack.

"Hey, guys—if we end up in combat, do your best to keep your backs facing the cliffs. I can support you with my skills if you do that."

""""Okay!""""

"Woof!"

Everyone responded in unison. Cion even seemed to understand what I meant, because she barked a reply as well, even if it was a bit delayed.

"Anna, do you mind waiting a bit to set the traps? I'd like you to show us how to set them," I said.

"……"

"You think you can set it, Theresia?"

She nodded. For whatever reason, she seemed capable. Just in case, I still had Anna show us how to set it, but it didn't seem like it'd be an issue.

"I guess Rogues can sort of handle traps," said Igarashi.

"She can also learn skills to disable traps," I added. "At higher levels, she might even be able to learn how to set them. Even without a skill, though, I think Rogues might be better at handling traps than other jobs."

While we talked, Anna showed Theresia how to set the trap, which essentially consisted of putting together the cage, then setting the bait inside.

"You put the meat in here. Once the trap is set, if a monster tries to go after the meat, they'll activate the spring here. The trap will then close and set off these teeth, which are coated with a Weakening poison."

"……"

"…? Is something wrong, Theresia?"

Theresia was completely still, staring at the hunk of meat on a bone that was going to be used for the trap. I realized what was happening, pulled out some of the food I had on me, and held it out to her.

"It does look like very nice meat, but we need to use it for the trap. I'm sorry that all I have right now is this tasteless stuff, but once we set up the tents, we can have some real food."

She did seem to long for the meat, but she took the food I offered her, opened the package it was in, and started munching.

"...Mm..."

"Those food bars aren't that bad. They've got dried meat mixed in with vegetables and nuts. The meat we're using for the traps is fairly high quality to draw out the monsters. I understand why she'd want to eat it," said Anna. The trap was completely ready once we added the meat, and she started to dismantle it again to place elsewhere. Her movements were certain, which made it seem like she had some experience using traps like this before.

"Anna, do Thunder Heads like that kind of meat?" I asked.

"I've heard they do. They're apparently quite vicious and carnivorous. They can even eat the predators that try to eat them."

"Urgh... Sh-sheep are supposed to be gentle, but these ones sound so violent..."

"...Do they eat Aero Wolves? If they do, it might be easier to draw them in if I dissect the three we beat before and leave the meat out," suggested Melissa, but we'd get more time if they went for the meat in the traps and got caught than if they ate meat lying around and then ran away.

Out of the three Aero Wolves we'd defeated earlier, we'd found a magic stone on one of their foreheads. Appraising it told us that it was a "cyclone stone." It was a crystal that looked like a pale-green quartz, and I thought it was likely that it let you use the skill that the Aero Wolves had used. The meat didn't have any real use, so it would be possible to use it as bait.

"I just feel like it's rude to leave their meat scattered around a field. If we're not going to put it in the traps, we should think of a way to use it later," I said.

"Okay. Kyouka looks upset by it, too. I won't dissect them now. I'll probably skin them when we get back."

"N-no, it's fine... I know they're wolves, but they're similar to dogs, so I'm not sure how I feel about dissecting them," said Igarashi. "I'm not just gonna tell you to have at 'em or something like that."

It was probably better if the monsters actually looked monstrous. Having said that, there was always the possibility we'd run into a monster that just looked too terrifying. Even Cotton Balls had scary faces, but compared with the rest of the monsters in the labyrinths, they were actually on the cute side.

"If we put out a lot of food for the Aero Wolves, do you think we could make a giant army of wolves?" asked Misaki.

"It's pretty hard to tame monsters. Right now, we just have the Demi-Harpies..."

I remembered something as I replied to Misaki. There was the seed that was all that remained of the Vine Puppeteer. I needed to go to the Monster Ranch and make a contract with it. Its abilities could be very useful simply because they were so dangerous. "Anyway, we need to be on guard if these Thunder Heads are a monster that can hunt Aero Wolves. Let's stay focused."

♦Current Status♦

> Arihito activated Morale Support 1 ⟶ All party
  members' morale increased by 12
> Arihito activated Recovery Support 1 ⟶ All party
  members' vitality fully restored

Oh... Was everyone tired after this much seeking? I'll need to activate Recovery Support regularly since we're in for the long haul now.

I'd also used Morale Support a few times, which left everyone needing forty more morale points before they could use their Morale Discharge. I'd keep using it every time I could while I prepared for the night, and everyone readied the camps so that Misaki could use her Fortune Roll.

Part IV: Silvanus the Enchanter's Messenger

The darkness of night was about to fall as we finished setting up the three tents. In the past, there had apparently been someone who'd chosen Camper as their job, and they developed and started selling camping equipment for use in the labyrinth. That equipment was quite popular and available in most places. Cotton Ball fur was fairly similar to cotton, which made it the perfect material to use for a tent. That was one of the reasons why the prices of their fur remained so stagnant.

Some of the party members were on watch while the rest of us set up the tents. During their watch, they killed six Aero Wolves, and I was able to support them because my rearguard skills worked at a distance, as long as their backs were to me. Ibuki was helping me set up the tent, though I did make her worry that my back hurt if I sat down too long. After all, I kept getting up to move and make sure I was still facing toward the party members who were fighting.

I'd become much more physically fit ever since getting reincarnated. Sitting too much didn't make my joints hurt, nor did it make my back stiff. I actually couldn't help having a bit of fun setting up the camp. A long time ago, I'd go on camp outings with the other kids from the orphanage, where I learned how to pitch a tent, but I had to admit that the details had gotten fuzzy since. Thankfully, this camping equipment came with directions, and I slowly started to remember how to do it, so we didn't run into any problems.

"I was right to start calling you Teacher... I've never put a tent together before. I was worried I couldn't do it," said Ibuki.

"I was worried I couldn't, either. It's been a long time since I've put a tent together. I'm glad we could buy such handy camping equipment."

"Ibuki, you're strong so you could help set it up. I'm not... I wasn't really useful," said Anna, moping. Because she could attack from far away, she was keeping an eye on the surroundings to make sure no enemies came near. Certainly, she had been plenty helpful.

"Anna, you kept that monster at a distance with your serve earlier. You're helping out a lot. We might be used to fighting Aero Wolves now, but they're still dangerous if they can close in," I said.

"I can't attack from over here, and I didn't even see them coming because I was too busy doing this. You saved us. Thank you, Anna," said Ibuki.

"...I—I wasn't trying to fish for compliments or anything. You two are too nice."

Ibuki beamed as Anna blushed. Good to see they got along so well.

"Right, next, we can set the trap... Anna, would you mind letting my party set one of them? We might have a way of making it almost certain to succeed," I said.

"Oh... Do you have someone in the party with good trap-setting skills?"

"Well, Theresia seems like she'd be pretty good at it, but she's not specialized in that sort of thing. We can, though, combine some of our skills and improve the probability it'll work."

"S-so like a combo? Combos are great... It's a bit embarrassing to admit it, but I feel a rush of adrenaline when I can do that with the others," said Ibuki. She seemed like the kind of person who got pumped up from battle. She was a Karate Master, after all, but the fact that she used the word *combo* made it sound like she also enjoyed fighting games.

"Combos with Kaede as the lead attacker are sort of our bread and butter," said Anna.

"And we're lucky to have Elitia with us. Though, depending on the party, we could have someone defend against attacks, then we counterattack."

"I'm the receiver in our party... Oh, not *that* kind of receiving. I mean that I have a Counter skill as a Karate Master."

So Ibuki was their receiver... Though, that wasn't something I should really say about a girl more than ten years younger than me. I wouldn't have guessed she'd have known about the other kind she was talking about.

"Haaah… Ibuki, you can be such a blabbermouth sometimes. One of these days, you're going to give me a heart attack."

"I'm n-not a blabbermouth! Anna, you're embarrassing me in front of Arihito!"

"Look, my job's all about standing in the back and supporting everyone passively, so I guess I'm a receiving type, too," I said.

"…Um, a-are you sure you're not the more dominant type?" asked Ibuki. "That's what I'd expect from a mysterious man like you, Teacher…"

I tried to help smooth things out, but instead, it came back to bite me. Anna's face was as red as if Ibuki had addressed the question to her instead. I had no idea how to respond.

"Sheesh, Ibuki, you put Arihito in a real tough spot there," Kaede said. "Don't go secretly fantasizing about stuff like that."

"Ah, K-Kaede, you're finished…"

"Arihito did such a great job putting up our tent that I wanted to ask him about his hobbies. He got the whole thing done so quickly."

"Thanks for your help, Atobe. Sorry you had to put up our tent, too," said Ryouko.

"No, thank you for your help. We only managed it because we gave everyone their own responsibilities. Since the four of you are here, would you like to go in and test it out? I'll fix it if needed."

If we'd made any mistakes in how we set it up, that would definitely cause problems. They all went inside but didn't come back out. They stayed in there chattering away, which must have meant there were no issues.

"Ooh, it's super comfy... Arihito, you wanna come in here, too, while you've got the chance?" asked Kaede. "You're the one who put it up, so it might be a good idea for you to double-check it."

"Um, Kaede... It'll be far too cramped in here if he comes in, too," said Ibuki.

"That makes it even more fun," said Anna. "We'll need to huddle together for warmth in the cold nights."

"I-I'm not so sure about that... The only change of clothes I have is something really thin. That's not something I can let him see, even inside a tent," said Ryouko.

"It's not nighttime right now—just let him come in for a little bit. Though, he does look really embarrassed about the idea. He's so proper."

I felt pretty uncomfortable since they were talking about me, so I turned my attention to the other members of my party. I wasn't really trying to be proper; I just felt like if I did go into that tent, we'd lose our focus.

"Arihito, thank you for the help even though you were so far away," said Suzuna.

"Your skills have a long range... If the only requirement is that you're behind us, the range might even be unlimited," said Elitia.

"It seems I can use them as long as I can see you." And thanks to Hawk Eyes, I could see quite far, although not all the way to the edges of the labyrinth, of course.

My rearguard job wasn't the same as other jobs that were usually in the rearguard position. Mine was related to everything about being "behind" others. I even had a skill called Rear Stance that positioned me behind the target.

"It feels good knowing that even if we're separated and doing different things, we'll still get the benefits of your skills," said Igarashi.

"I know, riiiight? It's really comforting. Instead of a guardian angel or something, it's like I can always feel him behind me, protecting me," said Misaki.

"Woof!"

Since I used my support skills on Cion as well, her Trust Levels toward me were gradually increasing. She came over to me without my beckoning her, and she sat down, her tail wagging back and forth. I scratched her chin, and she closed her eyes happily.

"...You're lucky, Cion," said Madoka.

"If you want some scratches, I'm sure Arihito will do it if you ask," said Melissa.

"Ah... N-no, I'm all right. Cion just looks like she likes it so much that she's about to fall asleep, so I thought Arihito must be good at petting her... I w-wish I was as good at it as he is..."

"Want to try petting Cion, too, Madoka? ...Whoa, hey, are you getting attached to me, Cion?" I said. She was starting to sniff my shoes and nip at them. There wasn't actually anything wrong with her growing fond of me, but I was starting to feel Igarashi's jealous glare burning into me.

"Arihito, should we set the traps soon? We won't be able to see what we're doing once it gets dark," suggested Elitia.

"Yeah, you're right. Okay, let's go work on the one in front of the spring."

I called out to the four people still in the tent and got one of the traps from Anna, when she came out. I had Theresia set the trap so that it was hidden in the grass in front of the spring. But before that:

"Don't forget the important part I play! ...Morale Discharge, Fortune Roll!"

Misaki kept her voice down as she activated her Morale Discharge. Everyone stood watching with bated breath as Theresia set up the trap's cage.

"......"

◆Current Status◆
> MISAKI activated FORTUNE ROLL ⟶ Next action will succeed automatically
> THERESIA set BOX TRAP ⟶ Success

The moment Theresia finished with the trap, her entire body began to glow faintly—along with the trap itself.

"What...? Theresia, do you feel like anything changed?" asked Misaki, but Theresia just looked confused. She seemed to think she had set the trap normally, but it appeared different somehow from our perspective.

"...Looks like it'll be pretty reliable. Something about the way this trap was set seems different from usual," said Elitia.

"Um, ummm, Arihito, what was that thing Misaki just did...?" asked Madoka.

"It was her Morale Discharge. I think Melissa should be able to use hers now, too. You should be able to also if I raise your morale. I don't know if your Morale Discharges are battle-oriented, but they could come in handy. Just hold on to it for now, though."

"Okay. If I haven't used it by the time we leave the labyrinth, I'll test it then...," said Melissa.

"That's perfectly fine. I'm interested to see what it does."

If Cion had a Morale Discharge, too, I'd like to see what that entailed. If I could, I should also try to raise Four Seasons's morale using Outside Assist, but we didn't have a limitless supply of magic potions, so I decided to hold off on that.

It took quite a while to recover magic if you didn't use potions. I could recover as much as necessary with the Charge Assist and Energy Sync combo, but that wasn't something I could do at any time.

"All right... Should we start getting dinner ready? The camping equipment came with some cooking tools, so should we use those?" asked Igarashi.

"Yes. Since we're here, I'd like to try out what kind of food we can eat while camping," I said.

"Arihito, where should we do the cooking?" asked Madoka.

We'd have to choose a safe location since we'd be building a fire. The white, sandy beach by the spring would be a good spot, but it would defeat the purpose of setting the traps if we made our presence known.

"How about on the other side of those trees?" I suggested. "If we do it too close to the traps, the monsters will be on guard and won't come near."

Between camping and trapping monsters, our current strategy was full of new experiences. And since we'd likely be using these experiences later on, I wanted this all to succeed.

The portable stove we had was forged by blacksmiths, who used ores found in the labyrinths. It even folded flat, which made setup a cinch. The Labyrinth Country streets looked like something you might see in medieval Europe, but the quality of life was much higher thanks to magic stones and tools, as well as technologies that various reincarnates had developed. As a result, certain areas were surprisingly advanced, particularly camping equipment since almost all Seekers had to use it.

We'd found some form of solid fuel to use for the fire. Apparently, it wasn't that difficult to make and could be created from materials found in the labyrinths.

"Ahhh, it's been ages since I last felt like this! A nice li'l fire for one person, a li'l pot with meat sizzling away..."

"This world has camping kits, too...and rice."

Misaki and Suzuna were chatting happily away as they waited for the food to cook. It'd gotten quite dark, so I was holding my slingshot and keeping an eye out while the meal was being prepared. Cion and Theresia were also on watch since they had a wide scouting range. Every once in a while, an Aero Wolf would show itself in the distance, but there weren't any signs of anything else coming closer. But we still had to remain vigilant.

If there was some way we could camp safely without having to worry about enemies appearing, then we could really enjoy this whole experience. Can't exactly do that in our current situation.

"......"

"Oh, looks like food's gonna be ready soon. Theresia, you can take a short break from keeping watch. Go on."

Theresia was looking at me, so I waved her over. She walked toward me, staring at me like she was wondering what I'd do.

"I'll stay on watch for a bit. We can swap once you're done eating."

"……"

Theresia shook her head, but I could hear a small growl from her stomach. She must be pretty hungry.

"Don't worry about me. I'll be fine; I have some jerky. I should've given you some, though… Oh, uh, I see you already have some."

"……"

Theresia pulled some jerky out from inside her bodysuit—quite a weird place. She had slipped her hand in through the slit in the bodysuit that ran from her chest to her abdomen, which shocked me a bit. She held the jerky she pulled out toward me. I was actually quite moved that she would offer me food, since her own stomach was like a bottomless pit. But I guess I was reading into things too much.

"Are you sure? I could hold on to it for later…"

"……"

"O-okay. Thank you, Theresia."

Her expressions really never changed. Her mouth, which was the only part of her face visible from under the mask, almost always stayed a straight line. That's why I assumed it was just a trick of the imagination that I thought her footsteps were lighter as she walked toward the others.

Er...this jerky is a little warm...

I considered saving it instead of eating it, but I saw Theresia turn back to look at me. I felt like she was silently urging me, so I opened the wrapper and started gnawing on the jerky. It was pretty chewy meat, but being warm made it slightly easier to eat. Cion came back, and she looked like she wanted to eat some, so I gave her the jerky I'd had originally. I honestly didn't know if that was what Theresia would want me to do, but I at least wanted to eat the portion she gave me.

"Awoo..."

"What's wrong, Cion?"

The sky had started looking more and more menacing since the sun had set. It was overcast, and the only light available was from a lantern sitting near the stove.

Thunder Head... So lightning sheep. Could be quite dangerous if they appear along with thunderclouds.

I didn't see any lightning yet, but I was starting to worry about the weather, what with all the black clouds that were starting to appear. It wasn't raining, and I hoped it'd stay that way.

"...Woof!"

Cion had been resting her head on my boots, but she suddenly looked behind her and let out a bark. I glanced over, wondering what was going on...when I saw a few people watching us and trying to hide amid the darkness. I could hear panicked cries of "They saw us!" and "Crap, what do we do?!"

They looked like Seekers who were trying to go after someone else's trapped game and steal the profits. But if they'd managed to make it up to District Seven, they should be able to get by without resorting to such lowly tactics. Anyway, I couldn't just leave them, so I took Cion along as I went over to investigate.

We headed toward a hill a little way off from the spring, where the three Seekers revealed themselves as we came up—perhaps we'd been slow to approach. They were wearing strange suits with bits of grass glued all over them in an attempt to blend seamlessly into the environment, like ghillie suits. All three Seekers were men of average height and build, ranging in age from their midtwenties to their thirties. They seemed on edge, but they didn't run away.

"Uh... So what exactly are you all doing?" I asked.

"Hmm... Eh, guess we can just tell him. Right, guys? We're only here on orders anyway..." A bearded man who seemed to be the leader of the three asked his companions for their opinion. The weapons they carried between them were a machete, a bow gun, and thin spears for throwing—needless to say, they'd obviously come here to hunt monsters.

"We're members of Beyond Liberty. We're supposed to be tailing you."

"Whoa... H-hold up, you sure it's all right to tell this guy? If Gray gets wind of this..."

"There's not an idiot in this world who'd believe we just *happened* to find a monster stuck in a trap, and we just *happened* to hunt it... Either way, we're the bad guys at this point. I'd rather negotiate a bit so we don't rack up any karma."

There was the kind of burly guy with a beard, a slim man holding a pair of binoculars, and an incredibly calm man wearing a helmet that looked like a camo-colored biker's helmet—the last one gave me the impression that he was the brains of the party.

"So you're trying to take advantage of our traps? See, I'd rather avoid having you guys get in our way."

"Urgh… That stings, man. But we've got no choice. If the higher-ups tell us to jump, we just ask 'em how high."

"Could you at least show us what kind of monster you end up catching? I know Seekers try to avoid information leaks as much as possible, but…"

"N-no way he's gonna agree to that… It's way too convenient… You think so, too, right?" the slim man asked me, albeit without using his bow gun to threaten me.

I didn't actually sense any hostility from these guys, but at this point, I really didn't want any information getting back to Gray. There wasn't exactly anything against us just running into each other on this floor, though. If I tried to chase them out, it'd probably be considered putting a fellow Seeker in further danger, and my karma would go up.

"Grrrrr…"

"S-see? Even the giant dog is mad…"

"Don't worry; Cion only does what I say, so you don't need to be afraid of her. Look, I understand your situation…and if you're just going to observe us, then I can't really stop you."

"O-oh… And here I was prepared for you to tell us to get the hell out. But in this case…" The bearded man seemed relieved, but I wanted to push one point.

"If possible, could you just report that things didn't go well for us?" I asked. "You don't necessarily have to report the correct information, yes?"

"…Got it. I don't think it's right to rat you guys out anyway. Thanks for letting this whole thing slide."

"W-wow… Someone who'll listen to reason. You're a good guy; it's plain as day."

"Hey, hey… Sorry about him—he can be kinda glib. Anyway, we swear we won't get in your way. And if we do, you're free to retaliate against us for breaking the contract, and we'll be the ones to take the fall." The bearded man did something on his license, and it showed this display:

◆Interparty Pact◆
> Will not interfere with ARIHITO'S PARTY.
> Will not interfere with FOUR SEASONS.

"Huh? You lot don't have a party name yet… Us guys, we've just been working under the name *Triceratops* for now."

"I've been considering picking a name one of these days. Do you use *Triceratops* because you've got three members?"

"Yeah. We've been wondering what we're gonna do if we ever get four or more members. I dunno if this means anything coming from us, but you should be careful of Gray from Beyond Liberty. But you didn't hear that from me." Apparently, being a member of Beyond Liberty didn't mean that the organization was completely unified.

"…Oh, also—since I've got a lot of girls in my party, could you let me hold on to those binoculars for now?" I asked.

"Huh? Wh-wh-what're you talking about?! I'm no Peeping Tom!"

"Hey, Arihito's concerns are more important. We'll let him take them as proof that we mean to keep our word."

"S-sure, I guess that makes some sense... But they're valuable, so don't go breaking 'em, okay?"

```
◆★Owl Scope◆
> Greatly increases range of vision.
> Makes it easier to land direct hits using
  ranged weapons.
> Enables night vision.
> Can detect heat sources.
```

Are they like thermal imaging goggles...? How do you use them...?
You could set the scope up on a stand and use it while it sat on the ground, in which case, you'd have to lie on your stomach to operate it. But doing so would leave both your hands open to fire a long-range weapon while you used the scope to aim.

"We're good as long as you just let us watch. Be careful," said one of the men.

"Saying it like that makes me feel strange... You be careful as well."

The Triceratops members seemed to be struggling against the hierarchy of Beyond Liberty. Even so, I couldn't completely let down my guard with them. With my Hawk Eyes and this newly obtained Owl Scope, it wasn't likely they'd be able to escape my observation.

By the time I got back to the camp, everyone had divided the wonderful-smelling food onto individual plates.

"Ooooh… Campfire rice! Arihito, look at this steam! No need for a humidifier!" cried Misaki.

"I doubt this kind of steam has the effect you're looking for… but anyway, this looks delicious."

Melissa was stirring a pot that was on the camping stove. Inside the pot was some sort of bubbling stew.

…Wait. I know exactly what this is!

"…You used the meat and vegetables you bought this morning to make…curry?"

Apparently, there were spice mixes sold at the market in District Seven, and she was able to use those to make something that was very close to, if not exactly like, curry. The spices in the mix were limited to what was found in the labyrinths, meaning it wasn't quite the curry that I missed so much, but the aroma was very similar.

"Melissa said she heard about curry from her dad and made it once before," said Misaki.

"It's different from the curry we used to make at home, but it tastes very nice. Have some, Arihito," said Suzuna as she offered me a plate.

"Oh, thanks."

I'd feel bad for the Triceratops guys if they'd seen this through the binoculars.

A number of trees in the area had been chopped down, which left behind stumps that worked as convenient chairs. I sat on one and took a bite of the curry. The savory flavors of the meat and vegetables blended together, and it had a little heat that intensified as you ate. It made me realize how hungry I was, and it tasted so good that I didn't want the meal to end.

Madoka brought some water over to me and smiled as she watched me eat wholeheartedly. She had already finished her food.

"Melissa's curry is so good, isn't it? I pretty much gobbled it up, too."

"I can't believe we get to eat real food like this. It's all thanks to you, Madoka, for carrying all the equipment."

"Oh, n-no, that's not true... I mean, that's about all I can really do anyway..."

Madoka didn't think she contributed much to the party, but she was working so hard. I should let her know that whenever I did see her trying her best. It might embarrass her, but there were a lot of things I couldn't express if I never put them into words.

"You've been a huge help ever since you joined the party. Let's both keep up the good work."

"Ah... O-okay!"

She was young enough to be my little sister, or maybe even my daughter if I was really pushing it. Either way, I was the leader and needed to be fair with all the party members, regardless of their ages.

"......"

"Ah... T-Theresia. You surprised me since you don't make any sound when you walk."

"Theresia really seemed to enjoy the curry, but...she got really red when she ate it!"

The spicy curry might have made her body temperature rise... But if she wanted to eat it, well, there was no stopping her. I went to go get her some water since there was so much available drinking water nearby.

After we finished eating, we went to the three tents in the groups we decided before. I put Madoka in our party for the time being and raised her morale with Morale Support 1 as I sat outside the tent using the Owl Scope to keep an eye on the trap in front of the spring. But I didn't see any signs of monsters in it.

No point in trapping something only for it to get away... But thanks to that curry, I don't feel too tired.

I hadn't checked my license, but since Melissa had Cooking 1 and she was the one who made the curry, eating it should have given some additional effect. I did notice that my body felt warmer than usual, yet my mind felt clear, which was good. I moved the scope to look at the trap set on the east side of the spring.

"What?!"

What I saw there was something that quite simply shouldn't be happening. One of the other tents was set up on the east side of the spring as well, where it wasn't visible from the trap. Ryouko should have been near that tent, but instead, she was headed toward the spring. There was clearly something strange about how she was walking. She was wobbling and walking like something was drawing her forward—up ahead, where she had her gaze focused, was a bouncing Stray Sheep.

"Arihito, it's time to change watch—"

"Elitia, something's wrong with Ryouko!"

"What...?!" Elitia readied her sword and stood on the edge of the cliffs. She couldn't decide what to do right away and turned back to look at me for instruction with desperation on her face.

"I'll shoot that Stray Sheep and stop it in its tracks! Elitia, Theresia, you two go down the cliff to see what's going on! Madoka, use your Hide skill and wait to come out until it's safe!"

"Got it!"

"...!"

"O-okay!"

I removed Madoka from the party since she wasn't needed for battle and restructured the group to include seven people and one dog. I then retrieved my Black Magical Slingshot and peered through the Owl Scope, which was set up on the ground, to take aim.

"This better not miss!"

◆Current Status◆
> ARIHITO activated FORCE SHOT ⟶ Hit STRAY SHEEP H
> STRAY SHEEP H activated SIGNAL FLARE
> 1 STRAY SHEEP defeated

"BAAAAH...!"

I put everything I had into shooting the magical bullet, which struck the sheep—but the next moment, it let out a cry, and its entire body released a flash of light, blinding me for a brief moment. However, I could still see Ryouko's heat signature in the Owl Scope as she continued to walk toward the spring. I suddenly realized where she was headed—she was trying to get herself caught in the trap.

Misaki's Fortune Roll didn't work… No, this is something else; something I wasn't expecting!

We had to stop Ryouko somehow before she reached that trap. I couldn't stop her by attacking her…which left only one option.

"I need to hurry!"

◆Current Status◆
> Arihito activated Rear Stance ⟶ Target: Ryouko

The sheep was still emitting its flash of light when I teleported behind Ryouko and grappled her.

"Ryouko, snap out of it!"

"…Wh-what…? Why am I—?"

I managed to stop her with not much time to spare, and she finally returned to her senses. There was no longer any danger of her walking off like she was being controlled, but that didn't mean the situation was entirely positive. Quite the opposite, actually. Lightning flashed across the sky, followed by the roar of thunder as if it was responding to the flare that the Stray Sheep let out with its dying breath.

◆Current Status◆
> ★Silvanus the Enchanter's Messenger appeared
> 2 Thunder Heads appeared

"GROOOOAH!"

"GYAAAA!"

Three bolts of lightning raced across the sky. One struck to the east, and one to the west of the spring—near the traps and lightning rods we'd set up. The last bolt came down right in front of us, crashing into the spring. The electricity ran across the water's surface, then there was a moment of stillness. The ground began to tremble. Something appeared in the center of the spring, where there hadn't been anything before—the top half of a massive body burst from the surface.

"Whoooooa, wh-what the hell is that thing?!"

I heard the cry of the Triceratops's leader; they had continued to monitor us. I was just as confused, but the sound of his voice actually brought me down to reality. If we just killed the Thunder Heads and ran, someone would try to hunt the sheep in the same way, and someday, they could run into this monster. But we didn't have any obligation to fight this thing. We didn't have to risk anything, but the rewards for hunting a Named Monster were high, and we could get things we couldn't obtain otherwise.

"A-Atobe... This creature is a higher level than the Paradox Beetle from before. Even one level difference in Named Monsters means a huge difference in strength...," cautioned Ryouko.

"No doubt about it... Named Monsters are in a completely different league from normal monsters of the same level. If we're gonna run for it, we should get out before anything gets started... But we've come this far. I want to do what we can."

"...Yes, you're right. If we run now, then we'll have no choice but to do the same when we encounter an even stronger monster. And before long, we'd just end up stuck in one place."

"Ryouko, you can use water spells, right? That'd probably work against this enemy, but be careful you don't get yourself electrocuted."

Ryouko nodded and turned to her companions, who'd come out of the tent looking concerned. Even so, the three of them took their positions to fight and moved to where I could support them.

Igarashi and the others had already fallen into battle formation. They were in the west, facing off against the Thunder Head that appeared there. In the east were the other three members of Four Seasons, and then Elitia and Theresia arrived to join me and Ryouko.

"If only we could focus on one at a time, this would be much easier...but I don't think we'll be able to manage that," said Elitia.

Masses of Stray Sheep that had been lurking in the fields had appeared and were gathering onto the monster that appeared in the water. The Stray Sheep were either pieces of that creature or younger versions that were scattered throughout the labyrinth floor to bait Seekers. Their fluffy bodies covered the beast, whose head was that of a demonic-looking sheep. It was so massive that I had to crane my neck up to see all of it. It was about as big as the Giant Eagle-Headed Warrior, and the oppressive bloodthirst I sensed coming from its entire body was utterly supernatural.

◆Monsters Encountered◆
★SILVANUS THE ENCHANTER'S MESSENGER
Level 7
Hostile
Dropped Loot: ???
THUNDER HEAD A
Level 5

```
Hostile
Dropped Loot: ???
THUNDER HEAD B
Level 5
Hostile
Dropped Loot: ???
FLOCK OF STRAY SHEEP
```

"...OOOUGHHH... OOOUUGH..."

The beast let out a sound, not quite a voice, which was hard to believe came from a living creature as it lifted itself from the spring and began taking step after step.

"Elitia, can you keep this thing's attacks from hitting us by drawing it away?"

"Yeah, leave it to me. Theresia and I will get some quick strikes in."

"......"

Theresia readied her targe and throwing dirks. Elitia drew her sword and stepped to the front while the other parties were engaging in battle.

"—I'll crush you to pieces!"

Elitia wasn't going to let Silvanus's Messenger beat her when it came to bloodcurdling fierceness in battle.

"Elitia, I'll support you!"

"...OOOUUUGGH... OOOOUUGGGHH!"

Silvanus's Messenger raised one of its gigantic, wool-covered arms. Lightning crackled from the arm before suddenly turning black.

"—Elitia, don't get in too deep just yet!"

"...!!"

◆Current Status◆
> Arihito activated Attack Support 1
> ★Silvanus the Enchanter's Messenger activated Black
  Lightning Fist
> Elitia activated Rising Bolt
> Stage 1 hit Stray Sheep D
12 support damage
> Stage 2 hit Stray Sheep E
12 support damage
> 2 Stray Sheep defeated

Elitia leaped up, kicking sand back, and sliced the beast...only to hit two of the Stray Sheep stuck to the Messenger's surface. It didn't strike its main body, and it didn't have any effect against it. The Messenger swung its black-lightning-covered fist toward Elitia, but—

"Agh!"

"...!"

"Elitia!"

Theresia threw her dirks, and Ryouko attacked using a dolphin she formed out of the spring's water.

◆Current Status◆
> Theresia activated Double Throw
Threw 2 small dirks
> Stage 1 hit Stray Sheep R
12 support damage

```
> Stage 2 hit Stray Sheep N
12 support damage
> 2 Stray Sheep defeated
> Ryouko activated Aqua Dolphin ⟶ Hit ★Silvanus the
  Enchanter's Messenger
```

"—OOOOUUGGHH!"

Theresia's dirks didn't make it through to the enemy's body.
Ryouko's magic attack didn't have the support damage with it, but
it seemed to have some effect on the creature.

But that didn't stop the Messenger's fist. It continued with fierce
tenacity toward Elitia, and it was about to find its mark, when—

"Stooooooop!"

```
◆Current Status◆
> Arihito activated Force Shot (Stun) ⟶ Hit ★Silvanus
  the Enchanter's Messenger
> Elitia activated Air Raid
> Elitia evaded Black Lightning Fist
Hit by area damage
```

"OOOUUUGH!!"

"—Aaaaah!"

My magical bullet struck its face, throwing its fist off track
ever so slightly. Elitia used that moment to activate a skill in mid-
air and managed to evade the attack. Even though she did manage
to dodge the fist itself, the lightning it was surrounded by must
target an area, because she let out a screech of pain.

"I'm okay... This isn't enough...to stop me!" said Elitia, but my heart sank when I looked at my license. Her vitality had dropped by almost a quarter with one hit. "Our attacks will work if we can just manage to hit its actual body... Arihito, I'll cut off as many Stray Sheep as I can!"

"...Okay!"

She hadn't lost her fighting spirit, and she was right. There was an incredibly large amount of Stray Sheep, but they weren't infinite.

Silvanus's Messenger had remained expressionless until that moment. I clearly saw the corners of its mouth curl up in a smile—almost like it was sneering at our very hopes.

Part V: Kyouka's Perspective

Atobe and the others were facing off against the massive creature that had emerged from the spring. Our group was on the west side of the spring, where we'd set up our tent, when a bolt of lightning had struck the lightning rod near the trap we'd been monitoring. We guessed that was probably a monster and immediately got ready for a fight.

"Grrrrrr..."

"Wait, Cion... Don't attack yet. You might get electrocuted if you go too close."

The monster had fluffy fur and curled horns on its head. It looked like a massive Stray Sheep. Its face wasn't scary like a Cotton Ball's, but there was definitely hostility in its black eyes.

"...GIII..."

The Thunder Head almost smiled, baring rows of neatly lined teeth—and those teeth were definitely not meant for chewing grass. This was the face of a carnivorous beast that was going to try and devour us.

"Uuurgh... I can probably throw my dice at it from a distance...," said Misaki.

"Kyouka, let's reposition ourselves so that Arihito's at our back," suggested Suzuna.

"Yeah, good point... We need to make sure it doesn't go for him, either..."

There was still electricity crackling around the Thunder Head's body, but it didn't try to stop us from moving. We cautiously adjusted our position like Suzuna recommended, and while we were doing that—

"—Aaaaah!"

"Ellie!"

I couldn't take my eyes off the Thunder Head, but I guessed what happened from Suzuna's cry. Ellie had just taken a hit from that huge creature. But then, I heard her speak again.

"I'm okay... This isn't enough...to stop me!"

She'd managed to shout out to us despite having taken damage, probably in part to make sure we didn't worry too much.

"We need to beat this monster as fast as possible and then back up Atobe and the others!" I said.

"A-all right... Here I go! Arihito, I need your help!" called Suzuna with a note of tension in her voice. She put her trust in Atobe, who was at our backs. The next moment, I could practically feel him right behind Suzuna, fighting with her.

◆Current Status◆

> Suzuna activated Auto-Hit ⟶ Next two shots will
  automatically hit
> Arihito activated Attack Support 2 ⟶ Support
  Type: Force Shot (Hypnosis)
> Suzuna attacked Thunder Head A ⟶ Direct hit
> Attack Support 2 activated ⟶ Thunder Head A was
  Confused
> Arihito activated Attack Support 2 ⟶ Support
  Type: Force Shot (Stun)
> Suzuna attacked Thunder Head A ⟶ Direct hit
> Attack Support 2 activated ⟶ Thunder Head A was
  Stunned
> Thunder Head A discharged electricity ⟶ Thunder
  Head A's charge level dropped to 0

"BAAAH!"

Both of Suzuna's shots hit. When the second shot struck, the lightning surrounding the Thunder Head's body dissipated.

Incredible... Atobe used such helpful effects along with Suzuna's attacks!

But while he was supporting us over here, he still needed to support Ellie and Theresia as they stood against the giant monster over there. He'd always been good at juggling multiple tasks back when we worked together. No matter what project I asked him about, he'd know what was happening and be able to give me the right information. I accidentally ended up relying on him... and I still felt bad about it now when I remembered it.

But now, as a member of Atobe's party, I would do what I

could—whatever I had to do—so that I could fulfill my role. I would fight with everything I had so that we could all move forward.

"Cion, let's attack together!"

"Awooo!"

I brandished my cross spear and faced the Thunder Head. I wasn't going to let this chance go now that Suzuna's arrow had dispersed the lightning surrounding the enemy. Ever since I learned Wolf Pack, I'd been able to run so fast that I could hardly believe it was my own legs carrying me.

"—Hyaaaaa!"

◆Current Status◆
> ARIHITO activated ATTACK SUPPORT 1
> KYOUKA activated DOUBLE ATTACK
> 2 stages hit THUNDER HEAD A
24 support damage
> CION activated HEAT CLAW
> THUNDER HEAD A activated THERMAL ENERGY ⟶ THUNDER HEAD A's charge level increased to 1
> THUNDER HEAD A recovered vitality

"—BAAAAAAAH!!"

My spear attack definitely did something, but the Thunder Head didn't flinch when Cion struck it with her Heat Claw. Lightning once again started flickering across the Thunder Head's body.

...Wh-what...what just happened...?!

"—Igarashi! Tell Cion to use her normal attack!" came Atobe's voice. "That thing must have an ability that lets it turn heat into electricity!" Whatever he was doing was outside the range of my license and didn't show on the display, but he was still observing everything that was going on.

"—GIIIII!!"

An electrical current ran between the two horns on the Thunder Head's head, but it didn't use it for an attack. My best guess was that it didn't have enough electricity for an attack at only "charge level 1." But there was a chance that I'd get electrocuted if I attacked it with my spear. My Thunderbolt would almost certainly have the opposite effect from what I wanted, meaning I couldn't use it. I could risk ending it right away if I used my new Ambivalenz...but I would take damage when I attacked. I had no idea if I could survive both that and potentially getting electrocuted.

"Kyouka, let me go again. I'll fire another arrow with Arihito's support!"

"M-me too...! This doesn't always work, but here goes Lucky Seven!"

◆Current Status◆
> Misaki activated Lucky Seven 1
> Thunder Head A's status ailment resistance was reduced slightly

"Awww, a consolation prize... Oh no, am I having an unlucky day?!"

"No, you're not! We can do this... Atobe, support Suzuna with Stun again! It should discharge the enemy's electricity!"

"—Kyouka, look out!"

Right when I was starting to feel like we'd found a way through this, I saw something I never could have imagined.

"—!"

"Melissa?!"

Melissa had been watching the Thunder Head's movements, but she suddenly brandished her large butcher's knife and swung it at me. I was caught completely off guard by the attack, but I had my special move, Mirage Step, for moments like this.

I activated it, evading Melissa. The next moment, I heard the swish of air as the butcher's knife swung past me and gouged into the earth. She wouldn't do something like that without good reason.

Wait... I've been hearing a strange noise for a bit now. Is that giant monster...singing...?

"Everyone, cover your ears! Don't listen to that sound!" Atobe shouted in desperation, but I couldn't react in time. I'd already heard quite a bit of it.

I understood what had happened when I looked back through my license. I understood why Melissa had attacked me.

◆Current Status◆

> ★SILVANUS THE ENCHANTER'S MESSENGER activated HORN OF PLEASURE ⟶ Inflicts women with the CHARMED status

> MELISSA, RYOUKO, KAEDE, and ANNA were CHARMED

Morale decreased

> MELISSA followed ★SILVANUS THE ENCHANTER'S MESSENGER'S orders ⟶ Attacked KYOUKA

> KYOUKA activated MIRAGE STEP ⟶ Evaded attack

"Horn of Pleasure"... Is that monster something like the natural enemy of female Seekers...? But why were only some of us affected? ...Is it not guaranteed to work...?

"Huh, th-this sound kinda feels nice... Ah, is that what got to Melissa...?" asked Misaki.

"Melissa, please snap out of it! ...Be cleansed! Be purified!"

◆Current Status◆
> Suzuna activated Purification —→ Melissa's Charmed
  status was removed

"Ah... What...am I...?"

"Good job, Suzu! Whew, what a relief! I reeeally didn't wanna have to attack a friend!"

"I'm so sorry... I've caused you all this trouble..."

"Don't worry about that right now," I reassured Melissa. "I don't know why, but that sound didn't work on all of us, and that seems to have confused the enemy... Now's our chance!"

"Woof!"

The Thunder Head seemed to think that the sound that Silvanus the Enchanter's Messenger made should have been guaranteed to be effective. But for some reason, it hadn't worked on us, and the enemy couldn't make its next move.

"BAAH... BAAAAAAH..."

"It sounds kind of cute... Sorry. I have to defeat you and help my leader out," I said.

"—BAAAAH!"

The Thunder Head tried to use the electricity gathered

between its horns to attack, but by then, Suzuna had already activated Auto-Hit a second time and nocked an arrow in her bow.

Part VI: Arihito's Perspective

Silvanus's Messenger grinned, and a strange sound filled the air. It settled deep in my brain and gave me an indescribably unpleasant feeling.

"What is...this sound...? It's so sweet...and vile..."

"......"

Elitia, Theresia, and I heard the Messenger's sound and felt only slightly uneasy—but once I checked the display on my license, I felt another shiver run up my spine.

This ability... Oh—so that's why we didn't see it before!

I realized now that this sound might be what had lured Ryouko toward the spring earlier, when she was walking strangely and staring at the water.

◆Current Status◆
> ★Silvanus the Enchanter's Messenger activated Horn of Pleasure ⟶ Inflicts women with the Charmed status
> Melissa, Ryouko, Kaede, and Anna were Charmed
Morale decreased

"Ah..."

Nearby, Ryouko's body jerked strangely. She walked in my

direction, her expression vacant as she tried to activate a skill to use against me.

"Ryouko—!"

"Arihito, Theresia, you guys take care of her! You have to stop her somehow!" called Elitia.

Stop her...? It's not like I've got the cure for this sort of thing in my pocket. I could Stun her... No, I'll only attack an ally as an absolute last resort. But what should I do...? Think, Arihito, think...

"—Haaaaaah!"

◆Current Status◆
> Arihito activated Rear Stance —→ Target:
                                              Ryouko
> Ryouko's Aqua Dolphin was canceled

I moved around to Ryouko's rear and grappled her, just as I'd done before, in hopes I could get the same strategy to work twice.

"Ah..."

"I'm sorry... This is all I can do...!"

I was feeling the drain from using Rear Stance so much, but it was the only way I could think of to get her back to herself.

"—Ryouko, snap out of it!"

◆Current Status◆
> Arihito activated Outside Assist
> Arihito activated Morale Support 1 —→ Ryouko's
  morale increased by 12

"Urgh... Gahhh...!!"

Ryouko was far stronger than I could have ever guessed from her normally measured movements, and she tried to break from my grip. I was certain that Charmed people would attack their own companions.

I won't lose...a single person!

Ryouko stopped struggling for just a moment. Even though she was training her body every day, she likely couldn't keep up such violent movements for too long. I took advantage of the opportunity to call to her.

"—Pull it together, Ryouko! You're stronger than this!"

◆Current Status◆
> Ryouko expended morale to activate Morale Skill: Emergency Recovery ⟶ Ryouko recovered from Charmed status

There were some status ailments that people could use morale to recover from. It was a gamble that Charm was one of them, but it looked like my hunch was right.

"Ah... *Huff, huff...* Atobe, I'm sorry again..."

"It's okay, don't worry about it... The other Charmed people are still in danger!"

I didn't have time to explain how Charm worked to Ryouko. I checked my license and saw that Suzuna had used Purification in order to safely get rid of the status affliction without expending any morale.

"—OUUGHHH... OOOUUGHHH!"

"Arihito, watch out for stray attacks! It's about to launch something!" warned Elitia.

The Messenger hadn't done anything for a moment after activating Horn of Pleasure. There was no longer a smile on its face, perhaps because the number of people it managed to Charm was fewer than it'd expected.

"What…is that…?"

"The Stray Sheep are being killed by the big monster's lightning… No, wait… It's one of its attacks…"

The black lightning that danced across the surface of the Messenger's body coated a number of the Stray Sheep, turning them into balls of black lightning… And then:

"—OOOOOUUUGGGHHH!"

◆Current Status◆
> ★SILVANUS THE ENCHANTER'S MESSENGER transformed 4 STRAY SHEEP into DARKNESS BLITZES

Those level-1 Stray Sheep…it's going to use them as weapons!

I understood it instinctually before I had time to even think about it: Those four black balls of lightning were meant to decimate the four of us. Those cute Stray Sheep that had bounded through the plains were now horrifying tools of destruction—and they were aiming for us under the Messenger's command. It would be impossible to dodge, assuming they were still living creatures with intelligence despite having been turned into Darkness Blitzes.

Can we take the hit with Defense Support 1…? No, too risky.

We don't have someone with impenetrable defenses in the party like Seraphina...but we have something else!

Ariadne, I need your help!

"I, Ariadne, grant my devotee and his allies my protection!"

◆Current Status◆
> ARIADNE activated GUARD ARM
> DARKNESS BLITZ A hit GUARD ARM
> DARKNESS BLITZ B hit GUARD ARM
> DARKNESS BLITZ C hit GUARD ARM
> DARKNESS BLITZ D hit GUARD ARM
> GUARD ARM short-circuited

"Wha...?!"

As I'd anticipated, the Messenger launched off the Darkness Blitzes, which acted like guided missiles. The moment before they would have struck us, the Blitzes crashed into Ariadne's Guard Arm, which released a shower of sparks as it short-circuited.

"Magical lightning... As a Mechanical God lacking the proper defenses, I am unable to maintain my circuitry. Forty-five seconds remain until automatic repairs are complete and Guard Arm is once again ready for use."

"It's okay, you saved us... We'll take care of the rest. But we might need your help again in another thirty seconds..."

"...Murakumo's...Self-Defense Mechanism will not activate unless the situation is dire...but if you desperately need her...she will respond to my devotees..."

Ariadne's voice became distant. We'd have to survive some-how until we could use her Guard Arm again, which had become a sort of trump card for us.

"Elitia, Theresia, I need you to buy us time!"

"All right! Haaaah!"

"...!"

Theresia used her heat stone to activate Mirage and lure the Messenger's attacks. Elitia evaded, then tried to attack its head, which had become almost completely bare.

"—OOUUUGHHH!"

"I'll cut you to pieces!"

◆Current Status◆

> ELITIA activated BLADE RONDE ⟶ Hit 13 STRAY SHEEP
> ELITIA activated additional attack ⟶ Hit 9 STRAY SHEEP
> 22 STRAY SHEEP defeated

"Did she get it?!"

The increased number of attacks the Dexterity Gauntlets gave her was incredible. She sheared off the Stray Sheep that covered the Messenger's head like they were wool.

"OOOUUGH... OUUUGH!!"

◆Current Status◆

> ★SILVANUS THE ENCHANTER'S MESSENGER activated SHEPHERD'S HORN ⟶ Summoned flock of STRAY SHEEP

The Messenger let out a sound different from the one before. It rippled through the air, and countless Stray Sheep appeared before enveloping the Messenger again.

"…It wasn't even hurt…?"

How could it do something so absurd…? Actually, it's been plenty absurd this whole time. There's got to be a way we can survive this… There has to be!

"If that's how it wants to play this, I'll just keep slicing them off!"

"…!"

Elitia and Theresia went up against the Messenger again together, but the sheep-headed monster lifted its two arms, even though it shouldn't have been able to reach that far with an attack. It was like it was calling something down from the heavens…

I could almost see it—a scene completely different from the reality currently transpiring before my very eyes: my friends lying on the ground, monsters calmly approaching them. This scene flashed across my mind without any warning.

Are we…going to…die?

Just a moment's delay in reading the enemy's next move could spell our end. I made two decisions: the first, to shout out, and the second…

"—Come forth, Demi-Harpies!!"

◆Current Status◆

> Arihito summoned Asuka, Himiko, and Yayoi

"Arihito, what are you—?!"

"Demi-Harpies, take those three and escape to the sky! Hurry!"

"—Atobe, no! No, no, nooo!"

"—!!"

The Demi-Harpies grabbed Elitia, Ryouko, and Theresia before flying into the sky. I begged for them to get higher and higher, leaving me standing alone against Silvanus's Messenger.

There were two Thunder Heads, one to the east and one to the west. There was a clear reason why this monster brought two of them and not three. There was a reason why there weren't three. It was so the monsters could follow their instincts and feed on Seekers.

"—Atobe!"

"Teacher!"

I should have realized it. I should have realized that if we didn't completely stop the three from working together—

◆Current Status◆

> ★SILVANUS THE ENCHANTER'S MESSENGER coordinated with 2 THUNDER HEADS

> ★SILVANUS THE ENCHANTER'S MESSENGER and THUNDER HEADS activated SILVANUS'S LIGHTNING HAMMER

> ARIHITO activated DEFENSE SUPPORT 1

"GAAAAAAAAAH!!"

"...OOOOUUGHHH... OUUUGGH!"

Each of the Messenger's black-lightning-cloaked arms took a charge from one of the Thunder Heads, increasing their power, then it brought its fists down, slamming them into the earth. The black lightning arched out in waves to damage all its enemies in the vicinity, but Elitia and the other two were out of its range.

Just in case, I used Defense Support...but...I don't know if it'll do anything...

The intense pain as the black lightning ran through my body was more than I could have ever imagined. It jumped from my feet to the rest of my body in a flash, tearing me apart from the inside. I felt like it was boiling my blood.

And yet, I survived. As the rearguard, I was at quite a distance from the enemy. Perhaps you could just call it luck, but I was alive. However, I couldn't keep myself from falling to my knees. Before I collapsed, I managed a glance at each of the two other parties. They'd managed to stop the Thunder Heads that were trying to kill me.

"No... Arihito, you can't die! You can't!"

"These damn sheep... I won't take it anymore! Eat thiiiiis!"

"I let it bring you down... I'm so pathetic...!"

◆Current Status◆

> Kaede and Anna recovered from Charmed status
> Ibuki activated Flying Eagle Claw ⟶ 2 stages hit Thunder Head B
> Anna activated Spin Smash ⟶ Hit Thunder Head B
> Kaede activated Gyaku Ichi Moji ⟶ Hit Thunder Head B

"Why... Why won't it go down?!"

"Kaede, don't give up! Let's try again!"

"—Anna, watch out... Aaagh!"

The Thunder Head rampaged with a sweep of its horns. Ibuki couldn't evade and let out a screech of pain.

"Arihito… Arihito, come on… Stand up—stand up and run!"

"…!!"

Elitia shouted to me, and Theresia made a face like she was silently screaming.

I should be shouting for them to run. No point in fighting if it's just going to destroy us all.

"*—And yet, you, my master, are the least likely of anyone to give in. That is what I believe.*"

I heard a voice—it was Murakumo, the sword I carried on my back. I realized I was in a pitch-black space. I was still on my knees, and in front of me was Murakumo in her material form.

"…Right before organisms die, their mental processing speed and physical abilities increase greatly for a brief moment. I am using your quickened thoughts in order to speak with you," she said.

"Am I…dying? Was that attack enough to kill me…?"

"You are the one who should know that best. All monsters are a danger to Seekers. The probability at your current strength that this particular level-seven monster would destroy you is very high."

I chose to continue fighting because we'd been able to keep making definite steps forward, and we'd never lost to a Named Monster yet. And the result? Our attacks had no effect. The enemy kept throwing blow after powerful blow at us, and we were pushed to the edge.

"Your survival is my greatest priority. I have been analyzing the battle to see if you could strike the enemy's weakness if you used me."

"It might be possible if I used that skill, but…"

"You are at risk of destruction as long as the Thunder Heads remain undefeated... You should support your other companions more than you have been."

"More than I have been... Is that possible...?"

Murakumo nodded. She came over to me, crouched, and looked at me closely.

"...You, as well as many low-ranking Seekers, do not fully understand 'morale.' Those who have found themselves in life-or-death moments many times naturally gain an understanding of morale..."

"Life or death... Do you mean...?"

"When they want to win, even though it means risking their life... And encouraging your companions so that you can win. The amount morale can improve your skills is quite significant. However, you seem unaware that *your own* morale has also increased while you were seeking in the labyrinth..."

I had had no intention of risking my life. I just wanted to prioritize protecting my friends, even though as a rearguard, I was at the back of the party. But Murakumo was right. I could see something now that I'd been pushed to the very moment before death.

"You're saying I don't have to give up yet? But there's a problem first of all. I'm not sure I can even stand up."

"That is not a problem. I will support you. And...there are many ways in which you can be healed. One of those is already in progress."

By *support*, she meant literally. Murakumo, the physical embodiment of the Stellar Sword, and the one who wielded the katana, appeared behind me.

"I have gone a long time without showing my physical form, so I can maintain it now for about five minutes. You should decide quickly if you wish to retreat. Once a Named Monster has chosen its target, it will pursue it relentlessly until it is no longer on the same floor."

"That's scary...but I was chased enough last time—I'd rather not go through that again."

I let Murakumo support me as I stood. I could hear my friends calling me, but I was still literally on the verge of death and couldn't say anything loud enough to respond. The fact that we were still in a terrible situation shouldn't have changed. But almost like we were protected by some god, hope remained in the oddest of places.

"—Morale Discharge, Item Effects!"

I heard Madoka's voice. That was a Merchant's Morale Discharge. Its effect was pretty similar to what you might expect from the name. A ball of light appeared before my eyes. It split into a number of shards of light, which absorbed into my body. And then—

◆Current Status◆
> Madoka activated Item Effects ⟶ Target: Party members, subparty members
> Arihito received the effects of a Mid-grade Compound Recovery Potion
> Elitia received the effects of a Mid-grade Vitality Potion
> Theresia received the effects of a Mid-grade Mana Potion

The Merchant's Morale Discharge recreated the effects of the selected items and applied them to party members in the middle

of battle. Apparently, she could change which item effect it was for each person, and there wasn't even a need to actually drink a potion. Potions weren't considered very practical for use in the middle of battle, but this compensated for that and gave us yet another trump card in our hands.

Igarashi and her group also received some potion effects.

"Pheeew, wow... Is this, like, some sorta recovery spell? Man, Madoka's a really special girl..."

"And now...! Arihito, we can still fight!"

"Atobe, we'll be your backup! Just hold out a little while longer!"

They'd all gotten a second wind. Elitia and the others also recovered slightly, and the Demi-Harpies came down to set them on the ground.

"......"

"Arihito, maybe this isn't the time to tell you...but Theresia's expression says she thinks Murakumo's taken her place," said Elitia.

"......"

"T-Theresia, way to put me between a rock and a hard place... Let's talk about this later!"

I charged my slingshot with magic and let loose a magical bullet. Silvanus's Messenger had noticed Madoka and was going for her. I was trying to get its focus back on me.

◆Current Status◆
> Arihito activated Force Shot (Hypnosis) ⟶ Hit Stray Sheep A2
> 1 Stray Sheep defeated
> Madoka activated Hide ⟶ Became undetectable

No luck... Wait, no, it just didn't hit its actual body. How can we make it so the Stray Sheep don't block our attacks...?

"Arihito, I noticed something from watching it. When it's attacked, the Stray Sheep concentrate in that area, leaving other areas with less defense...or that's what it looks like." The fact that Elitia wasn't certain was a testament to how quickly and smoothly the Stray Sheep moved to concentrate the defense. But I unconditionally trusted the sharpness of her sight and intuition.

"In other words, we need to attack from multiple directions at the same time," I said.

"Yes. But it has more than one area attack that can take out its opponents... If we could just make an opening and all hit it at once, that should definitely..."

"...Atobe...," Ryouka said. "Oh, I'm so happy... I have no idea what I'd do if something had happened to you..."

I didn't tell her that this wasn't the place to be crying. Instead, I smiled at her, despite lacking the confidence to put my heart in it—our situation was still dire.

"Thanks to Madoka, I somehow managed to get through it. It's good to be alive."

"...How dare you just...smile and say a thing like that! What you did—"

"—was gutsy or maybe too insightful," interrupted Elitia. "So we're not just gonna sit and watch... I bet that's what Theresia's thinking."

"......"

Theresia's gaze stung. I wasn't surprised they were repri-
manding me. If Madoka hadn't saved me, I'd still be on the verge
of death, and we'd still be in an impossible situation. Everyone
was struggling with every ounce of strength they had. I didn't
know if my efforts would definitely get us through this...but I
had to try, like Madoka did when she took that one-in-a-million
chance.

"We have to turn this in our favor...or run away as fast as we
can. Either way, I'll guard the rear."

"Idiot... Don't think I'm going to keep letting you try to be
cool. No one's going to leave you behind," said Elitia.

If we weren't running away, then I could only pray that my last
option would work—a silver bullet to finally kill this sheep-headed
beast.

"It's all right...," I reassured her. "I've got Lady Luck herself
smiling on me—her name's Ariadne."

"If Misaki'd heard that, she'd probably say something like,
Oh, you mean me? ...So do you know what you'll do next?"

"Yeah. I'm not entirely sure what'll happen, but it's worth a
shot. Let's do this!"

There was a different world that only those who'd been faced
with death could see. Where would we be headed if we kept facing
it? The answer was clear: We'd turn Theresia back into a human
and save Elitia's friend. I needed to—no, *we* needed to grow stron-
ger and help bring out one another's strengths so we could clear
the path ahead.

"Morale Discharge...Complete Mutual Support!"

◆Current Status◆

> Arihito activated Complete Mutual Support

Time limit: 120 seconds

> Widened support effect range for Arihito's party and subparty

> All individual buff skills applied to entire party

> Entire party buffed by Wolf Pack

> Entire party buffed by Secrets of the Sword 2

> Entire party buffed by Knife Artistry

> Entire party buffed by Increased Drop Rate

> Entire party buffed by Child of Luck

> Entire party buffed by Secrets of Iai

> Entire party buffed by Secrets of the Strike

> Entire party buffed by Footwork

> Entire party buffed by Routine

So this is my Morale Discharge...Complete Mutual Support!

I had high hopes since everyone else's Morale Discharges were so powerful. My job was rearguard. It was normally a one-way road of support, from the rearguard to the vanguard, but this let it go the other way as well. It completely eliminated the major flaw of my job—the fact that I couldn't support myself—even if only in the most restricted circumstances. And that wasn't all. As the word *Mutual* in the name might imply, everyone's individual buffs were now applied to all party and subparty members. It wouldn't be active for a very long time, but it was likely enough to survive this situation.

My body feels so full of power... Is this how much of a difference

Wolf Pack makes? Footwork must be Anna's skill, and Routine is probably Ryouko's... I can do things now that I wouldn't normally be capable of. Even my focus is a level stronger!

And that still wasn't all. On top of these passive buffs was my usual support, plus Igarashi's and Theresia's Morale Discharges.

"...OOOUUUGGGHH... OOUGHHH!"

""—BAAAAAH!!""

Even the monsters could tell something had happened. The Thunder Heads let out battle cries and moved to attack the two parties facing them, but—

"With this...we can get to Atobe right away!"

"Woof!"

"Okay...! Misaki, Melissa!"

"Uh, ummm... Hope you guys are okay with a dice attack... Yah!"

"That horn...is mine...!"

◆Current Status◆
> ARIHITO activated ATTACK SUPPORT 2 ⟶ Support Type: FORCE SHOT (STUN)
> MISAKI attacked THUNDER HEAD A ⟶ THUNDER HEAD A was STUNNED
> ARIHITO activated ATTACK SUPPORT 1
> KYOUKA activated DOUBLE ATTACK
> CION activated WOLF RUSH
> Total of 6 stages hit THUNDER HEAD A
72 support damage
> SUZUNA's attack hit THUNDER HEAD A
12 support damage

> MELISSA activated LOP OFF ⟶ THUNDER HEAD A dropped
  materials
> 1 THUNDER HEAD defeated

"Yeah!"

The first hit stopped it in its tracks with Stun, letting everyone get their attacks in. They finished it off spectacularly, since even their normal blows were strengthened thanks to Complete Mutual Support. I chose Attack Support 1 for every strike after the first just because it used almost no magic and the twelve points of support damage was plenty effective right now.

"Hyaaa!"

Kaede, Ibuki, and Anna also finished off their Thunder Head. The fact that they did so as quickly as Igarashi's group despite having fewer people really showed how powerful their attacks were as a group of athlete-type jobs.

"We did it... Now let's go join Arihito!"

"Yes... We can help him, even just a little bit...!"

"Arihito, what should we do?!"

Ibuki, Anna, and Kaede rushed over at the speed of light. They looked like they may have attacked each other while they were Charmed, because their armor had some damage. But they weren't injured; they must have been healed by Madoka's Item Effects. Despite the damage they'd taken, they had never been more ready to fight.

"Ryouko, can you help with a joint attack?" I asked.

"Of course. There's no way I could face my girls if I ran now."

I wouldn't have been surprised if the men of Triceratops had run already. They were incredibly lucky that they weren't in the area hit by the black-lightning attack from just before, and if we lost this battle, they would be in danger of being next.

"Arihito... No, Captain, give your orders, while your Morale Discharge is still in effect." Elitia had guessed it had a time limit just because it was so powerful. Our window for attack was only going to be open for a short time.

"—We'll hit it in waves! First, we need to get the Stray Sheep off our backs for a minute... Suzuna, use your explosion stone! Any other long-range attackers, shoot at the same time, along with your mirage warrior! Close-range attackers, you'll be up next, in order...starting with Elitia!"

""""All right!"""""

Suzuna readied an arrow; Misaki gripped her dice; Theresia grabbed some dirks; Ryouko called forth a dolphin made of water; and Anna brandished her racket.

"Morale Discharge, Soul Mirage!"

"...!"

"—Strike your target!"

"—OOOUUGGGHH... OOUUUUGGHHHH!!"

◆Current Status◆

> Kyouka activated Soul Mirage ⟶ All party members and cooperating party members gained a Mirage Warrior

> Theresia activated Triple Steal ⟶ All party members and cooperating party members received Triple Steal effects

```
> Arihito activated Attack Support 1
> Suzuna activated Auto-Hit ⟶ Next two shots will
  automatically hit
> Suzuna activated Blast Arrow ⟶ Hit 16 Stray
  Sheep
Additional Mirage Warrior attack
192 total support damage
> 16 Stray Sheep defeated
> Misaki's attack hit ★Silvanus the Enchanter's
  Messenger
Additional Mirage Warrior attack
24 support damage
> Suzuna recovered vitality and magic
Successfully stole loot
> Misaki recovered vitality and magic
Successfully stole loot
```

"GOOUUGHH... OOOUGH!"

We penetrated its defenses...but it's not down yet!

"Whoooa, s-so cool... Suzu's arrow exploded!"

"—Your turn, everyone!"

Suzuna's explosion stone created a concussive force when it struck, sending Stray Sheep flying as they burned. Even so, they were still coming in unlimited droves. We couldn't let it summon them again.

"Theresia, aim for where its defense has weakened!"

"...!"

Theresia closed in using Accel Dash and leaped up in front of the beast's face with all the additional power she had in her. She flipped in midair, flinging out two of her dirks. Her attack was joined by blows from Anna and Ryouko. Add in the mirage warriors' help, and it was practically a shower of strikes.

◆Current Status◆
> Theresia activated Double Throw
Threw two small dirks
Additional Mirage Warrior attacks
> 2 stages hit ★Silvanus the Enchanter's Messenger
48 support damage
> Ryouko activated Aqua Dolphin ⟶ 2 stages hit
  ★Silvanus the Enchanter's Messenger
Additional Mirage Warrior attack
Defense decreased
> Anna and Mirage Warrior activated Spin Smash
  ⟶ 2 stages hit ★Silvanus the Enchanter's
  Messenger
Additional Mirage Warrior attack
Inflicted Concussion status
24 support damage
> Theresia, Ryouko, and Anna recovered vitality and
  magic

"GOOUGHH!!"

"—Theresia, avoid the counterattack with Mirage!"

"…!"

◆Current Status◆
> Theresia and Mirage Warrior activated Mirage, Accel Dash
Additional Mirage Warrior Attack
> ★Silvanus the Enchanter's Messenger activated Leveling
  Fists ⟶ Failed 4 times

The Messenger took a chain of attacks and tried frantically to counter. It crashed its fists down almost like it was trying to plow the land at its feet, but not a single strike hit despite the fact that it was aiming for Theresia, who was on the front line.

She can use Mirage for more than just reducing the enemy's hit rate... Both she and her mirage warrior keep using Accel Dash to lead its attacks and dodge every time!

"—Hyaaa!"

"Haaah!"

```
◆Current Status◆
> Kaede activated Soukouken ⟶ 2 stages hit
  ★Silvanus the Enchanter's Messenger
Additional Mirage Warrior attack
24 support damage
Subsequent attacks strengthened
> Ibuki activated Wave Thrust ⟶ Hit 2 Stray
  Sheep
Additional Mirage Warrior attack
24 support damage
> 2 Stray Sheep defeated
> Kaede and Ibuki recovered vitality and magic
Successfully stole loot
```

"Shit!"

"—BAAAAAAAH!"

Ibuki followed Kaede in for an attack, but the Messenger must have anticipated the blow because it brought its arm up to block. The shining energy that Ibuki launched from her fist simply hit a Stray Sheep, failing to get through to the Messenger's main body.

Regardless, the attack created an opening and drew the Messenger's attention to the right. Igarashi didn't hesitate to lead Cion and Melissa in to attack.

"—We're gonna defeat you! ...All of us!"

But she wasn't holding her cross spear—in her hands was the double-bladed spear she'd wanted to hold on to as a backup: Ambivalenz.

"Haaaah!"

"—Igarashi!"

"Wait, Kyouka! That weapon—!"

◆Current Status◆

> Kyouka activated Double Attack ⟶ 2 stages hit
  ★Silvanus the Enchanter's Messenger

24 support damage

> Kyouka took reverse damage

> Kyouka's armor broke

> Kyouka recovered vitality and magic

"GOOOOAAAAAAH!!"

"Argh...!"

Igarashi's vitality plummeted. Ambivalenz was frighteningly powerful, and she used it to strike the Messenger's arm where its Stray Sheep defense was thin. No attack we'd thrown at it thus far had done such obvious damage. But because of the reverse damage, I had to avert my eyes—her Ladies' Armor had burst open.

And even with her pale skin clearly exposed, she didn't so much as flinch.

"—Now, mirage warrior...! Join Cion and Melissa and give it everything you've got!"

"Woof!"

"...I'm gonna take both of those horns!"

◆Current Status◆
> Kyouka's and Mirage Warrior's attack rose as a result of Ambivalenz's special effects
> Kyouka's Mirage Warrior activated Double Attack
  ⟶ 2 stages hit ★Silvanus the Enchanter's Messenger

24 support damage
> Melissa and Mirage Warrior mounted Cion and Mirage Warrior

Used Wolf Rider
> Melissa and Mirage Warrior activated Lop Off
  ⟶ ★Silvanus the Enchanter's Messenger dropped 2 materials

"GOOOOOAAAAAAAAH... AAAHH!"

Melissa and her mirage warrior swung their butcher's knives in almost a cross, slicing off both of the Messenger's horns. Igarashi's mirage warrior, with its attack power buffed by the amount of damage Igarashi took, lashed out with its spear. It left a huge slash starting on the left side of the Messenger's head around to its forehead.

I can see something on its forehead... A weak spot, maybe? Even with Hawk Eyes, I can't quite tell...

That must've been Igarashi's strategy. She would use Ambivalenz to take damage, drawing out its true power, then her mirage warrior would attack. Melissa and her own mirage warrior then followed up, riding Cion and her guard-dog mirage warrior respectively to cut off both of the Messenger's horns in one go. That eliminated any possibility the Messenger had of Charming our party or calling reinforcements, meaning the tide of battle was in our favor.

But there was one major miscalculation—the consequence of such a powerful attack.

"...I'll...get past this... It's just...the sight of blood..."

"Elitia, hold on! We're here with you, even if you go Berserk! We're not afraid!"

"...Arihito..."

"Ellie, it'll be all right! No matter what happens, I'll bring you back to your senses...!"

Suzuna's and my calls reached Elitia, and she shook her head—but then, she was gone. She'd used Sonic Raid and dashed off, her speed increased from Berserk as well as everyone's support buffs.

"—Scatter like flower petals! *Blossom Blade!*"

The young blond swordswoman, followed by her equally light-footed mirage warrior, flashed their swords across the battlefield, like petals falling from a flower that bloomed out of season.

◆Current Status◆
> ELITIA activated BLOSSOM BLADE ⟶ Hit 7 STRAY SHEEP
25 stages hit ★SILVANUS THE ENCHANTER'S MESSENGER
Additional MIRAGE WARRIOR attack
384 support damage

The Messenger still didn't go down after taking a flurry of sword strikes. It did, however, seem to finally be overwhelmed as it fell to one knee. Those thirty-two total slashes were only the start. The rain of swords came back around to follow up with Elitia's counter-slashes.

"Soar high into the sky!"

◆Current Status◆
> Elitia activated additional attacks ⟶ 24 stages hit ★Silvanus the Enchanter's Messenger

Additional Mirage Warrior attack

288 support damage

> Elitia recovered vitality and magic

"GOOOOOUUUGGGH… OOOOUUUUUGGH!!"

The damage from her assault had increased because of the buff support—and then, there was the additional support damage. But the enemy still didn't go down. And even though Elitia was in Berserk mode, she was able to rein herself in.

"I…I…am a member of Arihito's party… I won't hurt any more of my friends!"

"As my master's sword, I respect those words. We will take care of the rest; you may pull back." Murakumo placed a hand on my shoulder. I knew that I'd see her fight again. At the same time, the knowledge of what I should do came to me.

Is this gonna go the way Murakumo thinks it will? …I just need to follow her lead. We'll finish things here!

The Messenger, close to its end, took the remaining Stray Sheep stuck to its body and cloaked them in black lightning. It was trying a final counterattack that would throw away the last of its defense.

—Auto-Blade System will now activate—

◆Current Status◆
> ★SILVANUS THE ENCHANTER'S MESSENGER transformed 15 STRAY SHEEP into DARKNESS BLITZES
> MURAKUMO activated BIRDCAGE

There was a ringing from somewhere, like a bell. The katana split into eight pieces, encircled the Messenger, and began to rotate.

"Master, my current manifestation is not enough to draw the enemy's attention... Fire a bullet at me...!"

"Okay, got it... Demi-Harpies, you join in!"

I charged my slingshot with magic while I gave an order to the harpies circling above. The Stray Sheep might have been turned into Darkness Blitzes, but so long as they still had characteristics of living creatures, it was possible the Demi-Harpies' special ability would work nonetheless.

"—Eat this!"

◆Current Status◆
> HIMIKO activated LULLABY
> ASUKA activated MUSICAL ROUND
> 3 DARKNESS BLITZES fell ASLEEP
> ARIHITO activated FORCE SHOT (BOUNCE)
Additional MIRAGE WARRIOR attack

> Force Shot bounced between Murakumo and
  ★Silvanus the Enchanter's Messenger ──→ Hit 4
  Darkness Blitzes
6 stages hit ★Silvanus the Enchanter's Messenger

Just as Murakumo said, a birdcage formed from the mass of her eight sword pieces. They rotated around the Messenger and ricocheted my bullet back at it, who could no longer even cry out. Its eyes flashed in defiance as it tried to counter, but—

"The bird can't leave its cage if it doesn't give the correct answer..."

◆Current Status◆
> 8 Darkness Blitzes attacked Arihito's party
> Murakumo activated Meteor Thrust ──→ Hit ★Silvanus the
  Enchanter's Messenger
Canceled actions of 8 Darkness Blitzes
> ★Silvanus the Enchanter's Messenger activated Demon's
  Blood
> ★Silvanus the Enchanter's Messenger's charge level
  reached maximum

The Messenger flung the Darkness Blitzes at the shards of Murakumo that made up Birdcage in an attempt to blast Murakumo away, but she took her physical form—that of a young girl—and dealt the monster a deadly blow from behind. Blue blood spurted out from the Messenger, and black lightning gathered around its demonic, ovine head while its entire body released a blue heat. It was aiming for me—but there was a different "me" in front of it.

"Raaaahhh!"

Full of resolve, I'd grabbed hold of Yayoi, the last Demi-Harpy who hadn't joined the song, and we swooped down, aiming right for the Messenger's forehead—between its missing horns.

The wound went all the way to its forehead when Igarashi attacked... I'm certain of it. This is the area it really wanted the Stray Sheep to keep protected!

"—Come forth, Murakumo!"

Once Murakumo had finished her attack, I had her appear—just like with the Guard Arm—in a specific location: within my raised hand.

◆Current Status◆
> Arihito activated Blade of Heaven and Earth ⟶ Hit
  ★Silvanus the Enchanter's Messenger
Weak spot attack

The only skill I could use with Murakumo was the one I'd seen before, but it was enough to bring the blade down into the Messenger's skull.

"...OUGH... OUGH..."

It fell to both its knees in the spring's shallows. I trusted in the ability of my strengthened body and leaped down from the Messenger's head, which was about ten feet above the ground. Huge waves rippled across the spring's surface. I steadied my feet so I wouldn't be dragged away by those waves as I looked at the Messenger again. On its knees, unmoving, it looked exactly as I had only minutes before.

◆Current Status◆
> 1 ★Silvanus the Enchanter's Messenger defeated
> All Darkness Blitzes extinguished
> Arihito's Complete Mutual Support has terminated
> Elitia grew to level 10
> Arihito grew to level 6
> Theresia grew to level 6
> Kyouka grew to level 5
> Suzuna grew to level 5
> Misaki grew to level 5
> Melissa grew to level 5
> Cion grew to level 5
> Elitia's Berserk has terminated with the end of
  combat
> Scarlet Emperor attained 1,000 total cuts,
  unlocking its inherent Cursed Blade skills

No doubt about it: This was an intense enough battle that the entire party leveled up. Hopefully, Madoka and Four Seasons had leveled up, too. The Scarlet Emperor display seemed ominous, but that could potentially be a benefit as well. Elitia had just come out of Berserk, heaving her shoulders with ragged breaths, and she hadn't noticed the display yet.

"Okay, but first— Aaah!" I turned around, trying to revel in our victory with the others, but someone suddenly leaped into my chest. Perhaps it was the relief of having won that made her take such a bold action. She was stuck to my chest, her eyes glistening as she looked at me. It was none other than Igarashi, who moments before had been showing us how courageous she was with her daring strategy.

"...Atobe... Thank goodness... I'm so happy..."

"I-Igarashi... Um, I—I am incredibly sorry for any concern I may have caused you, but the thing is, right now, how should I say this, there's still a serious issue that needs to be addressed..."

"What...? You can't just run off after doing something so crazy and reckless! Atobe, I seriously thought you were gonna die back there..."

Her armor was broken, leaving almost her entire top half exposed. I wasn't sure how I felt about armor that kept breaking in this way, but there was nothing we could do about it at this point. But with her so close to me, inevitably I'd catch a glimpse of something I'd normally only see in the bath. Not only was there a chance that I'd end up witnessing something I shouldn't...it felt like two oversized Cotton Balls were pressing against my chest.

Uh, I—I guess Cotton Ball *is a little rude... But I can't really think of anything more apt... They're not like slime. Crap, what should I do?!*

"K-Kyouka... I am painfully aware of how worried you were about Atobe, but don't you think you're being a little too forward?" asked Ryouko.

"Huh? ...Eeeeek!"

My twenty-five-year-old former boss let out a cute screech more suited to a college-aged girl, before pulling away from me. Ryouko took off her boa coat and put it on Igarashi.

"...He didn't see, did he? Because if he did, I...I'll have to change my job to 'Priest'..."

"Huh...? Wh-why Priest...?"

"B-because…I wouldn't be able to stay in the party without achieving enlightenment… Ughhh, why'd my armor have to break like that…?"

In other words, she hadn't noticed that it broke in the middle of battle. I hadn't thought things could end up like this, either. I had to admit that the Ambivalenz was a dangerous weapon…in more than one way. Its strengths and risks were equally jaw-dropping.

"Arihito…!" cried Kaede. "For real, I had no idea what was gonna happen to you! I suddenly snapped back to myself when you went down, like someone had smacked me upside the head…"

"…Me too. We would have caused Ibuki less trouble if we'd come to our senses quicker," said Anna.

"Ha-ha… I was definitely surprised, but I suppose there's all sorts of different monsters out there," replied Ibuki. "Although, I do wonder why it didn't work on me."

I was impressed by how fearless Ibuki was. She already didn't care that her Charmed companions had attacked her. I was also quite interested in the fact that there were some members who had been affected by Horn of Pleasure and some who hadn't been. I could go back a little bit in my license's display. I went back to around when Horn of Pleasure had been used.

…S-so that's what it was!

◆Status Record◆
> Theresia's and Kyouka's Trust Level bonus:
  Complete immunity to Charm 4 and below
> Suzuna's Trust Level bonus: Complete immunity
  to Charm 3 and below

> MISAKI'S, ELITIA'S, and MADOKA'S Trust
  Level bonus: Complete immunity to Charm 2
  and below

> IBUKI'S and CION'S Trust Level bonus: Complete
  immunity to Charm 1 and below

Each time I supported someone, their Trust Level toward me increased. That particular aspect of my skills was also having an effect here. I'd just met Ibuki, but perhaps the fact that she called me Teacher was a sign of her higher trust in me. Trust Levels probably didn't equate to affection levels, but there was something about it that made me blush. That said, she was more than ten years younger than me, so I should really just be grateful. It wasn't uncommon for people her age to call me an old man, being twenty-nine years old.

But...this is divided into four different levels. Do both Theresia and Igarashi trust me about the same, then...? Maybe that's because they've both been in my party from pretty much the beginning.

Anyway, this meant that the stronger our trust in each other was, the stronger the resistance against Charm. I felt like Ryouko had really changed how she saw me from when we first met, but it must be hard to build that much trust in one day. Melissa was also the only member of my party who didn't have the resistance. I wanted to work harder and gain her trust.

"Arihito...!"

"Ah... M-Madoka, there you are. I'm all right, thanks to the recovery medicine you used."

"Good... I had no idea my Morale Discharge would do that... but I wanted to help you somehow..." Fat tears ran down Madoka's face as she spoke. I really didn't think I could handle taking such a gentle girl into fierce battles, but I was genuinely so grateful to her. Her bravery back then was what kept me alive. It might be true that we gained a lot from this battle, but I was the leader, and I really needed to rethink my tendency to get too deep into the battle.

"Careful, but brave... Yep. Looks like I didn't understand you at all, Arihito," said Kaede.

"And that snap decision to protect everyone... That was thrilling. To be honest, I always thought you were a reliable man," said Ryouko.

"N-no... I wouldn't say it's about being reliable—it's just that we were about to die..."

"Honestly... Not this again! You did something incredible—don't get so worked up over a compliment. And..." Ryouko sort of sounded like she could be my older sister, even though I was older than her. She seemed to want to say something else, but her expression softened as she looked at my face. "...Thank you. If it hadn't been for you, we would've passed the point of no return."

"It was nothing... It looks like monsters think about certain things, too. If we run into any trouble, we'll support each other and work through it."

It was a tough battle, but in the end, our cooperation with Four Seasons was a success. I wanted to form a partnership with them until we moved up to District Six. We'd originally started working together in order to resist Beyond Liberty, and that goal hadn't been completed yet.

"Anna, the materials you needed were from the Thunder

Head, right? I imagine you'd be able to get something good from the Messenger as well," I said.

"I only heard about the Thunder Head's guts being good materials. I'd appreciate it if I could just have some of that. I imagine things will get complicated once you report this Named Monster to the Guild... I'd like all of you to consider whether you'd sell it or take it to a dissection center."

"Yeah, we'll do that. Okay, would you please take one of the Thunder Heads, then? Or we can have Melissa dissect it. Which would you prefer?"

"I can ask the workshop that's going to make the racket to do the dissection, too, so we'll take it there. I think Melissa's going to be busy dissecting the big one anyway..."

Melissa was standing, holding her butcher's knife that she'd used in battle and staring at Silvanus's Messenger...with an expression of ecstasy on her face.

"...You think a blue-blooded monster would be blue on the inside if I cut it open?"

"Um, uhhh... I mean, I guess that's a natural assumption to make... Melissa, can you send that to your Repository?" I asked her.

"I can make it fit. I'll need more people to dissect it. I'll get Dad to come, if he can."

It sounded like Rikerton would come to District Seven if his daughter asked. Were the Seekers who had retired and taken a support role allowed to move between the districts to a certain degree?

"Arihito, I don't know if this is because everyone's luck was increased, but there's one of *thooose* things in the shallow water," said Misaki.

"It's almost become customary for us to find one... Even though they're so rare and valuable," said Suzuna.

"We need to be very careful of any traps on a chest dropped by a monster like this. Should we take it to Falma, since we know she can definitely open it safely?" suggested Igarashi.

"Yeah, that's a good idea," I replied. "Madoka, can you please put it in our storage unit for safekeeping? Everyone else, let's look for dropped materials... Whoa, there's so many Stray Sheep."

I learned something by collecting a number of them: Stray Sheep and the Darkness Blitzes were actually separate entities—the former were bigger than a Cotton Ball, but still small enough that someone like Madoka could pick them up. We could probably get a lot of wool from these. I was looking forward to seeing the different traits the black wool had compared with the white wool. The Thunder Head's wool was yellowish, though I didn't know if maybe that was because they emitted light.

"Woof! Woof!"

Cion came over to me and gave a little woof while I was gathering materials. I looked up to see what it was and saw the members of Triceratops observing us from a distance. I let the others know that I was going away for a bit, then took Cion and headed to where the three Triceratops members were lurking. All of them were still in their ghillie suits, blending in with the fields around them. None of them stood as I approached.

"…Did you guys chicken out or something…?" I said.

"…We're as pathetic as they come. But man, you were seriously killer out there!" said the bearded man, raising only his face as he spoke. He wasn't pale or anything, but he looked like he was dreaming, not really looking at reality.

"Killer…? Do you mean dangerous?"

"N-nah, not like that… C'mon, have a little self-awareness!"

"Most folks couldn't pull off something like that even if they wanted to," said the helmeted man. "You had those Demi-Harpies scoop everyone up but yourself, and you just took the monster's attack… And then, you came back from the dead. That was the coolest thing I've ever seen. Haven't felt my heart race like that in forever." Even in his usual monotone, that sounded vaguely like admiration. Actually, it was probably rude to doubt his sincerity.

It sort of sounded like the word *killer* meant something along the lines of *cool* to these guys. I'd just been focused on fighting, so I was surprised they saw me that way, but I supposed it was better than being thought of as uncool.

"Phew… I've finally calmed down. Guess that battle really did happen… You guys are seriously blessed. I'm equal parts jealous and afraid," said one of the men.

"B-but you know… We're proud of how far we've come, too," said another. "We don't want to do anything to throw a damper on you and what you got from that battle."

"We didn't see nothin'. Those monsters will stay a secret, and we won't give any information to Gray. We don't want to destroy your image… Thanks for letting us watch all that."

"I'd appreciate it. I have a feeling that a fight between us and the Alliance is inevitable. When it comes to that, let's make it a great one," I replied. By *fight*, I merely meant a competition in ranking. We couldn't advance if we didn't make our way to the first rank. "I think you guys really held up your side of the deal. Sorry I had to take the Owl Scope as collateral. It was really helpful, though."

"D-don't worry about it. If it helped you out, you keep using it. You not running from that fight means it's less likely we'll get a stampede from this labyrinth, you know? We should be thanking you, or whatever..."

"There's no way we could've won against that Named Monster. And we don't have to beat it to know how you guys feel—what it's like to survive. But you won, and that's given us hope. Maybe this makes us pathetic, but we've got more fire in us now than we ever have before," said the bearded man, his eyes positively shining. We did really seem to be the spark that lit their fire. But that didn't mean I could just accept something as valuable as this scope.

"Okay... I'll buy it off you at its going rate. Would a thousand gold cover it?"

"Guh... *Cough, cough.* A thousand gold? It's not like we couldn't make that much ourselves, but you sure you can just throw that kinda cash around?"

"What sorta hell have you guys been through?! ...Geez, just hunt more Cotton Balls or something... The profits might not be so great, but District Seven's got a bunch of those kinds of monsters."

"Even one Grand Mole gives us a hard fight. Those things are a huge pain in the ass to hunt. One of those gets you fifty gold if you're lucky; a thousand gold would really give us a boost."

"All right, then that settles it," I replied. "If there's anything useful you're thinking of buying, come talk to us. More than likely, we can give you a better deal than what you get in the shops."

I decided to use the function on Madoka's license to send them the gold. They waved good-bye and left, then I headed back to help gather materials. Just a little longer, and we'd be able to go back home.

We took down the tents and headed back to town for a bit. There was a chance we'd be going back to that labyrinth if we found a key in the Black Box. I brought up the rear in a single-file line. Watching Igarashi in front of me had me worried. She had been full of surprises lately, including when she decided to use Ambivalenz.

"*Everyone in the party wishes to contribute, for your sake. I feel the same,*" came Murakumo's voice from the sword on my back. She'd once said a weapon should remain a weapon and shouldn't talk, but she seemed to be getting more talkative after this last battle. "*As a piece of the Mechanical God Ariadne, it is only natural that I became your sword, Master.*"

You saved me this time. You and Ariadne are both indispensable to our party.

"*...Mechanical God Ariadne should also be able to hear you. I* am nothing more than one of her parts. I will leave any response to her." Murakumo's presence faded; maybe she was trying to be considerate. Then, I could feel the presence of the girl who watched over us from her Sanctuary. She'd suddenly stopped speaking earlier, so I'd actually been concerned about whether or not she was all right.

Ariadne, thank you so much for saving us. We should look into short-circuit prevention...

"...*I almost let you, my devotee, die, simply because of my weakness to electrical attacks.*" Just like Igarashi and everyone else, Ariadne was concerned about me.

I'm sorry I worried you. But apparently, that was really the only way to let me use my Morale Discharge... We won't include that in our future strategy—we'll find a safer way...

"...*You've helped me learn anew how a Mechanical God's protection should work: If you protect your companions, I will protect you. That way, we can protect the entire party.*" Ariadne wasn't just fussing over me—she was looking at the future, guiding us in her own way. "*You must hurry and find a shield armament. I can overcome Guard Arm's weakness to electricity with a Guard Variant.*"

Sounds like some kind of divine providence. But maybe I shouldn't be saying that to an actual god.

"...*We are not all-knowing, nor are we the Founder. Sometimes, a human's potential can change the future we assume awaits us. With enough power, great beings can turn the tides of fate.*"

"*I want to hear you say you will carve your own fate using my power as the Stellar Sword as well as with Mechanical God Ariadne's power*," came Murakumo's voice. They were very similar in some ways, but I got the feeling that Ariadne was the more serious of the two. And that wasn't a bad thing—they each had their own lovable aspects.

"*...Love... Something that cannot be expressed in numbers. An emotion that we Mechanical Gods cannot comprehend.*"

"*I do not think what I feel from Master is love, but rather, simple emotional attachment. I must emphasize how well I, a weapon, fit with him. I wish to hear your own self-evaluation, Master.*"

Well, let's see... I'd give both of you 120 points. I'm not quite there yet, though.

Ariadne and Murakumo fell silent. They'd probably just tell me you can't score over a hundred points in something like this.

"*...I cannot evaluate you with mere points. There is no chance I could ever meet a greater devotee than you.*"

"*I agree with Mechanical God Ariadne. I will continue to serve as your sword, Master.*"

Ariadne's presence felt more and more distant, and Murakumo stopped talking. I wasn't sure how to respond.

"......"

Theresia was walking a little way ahead but turned back to look at me. I wondered what she was thinking. It seemed she'd gathered that I'd been talking to Ariadne and Murakumo. Then, she silently drew back to walk by my side. Even without words, that was enough to tell me that she was concerned about me.

"Sorry I worried you, Theresia. And thanks for always working so hard."

"......"

She didn't face me even when I spoke to her. Her mask just turned red little by little as we kept walking.

I didn't know it at the time, but as we made our way to the top of District Seven, something was about to shake the foundation of our awareness as Seekers forever.

The Rearguard and a Soothing Moment

When I suddenly awoke, I was lying on a bed, my head still spinning. I looked around but could only get a vague grasp of the situation.

"...Mr. Atobe...took care of me... And then..."

I sort of remembered drinking too much, which made me feel guilty, but I felt light and uninhibited. And not just because of the alcohol.

"Mr. Atobe was...so kind to me..."

I remembered when I'd first seen the job he'd selected and how concerned I'd been. My advice hadn't been appropriate, and he'd ended up in some strange job that the license couldn't even recognize. I would feel terrible if people treated him badly. That's what I thought then. I still hadn't asked him in detail about his job, but I did know that just him being behind me made me feel warm and happy. That might just mean I had a crush on him, though.

When I first came to the Labyrinth Country, I became a Seeker, then I retired and moved to a support role. I'd always been so busy and never really had any interest in romantic relationships. I'd seen so many of the Seekers I sent off get injured or become depressed that they never did very well. I'd thought that as

a Guild employee, it was my job to support them, and I shouldn't be thinking of anything else. But then, I was made Mr. Atobe's exclusive caseworker, and I found that I enjoyed spending time with the party. I even liked when he took care of me when I had too much to drink—a little guilty but still happy.

I thought that does happen sometimes, growing fond of someone you meet through work. Whenever he came to my mind, I just thought of how much I wanted to work hard to make everything go well for him.

"...Really...? Everything...?"

I'd thought about it for a while, and now I understood: The people in his party admired him as much as I did—if not even more so—and they'd spent far more time with him than I had. I'd never be anything more to him than a run-of-the-mill receptionist.

It made me so happy that I was able to gain his trust through my work. But surely, it wasn't wrong of me to express my gratitude in other ways. If Theresia was in the bath with him right now, then what was just one more person in there, too? Maybe that wasn't entirely okay, in truth, but I had a feeling it was fine in the moment.

"...Just you wait for me, Mr. Atobe... I'm really quite something..."

The entire way to the bath, and even after I entered, I couldn't stop my heart from racing. My head was swimming, but I thought I needed to appear calm, so I tried to say something that sounded logical.

"Mr. Atobe, may I just do a little something? What you did for me earlier made me so happy..."

I was thanking him for taking care of me. He stayed right where he was once I explained myself.

I'd chosen the job of Aesthetician upon my reincarnation. I'd only written that because I thought I had to put whatever my job from my past life was, but being an Aesthetician meant I was almost completely incapable of contributing anything to battle. I used to treat my lady friend who let me join her party, as a way of lifting her spirits.

"...L-Louisa... You don't have to do all this for me..."

I started massaging Mr. Atobe's scalp. He seemed to enjoy it despite his weak protest. I had a strong urge to tease him. I gripped his shoulders and started massaging them. When my robe came undone, my chest pressed against the back of his head, though I was wearing bathing clothes.

This is to show him how much I appreciate him... I can't help it if I have to press against him—it's for the procedure... Ahh, but... my head feels all warm, and I can't think straight...

Even though I was drunk, I did know what was acceptable and what was not. The problem was that the boundary between the two was a bit fuzzy.

"Ummm... L-Louisa, is this part of the procedure...?"

"Yes... Yes, it is. It's very relaxing to hold your head like this..."

"B-but you're not just holding it... Is this a head massage...?"

I felt even happier because of Mr. Atobe's innocent reaction. I glanced over to Theresia through the steam and saw she was bright red. I thought she must look that red because I was so drunk.

"Theresia, could I ask for your help...?" I said to her.

"......"

"Y-you don't have to if you don't want to, Theresia...," said Mr. Atobe nervously, but Theresia pattered over in her cute little swimsuit. I had her wash his back for me. I went around to his front and massaged him from his shoulders to his abdomen, releasing all the pent-up tension. It had been so long since I'd last used my skills.

◆Current Status◆
> Louisa activated Warm Bath Osteopathy ⟶ Target: Arihito
> Arihito recovered vitality and magic
> Arihito acquired Relaxation effect

I thought of the information that would likely display on my license and told myself it was all just a procedure. I massaged Mr. Atobe's pressure points and lymph nodes while looking at him. This was all so I could try and help him be less fatigued.

"...I-it is a little awkward, I guess... Uh... But it's certainly effective...," said Mr. Atobe.

"Yes... This is something you need. I could do this for you on the regular... If you could just let me take care of your health and well-being, too..."

"......"

"Hee-hee... You can join us, Theresia. It's going to be so much fun."

I started to sober up after continuing the procedure for a short while. Mr. Atobe was kind enough to allow me to go in the bathtub by myself to wash up, and I apologized profusely after getting out for causing him any trouble.

But if he didn't hate it this time around, then I wanted to think about how I could work with the rest of the party to express our appreciation for him. This would prove important for strengthening the party's bond—not to mention, some of my own personal feelings might be in there as well.

Nice to meet you all— My name is Tôwa. I mentioned this a little in the last volume, but I have nothing but the utmost appreciation for every single person who continues to read my work. I pretty much spend all my time now prostrating myself in gratitude.

Perhaps you've already noticed the large cast of characters in this series. It's incredibly difficult for me to decide which characters will be depicted in the illustrations. My lead editor will tell me, *"My money's on this character for this volume,"* and we'll choose a scene based on that, which then dictates what the book's illustrations will be. ※Note: My editor's tone is not what I have presented here. My editor always takes all aspects of the work very seriously and makes no compromises on delivering excellent work to (omitted due to space constraints).

…Anyway, what I'm trying to say here is, I would also love to see as many images of as many characters as possible, but there are just too many of them. Perhaps readers can have fun guessing who's going to show up in each volume's illustrations. I'd also really like to hear what you all have to say about that one scene where the kendo swordswoman, Kaede, was being quite cheeky. We writers are always eager to hear our readers' feedback.

I'm starting to run out of space now, so I'd like to thank Huuka Kazabana; my lead editor; everyone who helped get the book published; and most of all, my wonderful readers. I'm also looking forward to continuing to work with Rikizou on the manga version!

I hope to see you all again in the next volume of *The World's Strongest Rearguard*.

Tôwa

HAVE YOU BEEN TURNED ON TO LIGHT NOVELS YET?

IN STORES NOW!

SWORD ART ONLINE, VOL. 1–19
SWORD ART ONLINE PROGRESSIVE 1–6

The chart-topping light novel series that spawned the explosively popular anime and manga adaptations!

MANGA ADAPTATION AVAILABLE NOW!

SWORD ART ONLINE © Reki Kawahara ILLUSTRATION: abec
KADOKAWA CORPORATION ASCII MEDIA WORKS

ACCEL WORLD, VOL. 1–21

Prepare to accelerate with an action-packed cyber-thriller from the bestselling author of *Sword Art Online*.

MANGA ADAPTATION AVAILABLE NOW!

ACCEL WORLD © Reki Kawahara ILLUSTRATION: HIMA
KADOKAWA CORPORATION ASCII MEDIA WORKS

SPICE AND WOLF, VOL. 1–21

A disgruntled goddess joins a traveling merchant in this light novel series that inspired the *New York Times* bestselling manga.

MANGA ADAPTATION AVAILABLE NOW!

SPICE AND WOLF © Isuna Hasekura ILLUSTRATION: Jyuu Ayakura
KADOKAWA CORPORATION ASCII MEDIA WORKS

IS IT WRONG TO TRY TO PICK UP GIRLS IN A DUNGEON?, VOL. 1–14

A would-be hero turns damsel in distress in this hilarious send-up of sword-and-sorcery tropes.

MANGA ADAPTATION AVAILABLE NOW!

Is It Wrong to Try to Pick Up Girls in a Dungeon? © Fujino Omori / SB Creative Corp.

FUJINO OMORI
ILLUSTRATION BY SUZUHITO YASUDA

ANOTHER

The spine-chilling horror novel that took Japan by storm is now available in print for the first time in English—in a gorgeous hardcover edition.

MANGA ADAPTATION AVAILABLE NOW!

Another © Yukito Ayatsuji 2009/ KADOKAWA CORPORATION, Tokyo

A CERTAIN MAGICAL INDEX, VOL. 1–22

Science and magic collide as Japan's most popular light novel franchise makes its English-language debut.

MANGA ADAPTATION AVAILABLE NOW!

A CERTAIN MAGICAL INDEX © Kazuma Kamachi
ILLUSTRATION: Kiyotaka Haimura
KADOKAWA CORPORATION ASCII MEDIA WORKS

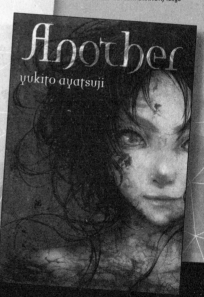

Another
yukito ayatsuji

1
KAZUMA KAMACHI
ILLUSTRATION BY
KIYOTAKA HAIMURA

A Certain Magical Index

VISIT YENPRESS.COM TO CHECK OUT ALL THE TITLES IN OUR NEW LIGHT NOVEL INITIATIVE AND...

GET YOUR YEN ON!

www.YenPress.com

Our Last CRUSADE
OR THE RISE OF A
New World

KIMI TO BOKU NO SAIGO NO SEN
ARUI WA SEKAI GA HAJIMARU SEIS
©okama 2019 / HAKUSENSHA, I
©2018 Kei Sazane · Ao Nekonabe / KADOKA
THE WAR ENDS THE WORLD / RAISES THE WOI
©Kei Sazane, Ao Nekonabe 20
/ KADOKAWA CORPORATI

LIGHT NOVEL

MANGA

LOVE IS A
BATTLEFIELD

When a princess and a knight from rival nations
fall in love, will they find a way to end a war
or remain star-crossed lovers forever...?

AVAILABLE NOV
WHEREVER BOOK
ARE SOLD

For more informati
visit www.yenpress.c